T5-AOU-629

As Mecan made his way back into the living room, Jeneva was still standing in the window, her arms wrapped tightly around her upper body. He sensed that there was something on her mind and it suddenly worried him. Mecan found himself struggling not to stare, unable to take his eyes off her. As she turned, her gaze meeting his, a tremor of heat flooded his body. He could feel the flames rising in his cheeks and he was grateful she could not see the raging color that flushed his dark face. He smiled, not wanting to appear overly eager. When Jeneva returned the smile, her eyes still locked on his, it was almost too much for him and he could feel the tightening of muscle below his waist wanting to take control. Mecan inhaled sharply.

"Are you okay?" Jeneva asked.

Closing his eyes, Mecan pushed his hands deep into the pockets of his khaki pants. He nodded his head. "I'm sorry. I . . . I . . ." he stammered nervously. "I'm making a complete fool of myself," he finally said.

Jeneva shook her head. "No. You're not."

"It's just that," Mecan paused, "you are extremely beautiful," he said finally, blowing warm breath past his full lips. "I am very attracted to you, Jeneva."

Jeneva lowered her gaze for a split second, then looked back up at Mecan. Before she could respond, the front door flew open as Natalia ushered Quincy inside.

Shocked by the words that had just spilled out of his mouth, Mecan turned away, embarrassed that he would say something so unprofessional. Looking from one to the other, Natalia sensed the sudden rise of tension between the couple. Sexual energy had filled the small space and the woman smiled at them all-knowingly.

Stepping into the room, Quincy ran straight into Jeneva's arms, dropping his head against his mother's shoulder. Hugging him tightly, Jeneva could feel the tears spilling down over her cheeks and she fought the desire to cry, not wanting to do anything that might upset her son. She held him close, her eyes shut tightly, and when she opened them, looking past the boy's shoulder, Mecan stood smiling at the two of them.

BOOK YOUR PLACE ON OUR WEBSITE AND MAKE THE ARABESQUE ROMANCE CONNECTION!

We've created a customized website just for our very special Arabesque readers, where you can get the inside scoop on everything that's going on with Arabesque romance novels.

When you come online, you'll have the exciting opportunity to:

- View covers of upcoming books

- Learn about our future publishing schedule (listed by publication month and author)

- Find out when your favorite authors will be visiting a city near you

- Search for and order backlist books

- Check out author bios and background information

- Send e-mail to your favorite authors

- Join us in weekly chats with authors, readers and other guests

- Get writing guidelines

- AND MUCH MORE!

Visit our website at
http://www.arabesquebooks.com

The RIGHT Side of
Love

DEBORAH
FLETCHER MELLO

Athens-Clarke County Library
2025 Baxter Street
Athens, GA 30606
(706) 613-3650
Member: Athens Regional Library System

Madison County Library
P O Box 38 1315 Hwy 98 West
Danielsville, GA 30633
(706)795-5597
Member: Athens Regional Library System

ARABESQUE

BET BOOKS

BET Publications, LLC
http://www.bet.com
http://www.arabesquebooks.com

ARABESQUE BOOKS are published by

BET Publications, LLC
c/o BET BOOKS
One BET Plaza
1900 W Place NE
Washington, D.C. 20018-1211

Copyright © 2004 by Deborah Fletcher Mello

All rights reserved. No part of this book may be reproduced, stored in a retrieval system, or transmitted in any form or by any means without the prior written consent of the Publisher.

If you purchased this book without a cover, you should be aware that this book is stolen property. It was reported as "unsold and destroyed" to the Publisher and neither the Author nor the Publisher has received any payment for this "stripped book."

All Kensington Titles, Imprints, and Distributed Lines are available at special quantity discounts for bulk purchases for sales promotion, premiums, fund-raising, and educational or institutional use. Special book excerpts or customized printings can also be created to fit specific needs. For details, write or phone the office of the Kensington special sales manager: Kensington Publishing Corp., 850 Third Avenue, New York, NY 10022, attn: Special Sales Department, Phone: 1-800-221-2647.

BET Books is a trademark of Black Entertainment Television, Inc. ARABESQUE, the ARABESQUE logo and the BET BOOKS logo are trademarks and registered trademarks.

First Printing: November 2004
10 9 8 7 6 5 4 3 2 1

Printed in the United States of America

For John and Gerri Roberson
You are proof that pure love
can overcome all obstacles.
Thank you for caring for mine as if he were yours,
and allowing me to care for yours as if they were mine.
Tamir and Alijah are truly blessed to have you as parents.
We are blessed to have you as friends.

ACKNOWLEDGEMENTS

As always, I must first give thanks to a loving and powerful God for His many blessings. It is because of Him that all of this has been possible.

Each time I do this, I imagine that it should be easier, but as my list of supporters grows longer and longer, the task begins to become more daunting. I have many people to thank. I fear that I may forget to give thanks to someone whose presence in my life has been invaluable, and such a slight would devastate me.

So, to my family and friends, I love you all. You each know how much you mean to me and how empty I would be without you. To those of you who have believed in my talent and have encouraged me at every step, there aren't enough words to say how much that has meant to me.

I value you all. I do not need to name you. You know who you are.

One

The Dynamic Divas, as Jeneva Douglas affectionately called them, were cutting up and acting a fool when a pitiful cry of "Party over here!" stopped them all dead in their tracks. Her best friends, Bridget Hinton and Roshawn Bradsher, both exchanged a look of blatant surprise as they spun around on their feet and turned to stare toward Jeneva as she leaned down over her son, Quincy. David Hunnicutt, a fourteen-year-old neighbor, and the only true friend Quincy had ever known, pulled the Xbox remote from Quincy's hand before reaching over to turn off the television set. Roshawn raced to turn the stereo down, muting the music the three women had just been lip-synching to.

"Quincy? What did you say, baby? Say it again for Mommy."

Thirteen-year-old Quincy Douglas rocked back and forth in his seat, staring out into space as if his mother weren't kneeling down before him, his face cupped in the palms of her hands. The young man said nothing, his gaze lost somewhere over Jeneva's left shoulder. She smiled warmly as she placed a damp kiss against his round cheek. "That's okay, baby. Mommy heard you. My baby said, 'Party over here'!" She looked up and smiled warmly at David, whose own bright blue eyes were shining with glee.

Behind her, the other two women burst into laughter. "I declare, Jay, one of these days Quincy's going to break out singing and send us all out of the room!" Roshawn exclaimed.

Bridget rocked her head from side to side. "That's twice this week, isn't it?"

Jeneva nodded. "He doesn't say anything for months, then all of a sudden we get a few words or a short sentence."

"That new school should help a lot, don't you think?" Roshawn asked.

Jeneva frowned. "I guess. I'm still not sure about this, though."

The other two women cut an eye at each other. "You made the right decision, Jeneva. Quincy will be fourteen years old in the spring and he needs to learn how to care for himself," Roshawn said.

Jeneva put out her hand, pushing her palm out toward her best friends. "Stop. I don't want to hear it. I know it's the best thing for Quincy, but I don't have to like it."

"It'll be okay, Miss Douglas. Quincy likes the new school. He'll do just fine there," David interjected, expressing genuine concern as he tried to comfort her.

Jeneva rolled her eyes. "Now, this is supposed to be Quincy's good-luck party. I told all of you not to come over here and do anything to make me cry," she said, shaking her index finger at them.

Bridget rose from her seat to go stand at the woman's side. She hugged her warmly, leaning to wrap her arms around her friend's petite frame. "We got your back, girlfriend. We'll be right here for you."

Jeneva smiled, sighing deeply as she reached out one hand to brush her palm against her son's cheek, and the other to squeeze young David's hand. The telephone ringing pulled her from the moment and sent her racing toward the kitchen to find the receiver.

"Hello?"

"Yes, hello. Jeneva Douglas, please."

"Who's calling?" she asked, not recognizing the male voice on the other end.

"My name's Mecan Tolliver. I'm calling from Hewitt House."

Jeneva paused. "This is Ms. Douglas. What can I do for you?"

"Ms. Douglas, I'm one of the directors here at Hewitt House and I was just calling to confirm that your son," the man paused, flipping through a pile of papers, "your son, Quincy, will be moving in tomorrow morning. I just wanted to make sure you didn't have any questions before you arrived."

"That's very nice of you, Mr. Tolliver, but I think we're fine. Everyone has been very helpful. Quincy and I are scheduled to be there around ten o'clock. I took the day off to make sure he gets settled in, and I'll be there to make sure he's okay with everything."

Jeneva could hear the man on the other end flipping papers as he spoke with her. "I'm sorry, but didn't they tell you that we preferred parents not remain once the resident has been checked in?" he asked. "We have found that it makes for an easier transition."

Jeneva bristled. "Well, Mrs. Montgomery did say it was easier, but I thought we had a choice." Jeneva could feel the man smiling into the receiver. "It is okay, isn't it?"

His voice was low and soothing as he responded. "It will be fine. Why don't we wait until you get here in the morning and see how things go. You may be surprised by how quickly Quincy settles into the routine. You may just find that you won't need a full day."

Jeneva hesitated as she pondered his comments. *Who is he to tell me what my son and I need?* she thought to herself. Aloud she said, "Thank you for calling, Mr. Tolliver." Irritation edged the tone of her words. "As I said, Quincy and I will be there in the morning, and I will be staying to make sure he gets settled in."

"I look forward to meeting you. Good night, Ms. Douglas."

"Good night, Mr. Tolliver."

Across the room, Quincy rose from his seat and headed into his bedroom, David leading the way. As David reached the room door, Quincy paused, stopping to turn up the music as he passed by the sound system. His head bobbed in time to the music.

Mecan Tolliver dropped the receiver back onto the hook, then leaned back into the leather of his desk chair. The upholstered fabric seemed to wrap around him as he settled his body comfortably in the seat, spinning his legs up to drop his feet against the desktop. The thick manila folder with its neatly typed label lay against his lap as he thumbed through the admittance application and all its supporting documentation. Pulling a cup of dark coffee to his full lips, he wanted to familiarize himself with young Mr. Douglas, and his family, before they arrived in the morning. Mecan wanted to make sure the boy's transition went smoothly, as much for his mother as for the student himself.

The file was proving to be an interesting read as he absorbed the details neatly packaged before him. The parents were divorced, the father noticeably absent from his son's life since the boy's birth and subsequent diagnosis. Working as an administrative assistant, Ms. Douglas had been the child's primary caregiver, but had successfully managed to provide her son with the best health services available in the state of Washington. From the many letters of reference, her devotion to the boy and his care had been substantial. Mecan bit his bottom lip, wondering if that attachment was going to prove to be a difficulty.

He'd been a director at Hewitt House for almost twelve years, and had a proven success record with the young adults entrusted to him. His unique approach to the family situations that came to the residential care facility was highly respected. Mecan was proud of that, though it had been many a parent and not the students who had proven to be his greatest challenges. The man stretched the length of his body, pulling his arms over his bald head.

On top of the folder, a photo of Quincy Douglas stared up at him, the young man's blank expression focused toward the ceiling. The attractive woman standing behind him, her hand resting against his shoulder, smiled brightly into the camera. The boy resembled his mother, both their complexions like pale honey. Old men would have called her a redbone, he thought to himself, admiring her soft, terra-cotta complexion, and the faint splattering of chocolate chip freckles against her full face. Mecan found himself staring into the woman's large round eyes, the ebony orbs shaping sensations that surprised him. Her eyes held the wisdom of a woman who had weathered many storms, yet they still held tight to an energy and laughter few possessed. As he shook the feelings from the pit of his stomach, dropping the folder back against the desk, its contents spilled out onto the thick, gray carpet, and the smiling woman continued to stare back at him from the floor.

* * *

With Quincy in bed, and their friends long gone, Jeneva dropped down into the silence that filled the room. The clock above the mantel read eleven-thirty, but she didn't feel tired, nervous tension dancing in the pit of her stomach. Turning on the television, she flipped channels on the remote, pausing when she came to a station that caught her attention. The show must be new, Jeneva thought, pushing the DETAIL button on the digital remote for the program's name. The neon lights flashed quickly, 1-800-MISSING, appearing in the lower left corner, the date and time right below it.

On the screen, that actress, Gloria Reuben, was wrapped up in the arms of the basketball player Rick Fox. Rick Fox definitely had her attention, Jeneva thought, sitting up straight in her seat to adjust the volume. She shifted a half-eaten bowl of popcorn and a bottle of flat cola out of her way as she leaned forward, pulling her legs up beneath the round of her buttocks. The music echoed subtly in the background. She watched as Rick leaned in for a kiss, noting that Gloria's expression was one of sheer bliss. The moment was surreal and Jeneva felt her breath quickening, her heartbeat racing. She couldn't remember the last time she'd been kissed like that, wondering if there had ever been a time in her thirty-three years that some man had kissed her with such complete abandon. A toothpaste commercial broke the moment and she was quick to remember that they were only Rick Fox the athlete and Gloria Reuben the actress, and the two of them weren't doing a thing but acting.

Jeneva turned off the television. After checking that the house was secured, she opened her son's bedroom door to peer inside. Quincy lay sleeping, clutching the yellow security blanket that was his constant companion. She smiled as she did an about-face and closed the door behind her.

Quincy was her pride and joy, despite the challenges fate had laid upon them. The night of his birth was burned heart-deep in her memory as she reflected back on thirteen years of history. She and Robert Lee Douglas had only been married six weeks when she found out she was pregnant. She'd been twenty years old at the time and Robert, her high school sweetheart, had been the love of her life, or so she'd thought. Robert had not welcomed fatherhood, challenged by the prospect of its inevitable responsibility. Jeneva had been sure he'd get past it once their baby boy was born. She'd been wrong. Four weeks before her due date, her water had broken, leaving her standing in a puddle of amniotic fluid as she watched Robert prance around their local bowling alley. It had been a Friday night, league night, and Robert's annoyance had been clear.

After eight hours of intense labor, Quincy Ira Douglas was delivered by an emergency cesarian section, the umbilical cord wrapped tightly around his tiny neck. Weighing in at four and a half pounds, they'd said he'd been starved of oxygen for well over a minute and the child's prognosis for survival had been dismal. Jeneva had told the doctors and nurses at Seattle Children's Hospital that God had a plan for Quincy, and nothing they said or did was going to interfere with that. Her son had beat the odds, surviving when most had given up hope. His father didn't, disappearing out of their lives before she could even get her new bundle of baby home.

Jeneva wiped the heaviness out of her eyes, staring at herself in the mirror. Time had been good to her, she thought, as she pulled her hands through the length of new growth atop her head. Two years ago

Roshawn had convinced her to cut her relaxed
tresses. Go natural, Roshawn had implored, dropping
natural-hairstyle books into her lap to review, shaking
her own shoulder-length dreadlocks at Jeneva when
she did. The ordeal had withstood the test of time and
Jeneva actually like the resulting flow of thick, tight,
russet-brown curls that framed her round face. The
style was complementary to her slight, five-foot, one-
inch stature.

Though tiny, she had meat on her bones and she
was comfortable with her full bust line, round hips,
and thick thighs. When she stepped outside her front
door, she still turned a head or two, though she
hadn't paid an ounce of attention to anyone since
Robert had left. Quincy had been all the male she had
wanted or thought she could handle. And now her
baby was going to live away from her. Thinking about
it suddenly made her want to cry. She and Quincy had
been together since day one. She had mothered him
every single second, sacrificing whatever it took to
take care of him. Her son had been her heart and the
thought of having to let him go tore at her spirit.

The man's voice, telling her that everything would
be just fine, danced across her memory. Mr. Tolliver's
tone had been soft, a gentle expression of concern.
Although the context of his straightforwardness had
annoyed her, she found his resonance comforting,
wanting to trust that whoever he was, he would safe-
guard her child since she no longer could. Dropping
down onto her knees, Jeneva whispered a prayer skyward, asking for strength to do what she had to do.
Laying her body down across the bed, she pulled her
knees into her chest and slowly let sleep consume her.

Two

As she exited the highway, Jeneva heaved a deep sigh. Their northern journey had started early in the morning, the three-hour ride from Seattle, Washington, to Hewitt House taking well over four hours. Quincy had been more restless than usual, and his discomfort had caused her to stop multiple times to let him walk around and ease the anxiety that plagued him. The ferry ride from their home to the heart of Seattle had been the most pleasant part of their trip. Quincy enjoyed the waves of water that had rushed beside them as they took in the skyline of rising architecture and the backdrop of Mt. Rainier over Elliott Bay. Back on the highway, though, his anxiety had kicked into nervous energy, and the car ride toward Vancouver and this side of the Canadian border had been annoying at best.

Hewitt House Adolescent Care Facility was situated on a twenty-acre estate of individual group homes for special-needs children with developmental disorders. Each distinct cottage housed two house parents and four to six students. There was a recreation center with a full-scale gymnasium, library, weight room, video arcade, and an Olympic-sized swimming pool. There was an educational building where students took their academic classes, and a fully staffed medical and

rehabilitation center. A private care facility, Hewitt
House was excessively expensive, but boasted an incredible success rate for the children with physical and
mental challenges it serviced. Jeneva had mortgaged
the modest Bainbridge Island home her parents had
left her to pay for two years of tuition and housing costs.

Quincy had barely been a year old when Jeneva ac-
cepted that he would never be like other children.
When other mothers were noting their children's beginning steps and first words, Quincy hadn't bothered
to lift his head yet or roll from side to side. He'd been
a quiet baby, rarely crying, never smiling, and always
staring out into space as if he saw something no one
else could visualize. Quincy's first steps came well after
his fifth birthday, his first words when he was almost
nine. The long list of labels each specialist and doctor
had tagged on his condition only reinforced Jeneva's
commitment to her son, serving to further cement
her parental bond. Now here he was, thirteen years
old, on the verge of manhood, and she knew she had
to let him go.

Standing almost five-feet, eight-inches tall, Quincy
had acquired his father's height. The changes from
child to adult were happening rapidly and Jeneva had
been forced to face that she no longer had the skills
to nurture her son's special needs to get him to adult-
hood. For the first time in a very long time, she had
needed to ask for help and Hewitt House had answered the call. In the seat beside her, Quincy
hummed, a monotone drone that had begun to grate
on Jeneva's worn nerves. Reaching a palm out to
stroke his forearm, she cooed softly, telling the boy
once again how much he was going to like living at
Hewitt House, assuring him and herself of her commitment to visit him weekly.

Turning off the main road, Jeneva looked from the

printed directions that rested atop the console toward each cottage, searching for number 29B. The small, white structure sat at the bottom of a cul-de-sac, the lawns around it perfectly manicured. Two houses sat to the right of it and a third to its left, each as meticulously landscaped. A potpourri of lush grass, blooming flowers, and shrubbery laid like a welcoming mat from the street to the front doors.

Parking her 1999 Ford Taurus in the driveway, Jeneva exited the vehicle, walking to the passenger side to help Quincy unlatch his seatbelt. Lifting his lean legs out of the car, she braced her feet beneath her as she helped to pull him out and onto his feet, then closed the door and watched as the young man raced across the lawn, dropping to the ground to roll his body against the carpet of green grass. Although his expression was stoic, the muscles in his face locked in a perpetual frown, Jeneva could sense that he was happy, and she smiled, knowing that in his own way, her son was smiling right back at her.

A voice calling her name pulled her from her thoughts and she looked around to see from where the sound had come.

"Ms. Douglas, hello!" Mecan called down to her, a raised hand waving excitedly as he stood atop the home's roof.

Jeneva raised her eyes toward the rising roofline, lifting the flat of her hand to shade her face from the sun.

"Hello!" she called back, trying to avoid the blinding rays of sunlight as she focused on the man who towered in the distance.

"I'll be right down!" he called back, lifting himself onto a ladder perched against the front of the building.

Jeneva watched as the handsome black man scaled the length of the ladder, strolling to where she stood. Quincy still lay playing in the grass.

"Hello," Mecan said, smiling widely, wiping his palms against his pant leg before extending his hand in greeting. "I'm Mecan Tolliver. Sorry about that. I was just checking the shingles. They say we've got rain coming and we had a leak a few weeks back. Wanted to make sure everything's okay," he said, gesturing toward where he'd been standing on the roof.

"That's quite all right. It's nice to meet you, Mr. Tolliver," she said as her own hand disappeared in the grip of his fingers. His other hand reached out to tap her shoulder, then fell against the back of her hand as he squeezed the appendage gently between his large palms.

"Please, it's Mecan," he said with a broad grin that filled his dark face. "Rhymes with pecan, but most folks just call me Mac."

Jeneva studied him, nodding her head as he spoke. Quincy had risen to his feet, coming to stand beside her. The boy rocked from side to side, humming softly to himself.

"This is my son, Quincy. Quincy, this is Mr. Tolliver. Can you say hello, please?"

Mecan extended his hand again, reaching to pull Quincy into a handshake. "Hello, Quincy. Call me Mac, okay? Welcome to your new home. We're very excited that you're going to be living with us."

Quincy's eyes rested on the man for one quick second before rising to that spot in the sky he liked so much.

"Why don't we go inside and get settled," Mecan said, reaching for the luggage Jeneva had pulled from the trunk of her car.

As Jeneva followed, she studied him intently. Mecan Tolliver was a large man, standing somewhere close to six feet tall. As she stood beside him, the top of Jeneva's head grazed a spot just above his biceps where the length of muscle ran into his shoulders. Everything about him was broad, beginning with the span of his shoulders and his thick chest. The sudden thought that his chest was probably as solid as stone touched Jeneva and she felt herself gasp lightly. His gray sport shirt with the Hewitt House logo was damp from perspiration. There was a circle of moisture in the dead center of his back, just above the waistband of his jeans where one article of clothing was tucked neatly into the other. Jeneva blushed as she found herself staring at his rear end, his jeans fitting like a second skin against his well-rounded behind.

Inside the home, they were greeted by a young man with Down syndrome, a wide grin filling the round, telltale features of his ivory complexion.

"Hello," he said loudly, his smile filling the room. "My name's Joel. Hello."

Jeneva smiled back. "Hello, Joel."

"Hello," he repeated, coming to take her hand to guide her toward the seats in the living room.

"Joel, this is Quincy. Quincy is going to be your new roommate," Mecan said, guiding Quincy toward Joel. Standing behind her son, Mecan lifted Quincy's arm so the two boys could shake hands. Jeneva thought her son responded admirably as the other boy pumped his arm up and down excitedly.

"Hello, Quincy," Joel said brightly. "I'm going to be your friend."

"Did you finish your chores, Joel?" Mecan asked, looking at the boy sternly.

Not breaking his grin, Joel nodded his head enthusiastically. "I did, Mac. I made the bed and put the trash in the big bag."

"Very good!" Mecan exclaimed, leaning to give the child a warm hug. "Joel, will you show Quincy where his room is? You can give him a tour around the house while I speak with Ms. Douglas."

"Okay, Mac," Joel responded, pulling Quincy along by the hand, still smiling brightly.

The two adults watched as the boys made their way out of the common living space toward the back of the home, Joel chattering as fast as he could form the words. Mecan gestured for Jeneva to take a seat, pointing to the brown chenille sofa in the center of the living room.

"I understand Mrs. Montgomery has given you the fifty-cent tour and of course detailed our programs, but do you have any questions for me, Ms. Douglas?"

"Please, call me Jeneva," she answered. The smile she'd been holding dimmed ever so slightly. "Are you one of the house parents here?"

"Only temporarily. I'll be here in the home for the next two months or so. My official title is director of student development and institutional advancement. I think you met Juan Santiago?"

Jeneva nodded her head. "At the last meeting with the administration," she responded.

Mecan continued. "Juan is the regular house father for this unit, but he's recovering from foot surgery and won't be back for a few weeks. His sister Natalia is still the house mother. She's with our two other boys at their swim lessons right now. You'll get to see her before you leave. I will be responsible for all decisions we make about Quincy. I'm his primary adviser. I will meet weekly with his teachers, his therapist, his doctors, and you, when necessary. I'll be monitoring his progress and making the appropriate recommendations as I see fit. If you ever have any concerns, then I'll be the one to get the answers for you."

"I thought Mrs. Montgomery was going to do that?"

"She was promoted to staff educational director since you were here last."

Jeneva nodded again, beginning to feel as if her head were a loose ball bearing on top of her neck. Looking around the warmly decorated room, she was pleased with what she saw. The walls were painted a bright yellow, framed geometric images in even brighter primary colors decorating the walls. A work-table sat in the corner, the top covered with an assortment of blocks, and there were two bookcases brimming over with books. The room was clean and the whole house smelled fresh, the faint scent of lemon and pine sweeping through the air.

"Do the boys have a television?" Jeneva asked.

Mecan shook his head. "No. I don't believe in television. I don't think it's good stimulus for them. There's a big screen in the main recreation center and we have movie night once a month. They're allowed to watch then if they've earned the credits."

"Quincy likes video games," Jeneva said aloud, thinking about the Xbox and assorted games she'd packed in the sports bag at her feet. She touched the canvas sack with the toe of her low-heeled pump.

Mecan smiled at her, the bend of his thick lips filling his face. Jeneva couldn't help but smile back.

"Quincy will have more than enough to keep him occupied. I assure you he won't miss the video games. We want him to learn to interact with other people. He can't do that if his only focus continues to be the television."

"He likes to be sung to at night and he's scared of thunder," she said, her top lip starting to quiver as she found herself fighting back tears.

Unconsciously, Mecan reached out toward her, dropping his hand against her bare knee. He squeezed it gently, the gesture intended to be comforting. Suddenly embarrassed, he pulled back as if burned. "I'm sorry. I didn't mean to be so forward."

Jeneva blushed. "No. I'm the one who should be apologizing. I didn't mean to get emotional. It's just that . . ." she paused, ". . . he's my baby," she said finally, dropping her chin against her chest.

Mecan nodded his head, rising to his feet. "Why don't we go see his room? You can help him get unpacked while Joel and I get lunch ready."

"The boys help with meals?" she asked, fighting to regain her composure.

"We teach our kids how to do a lot of things. By the time Quincy leaves us he'll be able to live independently and be totally self-sufficient."

Mecan continued to explain all the things Quincy would be involved in. The rules were stringent and he stressed that they were necessary to teach the students discipline. In the room, Quincy had lain his body across an unmade bed, rocking himself against the mattress. Jeneva reached out to draw a hand along his back, but Mecan stopped her.

His tone was authoritative as he began to give out instructions. "Ms. Douglas, that dresser under the window is Quincy's. If you'll please unpack his clothing for him. Socks go in the top drawer, briefs and T-shirts in the second, tops and sweaters in the third, and pants in the bottom drawer, please. His personal items can go on top of the desk over there. Quincy and I will put them away later."

He turned toward Joel. "I think grilled cheese sandwiches and tomato soup will be good for lunch. What do you think, Joel?" he asked.

"I want tuna fish," the young man responded.

Mecan turned toward Quincy. "Do you want tuna fish, Quincy, or would you prefer grilled cheese?"

Quincy continued to rock, not saying anything.

"He likes tuna fish," Jeneva said, nodding for him.

"Well, tuna it will be then. Joel, you get to go start lunch. I'll be right there to help."

"Okay, Mac," the young man said enthusiastically.

"Remember the rules for the can opener," Mecan said, tousling the boy's bright red hair.

"Be careful of your fingers and watch what you're doing," Joel replied.

"Very good, son."

Joel gave them all two thumbs up as he exited the room.

Turning back to Quincy, Mecan pulled him to his feet. "Quincy, you and I are going to make up the bed while your mom puts your clothes away. Then I'm going to show you where the bathroom is and where you will put all your personal stuff."

Jeneva watched as Mecan pulled a twin bedsheet into his hands. Standing behind her son once again, he guided the boy's hands as they made the bed together. Quincy still stared off into space as he allowed Mecan to pull him along from corner to corner. When they were through, he guided the boy and his toiletry bag down the hallway, leaving her to finish the last of the unpacking.

Dropping the last of her son's jeans and khakis into the bottom drawer, Jeneva ran her hands along the freshly washed fabric, still fighting not to let her tears fall. When she heard Mecan returning, still pulling Quincy along beside him, she wiped at the moisture in her eyes with the back of her hand.

"Are you hungry, Jeneva?" he asked, calling her by her first name. The sound of it carried by his deep voice was pleasant to her ears.

She shook her head, fearful that if she spoke, her voice would betray her sadness. Back in the living room, they heard the chatter of voices coming through the door and a woman calling out Mecan's name.

"In the back bedroom, Natalia," he answered, then turned back to where she and Quincy stood. "That's the rest of the family, Quincy. Why don't you come meet everyone."

As Mecan turned out of the doorway, Jeneva was surprised to see Quincy follow obediently behind. Pausing briefly, she turned to follow also.

Back in the living room, a robust Hispanic woman with deep black hair pulled into a tight ponytail greeted them. She smiled, reaching out to pull Jeneva into a warm hug. "Hello, Mama," she said. "It's very nice to see you again."

"It's good to see you, too, Natalia," Jeneva said, her newly found voice an octave lower.

"Hello, Quincy," the woman said, reaching to give him a warm hug, too. "It's so good to see you again. Welcome to your new home."

Quincy stood like deadweight within the woman's warm embrace. When she finally let him go, he strolled back over to Mecan and stood by the man's side.

"It's tuna fish for lunch. Joel picked this afternoon," the man said, pointing to the kitchen. "I was just about to help."

"I'll go do that," Natalia said, calling all the boys to follow her. "Michael, Billy, Quincy, let's go help with lunch."

Michael and Billy, the other two house residents, beat her into the kitchen. Quincy didn't budge. Mecan placed a broad hand on the boy's shoulder and pushed him in the direction of the kitchen. "Quincy, we need you to help us make lunch," he said, following behind the boy.

"Can I do something to help?" Jeneva asked.

Looking over his shoulder, Mecan shook his head.

"Just let me get Quincy started," he said. "I'll be right back."

A few minutes later, he had followed her out the front door as she stood in the yard staring out at the landscape. Walking up behind her, he appraised her warmly, taking in the feminine lines of her figure. The green plaid skirt she wore fit her nicely, accentuating the fullness of her hips. Her legs were thick, the toned muscle indicative of a faithful runner. As she turned to face him, her arms crossed over her chest, he was drawn to the abundance of her bustline, concealed behind a starched white blouse. The weak bend of her lips pulled at his heartstrings and he suddenly wanted to draw her close and hold her. He found the sensation disturbing.

"Are you all right?" he managed to ask, suddenly self-conscious.

"I didn't expect this to be so final."

"It's not. Quincy is going to be fine. He just doesn't need to be handled with kid gloves right now. You've always done everything for him and he's going to have to learn how to do things for himself."

The tears spilled from Jeneva's eyes. She wiped the moisture from her face, embarrassed. "I'm sorry."

Mecan smiled. "Right now Quincy is folding napkins. And he's doing a good job. Right after lunch he's going to meet his teachers and his speech therapist. Later I plan to take him and the boys fishing so they can have some time getting to know one another. He's going to be fine."

"He's never been fishing."

"He's going to love it." Mecan's smile caressed her. "What can I do?"

"Right now I want you to come sit and eat lunch with us. Afterward you and Quincy are going to say good-bye. Then you need to go to the admittance office and finish the last of the paperwork to officially register Quincy. I will call you tonight to give you a progress report, but you don't need to worry. Quincy is more than ready for this. He might not be able to express it, but you can see it in his eyes that he's excited." Mecan brushed his hand against her shoulder. "Do you have the contact numbers for our parents' support group?"

Jeneva nodded her head.

Mecan continued. "Don't be afraid to call them. We have a great group of parents who have already been through this. They're here to help you. I know it's hard. Your thirteen-year-old son is now in a position to assert his independence and you've never had to deal with it before. But trust me when I tell you that you will be fine, too. You've made the right choices for your son."

Jeneva met his gaze, staring deeply into his dark brown eyes. She could tell a lot about this man folks called Mac. The emotions brimming past his long lashes spoke volumes. Mecan Tolliver wore his emotions on his sleeve. She could feel the compassion he had for her and her child. She sensed his understanding of her hurt. Although he appeared hard with his coal-black complexion—that deep, blue-black some people feared—there was nothing hard about him. She could tell his heart was soft, even larger in stature than his body, and with few ills. She found herself drawn to his hands, massive paws of lightly callused tissue. The dark ebony skin was dry, visibly crying for moisture. She sensed he enjoyed manual labor and reasoned that he battled to keep his nails free from dirt, probably losing the fight more times than not. But his touch was soft, she thought to herself, remembering his hands holding on to hers, his palm resting against her knee. His touch was almost a whisper against the amber of her skin. As he led her back into the house, Jeneva couldn't help but think that some woman must ache for the feel of his hands against her skin, the wanting a sweet reminder of how Mecan Tolliver could fill her emptiness with the largess of himself.

Three

Jeneva's tears dropped like a rush of water from a broken faucet. She cried from the moment she pulled her car past the gates of Hewitt House and headed toward the highway until she reached her exit, turning left at the light toward home. She'd been away from Quincy for less than an average workday and the hurt of his absence felt almost intolerable. David and his mother standing in her driveway only added to her pain and she choked back the tears as she tried to compose herself. Shifting the car into park, she willed herself to smile as she exited the vehicle. David stood shyly behind his mother as MaryAnne Hunnicutt waved at her in greeting.

"MaryAnne, David. How are you?"

MaryAnne leaned to give her a warm hug, embracing her tightly. "We're fine. We came to see how you're doing."

Jeneva dropped the canvas bag of electronic toys to the ground beside her. She shrugged her shoulders. "As well as can be expected. Quincy's all settled in and when I left he was getting ready to go fishing."

David beamed, nodding the excessive length of his blond hair in her direction. "Cool. He'll like that."

Jeneva chuckled at the boy's enthusiasm. "That's what I was told. Are you okay, David?" she asked.

David shrugged, pushing his narrow shoulders up toward the bright blue sky. "I'm going to miss Quincy. Never got the chance to beat him at Halo."

"Well, he'll get to come home in a few weeks and if it's okay with your mom, you can go with me to visit him one weekend."

"I'd like that," David said as he bounced a basketball against the blacktop. "Can I, Mom?"

"It's 'May I' and, yes, you definitely may." MaryAnne nodded her own blond locks at her son. "Why don't you go on back home. I'll be there shortly."

"Okay." Pulling the basketball under his arm, David paused briefly, then strode over to stand beside Jeneva. "Quincy was real happy to be doing this, Ms. Douglas. He couldn't say it, but I knew." Standing taller than she did, David leaned to kiss the side of Jeneva's cheek, smiling sweetly as he turned from her to his mother, bouncing the basketball in his hands. The two women watched as the young man made his way across the connecting yards, stopping to throw his ball into the hoop attached to his garage. Jeneva wiped a tear against the back of her hand. MaryAnne turned her attention back to Jeneva. "If I can do anything for you, you'll let me know, won't you?"

Jeneva leaned to give the woman a hug. "Thank you, but I'll be fine."

"I know that. You're one of the strongest women I know, Jeneva, and I love you to death. Without you and Quincy I don't know how David and I would have made it when his father died. So whatever you need, anything, you let me know."

"I promise. Right now I'm going to go soak in a very hot tub, maybe have myself a glass of wine." She smiled, inhaling deeply. "I'm sorry you missed the party last night. Did David tell you Quincy talked?"

"He did and I wish I could have been there. Work-

ing double shifts at the hospital is about to wear me
down."

As the two women stood chatting, Bridget pulled
her silver BMW into the driveway, parking behind
Jeneva. She greeted them both cheerily as she made
her way to where they stood.

"Hey, girl. Hi, MaryAnne. How are you?"

"I'm fine, Bridget. How about you?"

"Good as gold. Just came to check on my girl here."

Jeneva rolled her eyes. "I keep telling you people
that I'm okay."

"Can't we worry about you?" Bridget asked. "Isn't
that what friends do?"

MaryAnne nodded. "That's what I was just telling
her."

Jeneva leaned to pick up her bags, adjusting her
purse under her arm as she clutched the rest of her
belongings in her left fist. "Okay, I'm going inside
now. You two are starting to gang up on me."

Bridget laughed. "Would we do that?"

MaryAnne hugged her one last time. "Let me go
make David some dinner. I will call and check on you
tomorrow, okay?"

"Thanks, MaryAnne. And tell David I said thank
you. He's been a good friend to Quincy and I really
appreciate that. He's a great kid."

MaryAnne winked, waving good-bye as she made
her way out of the yard. Bridget turned to Jeneva,
pulling a silk blazer off her narrow shoulders, her
bone-straight, shoulder-length hair falling against her
shoulders. "So, what's for dinner?"

Jeneva cut her eyes toward her friend. "Boone's
Farm strawberry wine and a hot bath. "

Bridget laughed heartily, the length of her five-foot,
six-inch body quivering with glee. "Boone's Farm?"

"What's wrong with that?" Jeneva asked as they

headed toward the front door and into the house. She dropped her keys and purse to the oak table in the entranceway, setting the canvas sports bag beside them.

Bridget followed behind her as they made their way through the living room and into the kitchen. "Not a thing except you don't drink. At least, not much. Boone's Farm is a little daring for you."

"That's why I'm drinking strawberry wine."

Bridget laughed. "Girl, you're a mess. So how did things go today?"

"They went well. Quincy took right to the place. I think he really likes the house parents," she said, pulling a wood bar stool beneath her rear end. Bridget took the seat across from her.

"Those are the two you were telling us about last time, right? The Santiagos?"

Jeneva shook her head. "Natalia is there, but he has a new house father for a short time. A man named Mecan. Mecan Tolliver. They call him Mac."

"Mac? Is he cute?"

"I declare, Bridget. What does his being cute have to do with anything?"

"I was just asking."

"He's very nice. I think he'll be a good influence on Quincy," she said, turning her gaze away from Bridget's.

Her friend studied her curiously and Jeneva could feel the color rising to her cheeks. "What are you staring at?" she asked.

"You."

"Please." Jeneva hopped off her seat to peer into the refrigerator. "You hungry?"

"No. Tell me more about Mac."

Pushing and pulling at the contents inside the fridge, Jeneva ignored the woman, pretending to be distracted by her search.

"Don't ignore me. You liked this man, didn't you?"

Closing the refrigerator door, Jeneva rolled her eyes at her friend. "Of course I liked him. I've entrusted my child to him. I should like him."

"No. Uh-uh. There's something you're not telling. Spill it." Bridget tapped at the empty seat before her. "I want all the details. What does he look like?"

Jeneva took a seat, amused by her friend's excitement. "He's okay, I guess."

"What does he look like?" Bridget asked again. "I want a detailed description."

"Look, counselor, this is not one of your courtrooms. Why the interrogation?"

"Don't get snippy with me. Just give up the facts. Does the man have two heads, four eyes, half a nose? What?"

Jeneva laughed. "No. One head and no obvious defects. But he's tall."

"How tall?"

"Six feet. Six feet—one, maybe."

"Okay. Go on," Bridget said, motioning with her hands for Jeneva to continue.

Jeneva grinned. "He was fine, okay. Is that what you want to hear? Brother is tall, dark, and to die for."

"I knew it," Bridget exclaimed, jumping to her feet. She snapped her fingers above her head.

"Girl, please. He's nice-looking and he was very pleasant. That's all."

"Is he single?"

"I didn't ask."

"Why not?"

"Bridget, I was there to drop off my son. I wasn't on the prowl for a man."

"You should be. It's been how long since you had a man in your life? Thirteen years? Jay, you are long overdue for a man. Need to get you a little somethin'-

somethin', now that Quincy's gone off to school. You can start acting like the single, available woman that you are."

"I do not need a man. I have a child to raise," Jeneva replied, reciting the mantra she had become known for. "My child is my only priority."

"Well, it's time you became a priority. Quincy's going to be fine. You, on the other hand, will probably dry up and wither away if you don't do something for yourself soon. I'm sure a big, fine man named Mac could be just the special treat you need."

Jeneva shook her head at her friend, a wide smile gracing her face. "Where's my Boone's Farm? You're talking crazy now."

Bridget laughed. "So does Mac have any unique qualities we need to know about? Anything else you might like to share?"

Jeneva pulled two tumblers down from an upper cabinet, then filled them both half full with the pink fluid that smelled of ripe strawberries. She passed one to Bridget who lifted it in a mock toast before pulling the glass to her lips.

Sitting back down, Jeneva's mind wandered momentarily. As a grin spread across her face, she found herself chuckling heartily. "Well," she said, taking a deep breath, "he sure knows how to work a ladder. And there's nothing like a man in a tight pair of jeans climbing up and down a ladder."

"Now that's what I'm talking about." Bridget giggled. "Tell me some more about Mr. Mac and them tight jeans!"

As Jeneva lay soaking in a hot tub, she was thankful for Bridget and the distraction her good friend had provided. They'd laughed for hours, and before

Jeneva realized it, the clock on her kitchen wall read ten forty-five. Bridget had hugged her before leaving, making her promise to join her and Roshawn for dinner Friday night.

Jeneva smiled. The three women had been the best of friends since grade school. Both had been in her wedding and she and Bridget had been in Roshawn's. They'd laughed and cried together more times than Jeneva cared to count. From their numerous relationship disasters to their career successes and everything else in between, they'd been three divas who stood firm in their support of one another.

When she had Quincy, both women had come to the hospital to drive her home. When Roshawn's daughter, Ming, was christened, the child was blessed with two godmothers who'd promised to be there for her whenever the need arose. Jeneva's mother had only given birth to one child, but Jeneva felt that she had two sisters who were closer than any blood relative could ever be.

She sighed, staring at the melting candle on the countertop. Mecan had promised to call her, to let her know how Quincy was doing. It was well after eleven and no call had come. Jeneva fought the urge to pick up the telephone to call the school herself. Just as she was berating the man under her breath, her telephone rang. Lifting her body out of the cooling water, she wrapped a plush towel around her naked frame and raced into the bedroom for the phone.

"Hello?" she said, breathing heavily.

"Jeneva. It's Mecan. I'm sorry. I didn't wake you, did I?"

"No. I'm glad you called. In fact, I was starting to get a major attitude that you hadn't."

Mecan laughed. "I'm sorry. Once the house quieted down, I wanted to finish some paperwork. The time got away from me."

"How's my son?"

"He's just fine. He went right to sleep. I think the day wore him out. You should have seen him. He caught two fish. We couldn't get him away from the pond, he was having such a good time."

"Wow. I wish I could have been there."

"You will, just be patient," Mecan said. Concern wrapped around his words as he asked, "How are you holding up?"

Jeneva dropped down against the side of her bed, pulling the towel tighter around her. "I don't know. I miss my child. And I feel like a horrible mother because I spent the evening laughing with my best friend. Does that make sense?"

Mecan nodded into the receiver. "It does. That's why I want you to contact the support group. I hope you don't mind but I called one of the members and asked her to contact you. Her name's Ivy Houston. She has a daughter who's been with us for five years and will be graduating this spring. I think she'll be a lot of help to you."

"Thank you. That was very nice of you."

"I don't want you to worry about Quincy. I promise I'll take good care of him."

Tears rose to Jeneva's eyes as she struggled to find her words.

"And don't cry," Mecan interjected, sensing the wave of emotion that washed over her. "If you need me, call anytime. Do you have my cell phone number?"

"I think so," Jeneva answered, knowing full well that she had circled the number in bright red ink on the business card he'd given her. "In fact, I'm positive you gave it to me," she said.

"Well, please feel free to use it. That's what I'm here for."

"I promised Quincy I'd be there to see him this weekend, but the office told me I should wait at least two weeks before I come back."

"I agree. He needs time to get comfortable with his new routine. It doesn't sound like it, but it will be much easier if you give him the opportunity to do that."

"May I call him at least?"

"Tell you what, I will let him call you Sunday morning. Will that work?"

"I guess. But I'm coming next weekend and I don't care what any of you people say," she said, her tone intense.

Mecan chuckled lightly under his breath. "I look forward to seeing you again, Jeneva."

She smiled. "Good night, Mac."

Mecan made one last sweep of the house, checking that all the boys were fast asleep and comfortable. Michael had kicked his blankets to the floor, and Mecan retrieved them, easing them back against the young man's body. Switching off the last of the lights, he retired to his room, and crawled into his own bed, wrapping a thick arm beneath his head as he lay staring out into the darkness.

The woman had gotten under his skin. Mecan didn't need to say it out loud or have anyone else point it out to him. He could feel it. He couldn't shake the feeling that Jeneva Douglas was crawling just below the surface of his flesh, caressing every nerve ending in his system. The feeling was unsettling, an emotion he'd never experienced in all his thirty-five years.

Whatever he was feeling was more than sexual attraction. It was nothing as basic as the contact that had sent a shimmer of warmth across his groin. This was more intimate, deeply personal, hitting him broadside like a jackhammer slamming into his heart and head. He took a deep breath, inhaling air into his bloodstream, wishing the sensation away. Rolling onto his side, he blew air back out, understanding that her presence still lingered along his muscles, holding tight, refusing to let go.

Four

Jeneva was grateful to be finished with her run as she made her last lap around the small high school track. Slowing down to a light jog and then to a brisk walk, she was pleased with her progress, sucking in oxygen like a well-deserved reward. She loved to run. She'd been a star athlete on her high school cross-country team, running circles around the competition. The last trimester of her pregnancy and that first year with her newborn son had been the only times in her life she'd not run religiously. When she'd resumed training, her body had become dependent on the regime to keep her stress levels balanced.

Jeneva came to a stop, bending forward at the waist as she reached her palms to the top of her toes, stretching the muscles down the back of her legs. Standing upright, she pulled her right heel toward her buttocks, grasping her foot in her hand as she pulled the appendage backward, stretching her thigh. She repeated the gesture on the other side, then rotated her shoulders skyward. She felt energized, leaning her head from one side to the other. Glancing down at her watch, Jeneva realized she was just minutes away from missing Quincy's first call home. Turning an about-face, she sprinted to her car and headed for home.

The telephone was ringing as Jeneva entered the house. She dropped her keys and a sweat-stained towel onto the floor in the entranceway.

"Hello?"

"Jeneva, good morning. It's Mecan Tolliver."

"Mecan, hello. How are you?"

"I'm doing very well this morning. How about yourself?"

"Anxious. How's my son?"

Mecan laughed. "Quincy's just fine. He's right here. Hold on while I give him the telephone."

Jeneva dropped onto the sofa, kicking off her sneakers as she pulled her legs beneath her. In the background, she could hear Mecan encouraging Quincy to speak into the telephone. She could hear her son breathing excitedly into the receiver.

"Hi, Quincy. It's Mommy. How's my baby?"

Quincy gurgled on the other end.

"Mommy misses you. Mommy misses you very much. I promise I'm coming to see you next week. Okay? Mommy loves you, baby."

Her son hummed on the other end, then dropped the receiver to the ground as he bolted outside to join the other students.

"Jeneva? Are you there?" Mecan asked.

"I am. What happened?"

"The boys are playing frisbee. Quincy's gone out to play."

Jeneva smiled, shaking her head from side to side. "You must think I'm crazy."

"Not at all. You're not the first mother who's wanted to speak to her child."

"But mine can't talk back."

"Neither could the others," Mecan say with a wry laugh. "Doesn't mean you shouldn't try."

"Well, thank you. I appreciate you calling me."

"It was my pleasure. Please feel free to call me if you have any concerns."

"I appreciate that. I'm actually coming up on Wednesday evening for one of those parent meetings. Ivy Houston called and invited me for a new-parent potluck dinner."

On the other end, Mecan beamed. "That's great. I'm bringing beanie-weenies. They're my specialty. I'll be sure to look for you."

"Beanie-weenies?" Jeneva said, laughing boldly.

"Wait until you taste them. You'll want the recipe."

Jeneva nodded into the receiver. "I'm sure I will. Good-bye, Mecan. I'll see you Wednesday."

"Bye."

The ride seemed shorter, Jeneva thought, as she parked her car in the side lot by the Hewitt House recreation building. Stepping out of the vehicle, she adjusted the line of her black wool slacks and matching sweater and reached into the rear seat for a dish of candied yams adorned with mini marshmallows, one of her mother's favorite recipes. The metal container was still warm and her hands felt good wrapped around the dish, warding off the chill beginning to blow outside. Nervous energy guided Jeneva into the brightly decorated recreation room, the walls and ceiling covered with red and yellow crepe-paper streamers.

From behind a small folding table, Ivy Houston greeted Jeneva cheerfully, a large smile filling the woman's round face.

"Hello. You must be Ms. Douglas," she said, rising from her seat to extend her hand in Jeneva's direction. "I'm Ivy." She pointed to the nametag on her suit jacket.

"Hello, Ivy. Please, call me Jeneva."

Taking the dish from Jeneva's hands, Ivy passed it to another parent as she gestured for someone to come relieve her at the welcome table. "Let me introduce you to everyone," she said, pulling Jeneva along by the hand as she guided her into the main room.

A smile was frozen upon Jeneva's face as she shook hands and greeted the other parents, who welcomed her warmly. Before she knew it, she was engaged in animated conversation with a couple whose son was in Quincy's educational class and a woman whose daughter had started the program the same week as her son. Ivy had pressed a cup of hot apple cider in her hand before returning to her duties as greeter. It wasn't until Jeneva heard his name being called across the room that she realized Mecan Tolliver had arrived, filling the space with his presence. She smiled shyly as turned to watch him enter. He greeted each of the parents personally as he exchanged pleasantries and passed out hugs.

Turning back to her conversation, Jeneva tried not to appear excited as he made his way over to where she stood in discussion. Her heart was beating fast as she balled up her hands into tight fists at her sides, perspiration rising to her palms.

"Mecan, how's it going?" Brian Wills said, extending his hand to Mecan. "It's good to see you."

"You, too, Brian," Mecan responded, the duo pumping palms quickly. Mecan leaned to kiss Susan Wills's cheek. "How are you, Susan?"

"Just fine," the woman responded.

Mecan turned to face Jeneva. "Ms. Douglas, welcome," he said politely, a touch of formality to his tone. "It's good to see you again."

"Thank you, Mr. Tolliver. I'm glad I was able to make it."

Mecan could feel a pool of nervousness rising in his stomach. He smiled widely, fighting to shake the feeling. "Did you have an opportunity to see Quincy when you arrived?" he asked.

"I did. I stopped by the house before I came here. Natalia had the boys preparing dinner. Quincy was stirring the potatoes."

Mecan nodded. "I offered to leave them some of my famous beans but they declined."

Brian laughed. "Obviously they've had those beans of yours, Mecan."

"What's wrong with my beans?"

Susan giggled. "Nothing a stomach pump won't cure. Avoid them at all costs," she said, tilting her head toward Jeneva.

"You people are giving this poor woman a bad impression of me."

"Would we do that?" Brian said, still laughing. "We were just trying to warn her about your cooking."

"I'm insulted."

Jeneva smiled as she glanced from one to the other, enjoying the exchange between them. Occasionally her gaze would fall on Mecan, and she fought not to stare at the man.

"Well, let me finish saying hello," he finally said, reaching out a large hand to squeeze Jeneva's arm. "I'm sure we'll talk again before the evening is over." His eyes were hopeful.

Jeneva could not help but stare into them. "I'm sure," she said, smiling sweetly, then watching as he turned and walked away.

"He's quite the character," Brian said, drawing Jeneva back into the conversation.

"Mecan's a sweetheart," his wife added.

"Mr. Tolliver's been a great help," Jeneva replied.

Brian winked. "And his beans really aren't that bad.

Not bad at all," he said with a deep chuckle. "We just love to give him a hard time. Beans are all Mecan ever brings to these potluck dinners."

The trio continued conversing, making room as two other couples came to join them. Jeneva enjoyed the fellowship of the other parents, but she could not stop herself from searching out Mecan across the room. She watched as he cajoled and kidded from one conversation to another, noting how well liked he was. The parents had great respect for him and they shared this eagerly, wanting Jeneva to know how much they valued him and the other staff at Hewitt House.

For a quick moment, her eyes caught his gaze. His stare was piercing, she thought, even if the intriguing man was standing some fifty feet away from her. The eye contact did not last long as Jeneva dropped her gaze to the ground, acutely aware of a rise in her body temperature. Caught off guard himself, Mecan heaved a deep breath, forcing a laugh at a bad joke a parent had just shared with them.

He caught up with her as she was preparing to make her departure, stopping first to thank Ivy Houston for inviting her. The woman had pulled Jeneva into a warm hug as Mecan approached. Mecan clasped her elbow.

"Are you leaving so soon, Jeneva?" Mecan asked.

Jeneva nodded. "Yes. I have a bit of a ride back home. I've had a great time, though. I was just telling Ivy how pleased I am that she called me."

Ivy smiled. "We parents have to support each other. Call me anytime. No matter what."

"Thank you," Jeneva said as the woman scurried off to say good-bye to another family who was leaving.

A painful silence filled the space between Mecan and Jeneva. Jeneva's gaze flickered around the room as she struggled with the sudden awkwardness, averting her stare from his.

Mecan cleared his throat and looked over his shoulder, then back to Jeneva. "I'm sorry," he said, "I'm not usually at a loss for words."

Jeneva smiled, turning to glance up at him. "Neither am I."

"May I walk you to your car?"

"I'd like that. Thank you."

Reaching for her elbow a second time, Mecan guided her out the door and down the front steps of the building. His touch sent a shiver of excitement through her body.

"What a beautiful night," Jeneva said, shaking the sensation that was consuming her. She stared up at the dark sky and the full moon reigning in the distance.

Mecan nodded. "It is nice. Feels more like the end of spring than the beginning of winter."

As they approached her vehicle, Jeneva found herself staring at him again, their eyes locked. A rise of red-toned clouds had filled the sky, masking the glow of the moon, and Jeneva thought it looked like the sky had turned into one large shimmering candle. The moment was enchanting and Mecan's presence made her feel giddy.

"Thank you," she muttered, searching for her voice as she eased her car keys into the door and unlocked it.

Mecan nodded. "Drive safely," he said as he held the door open for her.

Jeneva smiled. "I will. Thank you." She paused, her hand resting on the edge of the car window. "Will you call me?" she asked. "To keep me posted about Quincy," she added, as if her question needed clarifying.

"No problem. It would be my pleasure."

Jeneva gave him one last smile, her expression gently caressing his face. "Good night, Mac."

* * *

Opening the front door, Jeneva was glad to finally be home. The ride back to the empty house seemed to have taken longer and her tired body was feeling the effects. After a quick check of the answering machine, Jeneva dragged her body into her bedroom. Her clothes lay sprawled across the floor as she dropped herself into bed, pulling the covers up beneath her chin.

Hours later, Jeneva sat up in the bed and reached for the television remote. The credits for the movie she'd watched were scrolling across the screen, so she flipped stations, stopping on an old *Good Times* rerun she'd seen so many times, she knew the dialogue by heart. The screen faded to black as she hit the OFF button and lay back against the pillows.

She reflected on the evening, and Mecan, and how the man had fascinated her. She was surprised by how she'd reacted when he'd arrived. She'd been like a schoolgirl in the presence of her first crush. When he'd walked her to her car, she'd been grateful for the dusk, embarrassed that he would see the blush of color that filled her face. She sighed deeply, blowing air past her full lips. As she thought about him, the sensation of his fingers against her arm still burned within her memory. She imagined his touch still lingering along her skin and the thought caused her to breathe heavily with wanting. Jeneva felt her own hands brush the length of her body. Rolling onto her side, she pulled her knees into her chest, clasping her arms around her body. Dropping herself into a fantasy, Jeneva let visions of Mecan Tolliver fill her dreams.

Five

The house was quiet when Mecan came through the door, tiptoeing into the living room so as not to disturb anyone. He slipped out of his leather loafers and left his shoes in the entrance, then eased his way down the narrow hallway. Peeking into each room, he noted that all the boys lay sleeping peacefully. From behind a closed door, he could hear the low volume of Natalia's radio playing softly. Making his way back to the other side of the home, he entered the office, closing the door behind him.

The digital clock on his desk read eleven-fifty. Mecan tapped a pencil against the desktop as he pondered what he wanted to do. Jeneva Douglas had been on his mind most of the day. An off-site conference had taken him away from the house and he had missed her visit with her son. He had missed her. Pulling the telephone receiver to his ear, he dialed quickly before the strength of a second thought made him change his mind.

"Hello?"

"Jeneva, it's Mecan. I didn't wake you, did I?"

Surprise graced Jeneva's face as she tightened her grip around the telephone. She pulled her body upright against the headboard of her bed. "Mecan, no. Not at all. This is a surprise."

"I just got in and wanted to check how your visit went with Quincy."

Jeneva smiled into the receiver. "We had a great time. It was good to see him. I'm sorry I missed you, though. Natalia said you were at a conference?"

"Yes. One of those long, boring things I have to do to ensure we continue to receive government funding for some of our programs."

"That sounds like it was fun."

Mecan laughed. "Like getting a tooth pulled."

Jeneva laughed with him. They both fell silent, searching for something to say. "So," she started, as the pregnant pause billowed between them, "what are you guys going to do tomorrow?"

"The kids are going to the circus in the afternoon. I actually have a day off and will probably head home for a few hours."

"Where's home?"

"San Juan Island."

Jeneva nodded, filing the slip of information away. "That should make up for today."

"I'm sure it will. How about yourself? Any plans?"

"Not really. Church and probably lunch with a friend. Nothing special."

"It sounds like a good time to me." Mecan took a deep breath. "Well, I know it's late so I won't keep you. I just wanted to make sure everything went smoothly and that you didn't have any problems today."

"Thank you. I'm glad you called."

"So am I. I'll give you a call later in the week," he said, "to update you on Quincy."

Jeneva blushed. "Good night, Mecan."

Replacing the receiver, Mecan grinned, shaking his head. He was glad he called. Having heard her voice would make sleep come easier and he relished the prospect of meeting Jeneva in his dreams.

Bridget giggled as the two women sat gossiping over two cups of chocolate latte. "And you two didn't talk about anything else?"

"Nope," Jeneva responded, blowing against the edge of her cup before taking a sip of the hot liquid.

"You are too funny," her friend said, setting her own mug down against the tabletop. "It's obvious you like him and he likes you. What's the problem?"

Jeneva shrugged. "I don't know how to do this, Bridget. Flirting and dating is like a new language for me. I can't seem to translate any of the words."

"Girl, please. It's like that bike-riding thing. Just get back up on them wheels and you'll remember what to do."

Jeneva rolled her eyes. "It should be so easy. Girl, he is just so incredible. The man is good-looking, intelligent, and sexy as sin. He gives me goose bumps every time I hear his voice. Then my mind goes blank."

"Well, first thing you need to do is ask him about himself. His family, his history, his preferences. Find out what he likes."

Jeneva nodded. "But maybe we shouldn't be doing this, Bridget. I wouldn't doubt Hewitt House has some policy about him fraternizing with a parent."

Bridget flipped a hand at her friend. "You haven't fraternized yet. You're just getting to know one another. What can be the harm in that?"

Jeneva took another sip of her drink. She sighed, a wistful exchange of breath that eased past her lips. "You're right, but, girl, what I wouldn't give for just one kiss."

Six

They were all milling around, chatting easily, when Mecan entered the conference room, pulling anxiously at the gray, silk necktie around his thick neck. As he twisted his head from side to side, he couldn't help but think how much more comfortable he would be once he could get out of the suit and tie that draped his body. Natalia waved anxiously in his direction, gesturing for him to join her as she stood talking with Dr. Simon Hull, the senior speech therapist at Hewitt House. They greeted him warmly.

"Mecan, good to see you," Simon said, extending his hand.

"Hello, Simon. Natalia. I'm not too late, am I?"

Natalia shook her head. "No. We're still waiting for Dr. Abernathy."

Mecan smiled, knowing the good doctor's notorious reputation for never being on time. He glanced down at his watch. "Well, why don't we get started?" he said, dropping the folders in his arms onto the conference table and gesturing for the others to join him. Simon and Natalia took the two cushioned business chairs at his left. Dr. James Burton, pediatric intensivist, and Talbot Lomas, the director of primary instruction, took the two seats at Mecan's right.

"They've had you busy today," Talbot said with a smile, directing his comments at Mecan.

"It's been one meeting after another," he replied, "but you'll be pleased to know that we were able to secure almost two million dollars in additional funding."

"That's great," Natalia exclaimed.

"Congratulations," James added.

"Where's it going to be spent?" Talbot asked.

Mecan smiled in the man's direction, waving his head from side to side. "You and Simon are the lucky recipients this time, Talbot. The funds have been earmarked for educational materials and additional staff."

Both men beamed, Talbot sitting back comfortably in his seat as he folded his hands neatly over his bulging potbelly. "Very nice," he said. "Very nice indeed."

As Mecan opened the folder in front of him, the door swung open. Dr. Rachel Abernathy rushed inside, dropping onto the empty seat beside Talbot. "Hello, everyone. Sorry I'm late."

Mecan nodded his head. "Good to see you, Rachel. We were just about to get started," he said as they all spread files and folders before them, pens and paper in hand. Mecan started. "Mr. Quincy Douglas checked in six weeks ago. Initial orientations have gone exceptionally well. He has adjusted to the programs and I believe at this point everyone should have completed all their assessments. His mother has visited faithfully since his arrival, and he hasn't had any separation anxiety that we've been aware of. There have been some difficulties with him the past two days, though."

Natalia nodded her head, speaking to all of them at the table. "Quincy's been extremely agitated since Tuesday. He didn't sleep well at all last night. Both Mecan and I were up repeatedly trying to calm him down. We sent him to the infirmary this morning to be evaluated.

He's been doing extremely well since his mother checked him in, so I don't know what has set him off."

"I do," Rachel said. "Quincy has a massive ear infection. He had some minor fluid built up in his middle ear. I don't doubt that he was probably in extreme pain and just wasn't able to communicate such. I've started him on antibiotics and we were able to get some drops in his ears for the pain. He's calmed right down. I will probably keep him overnight and send him back in the morning."

"Is that necessary?" Mecan asked.

"I just want to be safe. His records show that he's had a number of ear infections. We may consider placing tubes into his ears if they continue to be a problem."

Mecan took a deep breath. "How did your evaluations go, James?"

"Quincy's an intelligent young man. He's quite perceptive and appears to learn quite quickly. I think our challenge is going to be determining which programs will best suit his needs."

Simon interjected. "I agree. I believe the young man's primary deficit at this stage is his lack of appropriate communication skills. Acquisition of language needs to be our initial goal for him."

"His vocalization has been minimal at best. Have we found a physical cause for his lack of speech?" Mecan asked.

James nodded his head. "To put it simply, there is a flaw in the switch between his brain and his mouth. I don't doubt Quincy has a strong word bank stored up there, but he needs to get past a bad wire to get them out and he hasn't figured out how to do that. Every so often he can get past the dip, but not as often as we would like him to."

"James and I have put together a very intensive

speech plan for the boy," Simon interjected. "I think once he can express his needs better, then he'll fly right through the rest of our programs."

"What do we need to do?" Natalia asked.

"First, we need to give him a means to express basic needs like pain and hunger," the man responded. "I think the use of word and image placards will do the trick. I'll start working with him this afternoon. If he's hurting, then he needs to be able to tell us. The ear infection is probably a good catalyst to get that started. Right now, he knows his ears hurt. If I can show him how to express that, then he should be able to transfer that to his other emotions as well.

"We also want to start imitation vocalization," Simon continued. "I want anyone involved in Quincy's care to be retrained on it if they've not worked with a student who has used it in the last six months."

Talbot shook his head. "I've heard you talk about it, but I've never done it before," he said. "Is it difficult?"

Simon shook his head. "No. And you in particular will need to be trained. From now on, everyone who has to speak to Quincy will need to do hands-on therapy. When you speak, you'll place his fingertips on your throat so that he can feel the vibrations." Simon pulled Talbot's fingers to his throat as he spoke. "Then you'll repeat your words with his hands on your lips so that he has tactile sensory perception of how the mouth should move. Comments should be very simple at first until he adjusts. As we work with him more, we hope he'll start to imitate the vocalization and figure out how to ease his way past that bad switch."

Mecan jotted notes down as he took in the comments being passed around the table. Blue ink flowed hastily onto the lined yellow notepad before him. "Anything else?" he asked.

James answered. "I want to start him on physical therapy four times a week. Let's get him into the pool. There's far too much muscle degeneration for a boy his age. We need to build him up before it becomes problematic. He's not as steady on his feet as he should be."

"Could his unsteadiness be related to his ear problems?" Mecan asked.

"Possibly, but the exercise will still be good for him."

"How has he interacted with the other children in the home?" Rachel asked.

Mecan laid his pen onto the table. "I get the impression he likes being in the house with them. He's started to follow Joel around more and I've noticed that he will occasionally focus on one of them when they're playing."

"He's become quite attached to Mac," Natalia interjected. She reached out to pat the man's hand. "My impression is that he's starved for a father figure, which of course he's never had."

"How has he reacted with you, Natalia?" Rachel questioned.

"For the most part he seems to keep his distance from me, but he's mindful when spoken to. The first few weeks I felt like he wanted me close only at bedtime, but I think that's because he was missing his mother. It seems to have passed, though."

"I agree," Mecan said. "I also noticed that when he wasn't feeling well yesterday, he responded to Natalia more than he did to me."

James nodded his head. "That's good to know. We can use that as a barometer to diagnose if he's feeling any discomforts until he can express it himself. Just be aware of it. If he's clinging to you more, Natalia, that may be our signal that something's not quite right."

Both Natalia and Mecan nodded their heads in agreement. "His mother will be visiting again this weekend. I would like you to give her a brief lesson on imitation vocalization, Simon," Mecan said.

Simon jotted down a note on his calendar. "I'm free at one o'clock."

"That should be fine. I will let Ms. Douglas know. I will also call and let her know about his ear infection. Anything else?" he asked. His eyes dashed around the table from face to face as he made some last notations. "Good. Who's next?" Glancing at his watch as they started reviewing notes on other students, Mecan was anxious to be finished. He wanted to call Jeneva, grateful for any excuse to talk to the woman.

Jeneva had crawled home from work late, exhaustion pulling at every muscle in her body. She'd started her day running an extra mile around the track and hadn't stopped since. It was the end of a fiscal quarter and the twenty salesmen, who relied heavily on her skills to help them meet their quotas, had been like a swarm of vultures. They'd pulled and torn at her all day until she felt as if there were nothing left of her but a pile of bones. With the telephone ringing incessantly, she'd not even had a moment to grab something to eat. So now not only was she exhausted, but she was also famished, and the lethal combination had put her in an exceptionally foul mood.

The telephone ringing as she entered the door of her home was not at all welcome, and she ignored it, allowing the answering machine to pick up the call as she kicked off her shoes in the doorway. Listening for the message, she was even further annoyed when the party on the other end hung up, not bothering to say a word. Crossing through the living room into the kitchen, she peered down at the indicator button, which showed six messages had come for her since

THE RIGHT SIDE OF LOVE   55

she'd left that morning. She pushed the PLAY button. Six hang-ups welcomed her home. As the tape on the machine rewound, she opened the refrigerator door, searching for something to eat, then cursed when she realized she'd not bothered to shop for food since Quincy had gone to Hewitt House.

The cool interior of her GE refrigerator hosted a half-empty bottle of ginger ale, a bag of baby carrots, and something that had so much mold across its surface, someone probably could have made enough penicillin to cure a boatload of sickness. Jeneva frowned, twisting her face in disgust. Pulling everything from the cool cavity, she dropped the soda bottle, rabbit food, and fungus into the trash, then slammed the container door closed. On the counter, two packages of ramen noodles were calling her name so she dropped them into a pot of warm water and turned on the stove.

The telephone rang again just as she had finished adjusting the gas flame to low and was headed into the bedroom to fall out of her clothes. She pulled at the zipper of her silk skirt as she reached for the receiver.

"Hello?"

Silence greeted her on the other end.

"Hello?" she said, annoyance taking full control.

"Hello, Jeneva," the male voice on the other end said. "How are you?"

Jeneva's grip on the receiver tightened. She inhaled deeply, shock registered on her face. "Who's calling?" she asked, her voice low, the words catching against the back of her throat.

The deep voice laughed. "Oh, you know who's calling, Jay. I know you haven't forgotten my voice."

Jeneva closed her eyes. Her legs quivered, threatening to give out on her, so she dropped her body to the brick-tiled floor, pressing her back against the white oak cabinets. She pulled her knees to her chest as she clutched the receiver to her ear. Silence danced across the telephone line, neither party saying anything. Jeneva suddenly felt as if time had stopped, and she fought to catch her breath, not wanting him to know he had surprised her.

"What do you want, Robert?" she asked her ex-husband, finally finding a voice to respond with.

"I just wanted to say hello. Wanted to know how you're doing, is all."

"Well, I'm fine. I've been doing fine for thirteen years. Thanks for asking. And now that you know, you don't need to call again."

Robert Douglas laughed into the receiver, the familiar lilt to his voice causing Jeneva's heart to race. "How's my son?"

"Your son? Your son? Oh, no, you didn't!" Jeneva could feel her anger rising.

"Well, have you been getting my checks?"

"No thanks to you."

"I've been sending money, Jeneva. You know I've been sending good money every month."

"Thanks to the state of Washington and child-support enforcement. We know we can't trust you to do what's right, now, don't we?"

"You're not right, Jay."

"Don't call me Jay."

The man took a deep breath. "I'm sorry, Jeneva. I just called because I wanted to apologize for hurting you."

"You give yourself far too much credit where I'm concerned, Robert. Trust me, you have no influence on my emotions, so don't think there was that much between us that you could possibly have hurt me. There wasn't."

"We both know better than that, Jeneva," he said smugly.

"What do you want, Robert, because I'm busy. I've

got more important things to do than sit here listening to you try to make amends for only being half a man, and a poor half at that."

"That wasn't necessary, Jeneva."

"Wasn't it? You know, Robert, it took some time for me to come to my senses, but when I did, I saw you for what you were. Nothing. Now, I warn other women about men like you. I let them know what bad sperm can produce."

She could feel the man bristle, his own anger rising to meet hers.

"You still have that smart mouth, I see."

"What do you want, Robert? And this is the last time I'm asking before I hang up."

"I want to see my child."

This time, Jeneva laughed. "Good-bye, Robert. Don't call my house again. You don't have a child here to see. You abandoned him nearly fourteen years ago. I'm sure the statute of limitations ran out a long time ago on any claims you might have had to being someone's daddy."

"Please, Jeneva—"

Jeneva slammed the telephone down onto the cradle, disconnecting the line before Robert could spit his last words into the receiver. Tension exploded down her arms, across her shoulders, and up into the back of her skull. The mounting pressure pulsed through the woman's eyes, the throbbing in her head causing the room to spin as she lay down across the kitchen floor. Jeneva struggled to gain control of her breathing, her lungs gasping for oxygen, feeling as if she'd not taken a breath since she'd picked up the phone.

The last time she and Robert Douglas had had a conversation, Quincy had been two weeks old. Spending every minute in the neonatal intensive-care unit of the hospital had consumed all Jeneva's time and energy, and when she saw Robert strolling in her direction, easing down the hospital hallway with that confident gait that was all his, Jeneva had welcomed him excitedly. That excitement quickly had turned into despair.

"How's the kid?" Robert had asked, leaning to peer down into the incubator that housed their son. Tubes ran from one end of the child's body to the other, his tiny chocolate figure barely visible.

"The doctors say there's been dramatic improvement," Jeneva exclaimed, smiling up at her husband. "They think they're going to be able to take him off the ventilator by the end of the week and then he'll be able to breathe on his own."

Robert tapped a finger lightly against the glass enclosure.

Jeneva continued speaking. "He's got a low-grade fever, but they say that's normal. And he seems to be fighting infection. Our baby boy's a fighter." She smiled again.

Robert nodded his head, then raised his eyes to stare into Jeneva's face.

"I can't do this, Jay."

Jeneva met his gaze with her own. "Can't do what, Robert?"

"This. I can't be no daddy. I didn't want this. I thought I could 'cause you wanted me to but I can't. Not with him being sick like he is."

"So what does that mean, Robert? Quincy's here. He's our son and we're responsible for him."

"What's going to happen if he doesn't get well? What then? I don't want to be spending every day running back and forth to hospitals and doctors. And what if he ain't normal?"

"How can you say that? He's beautiful. We couldn't have asked for a more perfect baby."

"Jeneva, you're crazy. This boy ain't perfect. He might not never be perfect. Then what you gon' do?"

Tears filled Jeneva's eyes. "I'm going to love my son. What else would you expect me to do?"

Robert glanced around the small room, finally noticing the babies in the other incubators and the staff of nurses and doctors that flitted from one small infant to the other. The nurse monitoring his own child gave him an icy stare as she read the monitors connected to Quincy's small body and jotted the figures down onto a clipboard of papers.

The whole room had overheard their conversation and he could feel their distaste with him spreading throughout the air. He looked back down at his son, then turned to the child's mother.

"Look. I left some money in the bank. I took just enough out to get me a bus ticket to California. My brother said he had some work for me out there so I'm gon' go see what I can do. When I get settled I'll send you some cash to help out."

"You're leaving us?" Jeneva's expression was incredulous. "How can you do this, Robert? How can you just leave us like this?"

The man took a deep breath, resolve settling over his expression.

"I'm sorry, Jay. I gotta go."

Brushing a palm down the side of her face, Robert spun out of the room and her life, gliding back down the hospital hallway just as easily as he'd come in. Two attorneys had facilitated all the other conversations they had needed to have, relaying messages back and forth at a rate of one hundred dollars per hour of billable time.

* * *

Realizing that she'd forgotten her dinner, Jeneva pushed herself up from the floor and onto her feet. She dropped the pot of burned mush into the sink, filling the charred substance with cold water. Her head still throbbed, the pain a dull ache that was determined to hang on.

When the telephone rang, Jeneva resisted the sudden urge to kick it across the room and through the closed window. Instead, she allowed the answering machine to pick up the call.

"You've reached the Douglas residence. We're unable to take your call at the moment, but if you'll leave your name, number, and a brief message, someone will get back to you." *Beep.*

"Jeneva, hello. It's Mecan Tolliver. Would you please give me a call when you have an opportunity? I need to speak to you about—"

"Hello?" She put the telephone to her ear, banging it against her knee as she pulled it from the floor.

"Jeneva?"

"Mecan, hello. Sorry about that. The machine beat me to the punch."

The man nodded into the receiver. "Are you okay? You don't sound well."

Jeneva paused, wanting to contain the tone of her voice. "I'm fine. Is Quincy all right?"

"He's fine. I wanted you to know, though, that he's in the infirmary."

Panic swept up and over her. The tension flew past her lips with the flow of her words. "What's happened? What's wrong with Quincy?"

"Don't panic. Quincy's fine. He has an ear infection. It took us a day or so to recognize that there was a problem, but the doctor says he's going to be just fine. She wanted to keep him in the infirmary tonight to keep an eye on him. I just left him and he was sound asleep. I'm going to pick him up first thing in the morning. He'll be on antibiotics for a few days, but the doctor says he's not in any more pain."

Jeneva breathed a sigh of relief, tears starting to flow down over her cheeks. "He's had them before. He gets very irritable." Jeneva broke down into sobs. "I should have been there," she cried into the telephone.

Mecan could feel his own tears pressing against his eyes. "Jeneva, don't. It's okay. Quincy's fine. Don't upset yourself like this." He suddenly wished he could pull her through the telephone and into his arms. "Darling, please don't cry," he heard himself say, the words falling easily from his mouth.

Jeneva fought to stifle her sobs, trying to regain control. She was embarrassed to be behaving so shamefully. "I'm sorry," she gasped. "I'm so sorry."

"You have nothing to be sorry for, Jeneva. Nothing."

They both paused, wanting the other to say something to ease the rise of nervousness that had risen between them.

Mecan finally spoke. "Are you still coming to visit Saturday?"

"I think I should come tomorrow. Quincy needs me."

"No. Quincy needs to see you on Saturday. You can't rush up here each time he catches a cold or has a stomachache. This is not major. He and I had dinner together and he's almost back to normal. You wouldn't know anything was wrong if I didn't tell you."

"Are you sure?"

"I'm positive. What time are you coming Saturday?"

"I'll be there first thing in the morning."

"Good. We've got a full day of activities planned for both of you."

Jeneva felt herself smile. "I miss my baby," she said out loud, not really meaning for him to hear.

"I know you do. And he misses you. But you'll be together again on Saturday and everything will be just fine."

"Thank you. I really appreciate everything you're doing."

"You're welcome. If you just need someone to talk to, please call me. If you just want to ask how Quincy is doing, I'm always here. Okay?"

She nodded her head, forgetting that he couldn't see her. "Good-bye, Mac."

"Good night, Jeneva. Sweet dreams."

"What was that all about?" Natalia asked, standing in the door of the home's small office, her hands pressed against her hips.

Mecan looked up at her in surprise. "What?"

"That was Quincy's mother you were speaking with, wasn't it? You called her 'darling.'"

Mecan looked away, embarrassed.

Natalia smiled, winking in his direction. "Sounds like you got a crush, Mr. Tolliver."

"Please."

"'Darling'?"

"You must have heard me wrong."

"I know what I heard." Natalia made her way into the room, taking a seat on the chair at the opposite side of the desk. "She's very pretty, Ms. Douglas is."

Mecan eyed his friend cautiously. "Yes. She's very attractive."

"You like her a lot, no?"

"I like her, yes."

"I think Ms. Douglas likes you, too."

Mecan smiled. "It's nothing like that, Natalia."

The woman laughed, shaking a finger in his direction. "You men are so dense sometimes."

"Well, it wouldn't work. It would be very unprofessional of me to become involved with a client. Ms. Douglas is paying us to take care of her son. That's all I'm here to do."

"Who are you trying to convince?" she asked. "Me or you?"

"Why are you bothering me?"

Natalia laughed again. "I've been watching you, Mecan. I see how much attention you've been giving to Quincy. I see how you get when you speak with his mother. I see things you don't even see." She rose from her seat.

"And?" Mecan asked, rising from his own seat. He walked around the desk and leaned back against the desktop in front of her.

"What will happen when Juan returns and you go back to that big fancy office of yours?"

Mecan shrugged his shoulders, not sure he had an answer to respond with.

"You've been here a long time. You've loved each one of these kids like they were your own, but they're not. Since I've known you, I can't remember you ever dating anyone seriously, but I can see it in your eyes."

"See what?"

"I can see how much you want a family of your own. Your own child to love. A woman to be by your side. Yes. I see this in your eyes. I see it more now when you're with Quincy and when you speak on the telephone with his mother. It's like they're the family you want, but haven't been able to have."

Natalia's gaze was intense, and as the truth of her words reached out to slap him, he had to turn his face away from her, not wanting her to see the wave of water that rose in his eyes. She reached out to tap her hand against his, clucking under her breath.

"Good night, Mecan."

"Good night, Natalia, and thank you."

Seven

From his eighteenth-floor room at the Elliott Grand Hyatt hotel, Robert Douglas stared out the large windows, taking in the expansive view of the city. In the distance he could see the Space Needle, Elliott Bay, and Lake Union. He could also see the onslaught of dark clouds filling the sky and could feel deep down in his bones the brunt of rain they carried in their shadowy mist. The first drops of precipitation against the glass reminded him why he'd not missed Seattle. The winter months brought the rain, so much of it at times that a man would have to fight the onslaught of flooded streets and roadways in threat of landslides just to get to work or go check on family. The sheer dreariness of it had kept him in a foul funk for half a year.

Right before he'd left, Robert had felt as if the six months of spring and summer were not nearly enough to move him out of the blue moods that consumed him from day to day before the vicious cycle would overtake him once again. Staring out over the city made him realize how ready he was to go back home. How ready he was to leave Seattle and all his baggage behind, again.

He sighed, taking a seat on the richly cushioned sofa in his suite. He sat staring at the telephone on the tableside, contemplating whether he should try to call

Jeneva back. He'd not known what to expect from the woman. But her obvious hatred had actually surprised him. He hadn't expected her to welcome him back with open arms, but he had half hoped that with all the time that had passed between them, she would at least have been willing to be civil.

Maybe he had abandoned her and their son. So what if he'd been a coward at the age of twenty-one? He had at least been there to financially support the boy. Maybe it hadn't been much in the beginning, but when his business took off and his investments were lucrative, he'd increased the court-ordered fifty dollars per week voluntarily. When Jeneva's parents died, he'd been the one to pay the taxes on that old house she loved so much, ensuring that she and Quincy would always have a roof over their heads. He'd done the best he could do. That had to count for something.

Even as Robert mulled his numerous excuses over in his mind, bland fodder to defend his actions, he knew that signing his name to a check didn't give him a whole lot of right to come back into their lives as if nothing had happened. He heaved a deep sigh.

He had no excuses for what he'd done, other than to say that he'd run scared, and gone as fast and as far as his feet could carry him. Time had taught him many lessons, and he would be the first to admit that he'd made some wrong decisions in his life. Destroying his family and deserting his child had been his greatest mistake. But despite it all, he now needed to see his first-born son. He wanted to know the boy that was half his blood. He'd been thinking about the child since forever, even longer than he'd been willing to admit to himself. This was something he felt he had to do, or at least die having tried.

Robert rose to his feet, falling down against the king-size bed. Flipping through the pile of images that

lay atop the paisley comforter, he pulled from the lot
a photo of him and Jeneva standing side by side.
She'd been pregnant, grinning from ear to ear. His
expression had been hard. Looking back into his own
eyes, he could see how lost he'd felt. He dropped the
photo back down against the others. She would not
make this easy for him, nor did he want her to. But no
matter the challenge, he knew in his heart that nothing, and no one, was going to keep him from his son.

Jeneva had never mourned the loss of Robert Douglas. There had been no time. On the heels of his
departure, she had a child to be responsible for, and
crying over the loss of a man had not been on her
schedule of things to do. While fighting to be a good
mother who was plagued with massive medical bills
and a sick infant, she'd simply suppressed her feelings
for Robert, shoving them deep down into some internal space she could ignore and forget at will. The
anger and hurt of losing someone you loved had not
touched her, not until she'd picked up the phone and
his voice had been on the other end. Then the doors
of that internal spot opened like floodgates, spilling
out over her spirit.

She lay across the bed, sobbing. Her child was sick
and needing her and here she was bemoaning the
loss of a man who'd made it perfectly clear that he
didn't care. Jeneva tried to focus on the music that
spilled out from the speakers on the floor. Her taste
in music had always been different, and she could just
hear Roshawn and Bridget laughing at her choices.
They would have chosen some dated, sultry, rhythm
and blues, Motown selection. Someone crying about
a bad man doing them wrong. She preferred more ex-

otic tunes. Easy, sensual instrumentals and ballads that were quick to calm.

The CD player had just finished spinning tracks by Cesaria Evora, the Cape Verde songstress with the voice like thick honey. The Portuguese lyrics were a soothing balm against Jeneva's ears. With the brief pause between one disc ending and another beginning, Jeneva realized that her breathing had finally returned to normal, the heaving wails having subsided. She pulled a thick pillow under her head, turning to lie on her back as she stared up at the ceiling.

The second CD was meditational, soothing to her spirit. Entitled *Transparency* by a group called Circle in the Round, she found the mystical collaborations of the koto and zither instruments relaxing. Reaching above her head, Jeneva pulled the CD cover into her hand, staring at the husband-and-wife duo who composed the group. The couple smiled warmly, seemingly excited to be where they were, doing what they were doing. She found herself fascinated by their biography, wondering what possessed two black, Duke University law graduates to give up promising law careers to pursue musical instruction in Japan for eight years. Especially musical instruction on instruments with names the average person would never be able to pronounce. She imagined they led a charmed life, doing what they loved to do most, and having a family to share that with.

Jeneva heaved a deep sigh. After her parents died, her father from a heart attack, and her mother from heartbreak three months later, Quincy had been all the family she had. For the most part, life had been good to them both and though she'd not been unhappy, she realized she'd not been fully complete. The thought hit her suddenly, knocking the wind from beneath her wings. She missed companionship. She missed a partner to laugh with and debate with,

someone she could turn to for guidance, and offer a
shoulder to when his burdens were heavy. She missed
the warmth of a man's hand caressing a day's tension
away, or that same hand inciting passion throughout
her body. While caring for Quincy, she'd been too
busy to miss what she'd never really had. With the boy
now gone, the list of things that had passed her by un-
folded like rancid sewage at her feet.

Crossing her arms over her chest, Jeneva hugged
herself tightly. Robert Douglas had stolen her dreams
the day he walked out of her life, stripping promises
of lasting love from the lining of her heart. And now
he had the audacity to come calling like they were still
the best of friends. Jeneva chuckled at the absurdity.

Turning toward the nightstand, she reached for the
digital clock beside the bed. It was well after three
o'clock in the morning. She was past the point of exhaustion, but sleep seemed to elude her. She couldn't
get Robert off her mind, and the fact that Quincy had
been sick and she'd not been there to care for him
just compounded her agitation. She thought back to
her conversation with Mecan. There was something
about that man Jeneva found refreshing. He had an
easy energy, a calming spirit that made her feel better.
She trusted him with her son, trusted him when he
said Quincy would be well without her by his side. She
felt comfortable that he was personally taking care of
her child, despite his responsibilities to the other children residing at Hewitt House.

Closing her eyes, Jeneva wished for sleep to take the
memories and reflections from her mind, and just as
she began to doze lightly, playing the conversation
with Mecan over and over in her head, it suddenly
dawned on her: the man had called her "darling."

Eight

Jeneva and Bridget were already seated at a table when Roshawn walked through the doors of the Dahlia Lounge. She waved excitedly in their direction as she gestured to the hostess that she'd located her party. She leaned to kiss them both on the cheek before dropping down onto the remaining upholstered seat between them.

"Girl, what took you so long?" Bridget asked.

"My last client of the day decided, after I cut her hair, that she wanted me to color it, too. Decided she didn't want to be a brunette anymore. She wanted to go blond."

Jeneva shook her head as Bridget laughed.

"It's not funny. After I bleached her hair, it took me two tries to get just the shade of blond she was looking for."

"Was she happy?" Jeneva asked.

"Does a fat kid like cake?"

The trio laughed.

"Well, we ordered you a chocolate martini," Bridget said.

"Somebody loves me!" Roshawn exclaimed.

"We ordered appetizers, too," Jeneva interjected. "The smoked salmon and the shrimp-scallion pot stickers. Figured we'd share them."

Roshawn nodded her head. "That works for me."

Their waitress, a young woman named Mindy, came to the table, her wide smile as large as the deep green eyes that filled her petite face. She deposited three chocolate martinis in front of them. "Are you ladies ready to order yet?"

Jeneva and Bridget looked toward Roshawn, who had pulled the menu into her hands. She nodded her head. "You two go first," she said. "I'll be ready by the time she gets to me."

"I want the crabs," Bridget said, passing her menu to the young woman. Mindy nodded her head as Bridget rolled off the rest of her dinner order.

"Well, I need meat, tonight," Jeneva said when it was her turn. "I'll take the rib-eye steak, rare."

"That's not the kind of meat you need." Bridget laughed as she and Roshawn gave each other a high five. "You need some beefcake!"

Jeneva rolled her eyes at the two of them, shaking her head. "Ignore them. They're rude," she said to Mindy, who was giggling also. "Would you please ask the chef if he has any of that potato and pancetta hash? If he does, I'd like a side order."

"That shouldn't be a problem at all," Mindy responded. She turned toward Roshawn.

"Well, I don't need any meat. So, I'll have the king salmon, please."

Gathering the last of the menus, Mindy headed to the kitchen with their orders, promising to be right back with their appetizers.

"So, how are you doing, girl?" Roshawn asked, adjusting her napkin in her lap before pulling her drink to her lips.

Jeneva shrugged. "I've been better."

"Have you heard from the school about Quincy?"

"Mac called me last night. He's got an ear infection."

"Ouch," Bridget said, squinting her face into a mock grimace. "Poor baby."

"Who's Mac?" Roshawn asked.

Bridget squealed excitedly. "That's right! Roshawn doesn't know. Tell your girl about Mr. Mac!"

Jeneva rolled her eyes again, lifting her own glass to her mouth. "He's one of the program directors, and he's the house father for Quincy right now. That's all."

Bridget laughed. "I hear he's fine, too."

Roshawn joined her. "Maybe you will get yourself some real meat after all."

Jeneva giggled. "You need to stop."

Mindy placed their appetizers on the table, then excused herself to go check on their dinner orders.

"Say grace," Roshawn commanded, her gaze pointing at Bridget.

They all bowed their heads as Bridget blessed the table and sent up good wishes for each of them.

"Amen," the trio said in unison.

"So what else is going on with you women?" Bridget asked, watching as Roshawn pulled two pot stickers onto her plate.

"Not much here," Roshawn said. "What about you, Jeneva?"

"Well, last night . . ." she started to say before Bridget hushed her, the woman's eyes widening in shock.

"Oh, my Lord," Bridget exclaimed, gesturing toward the door with her eyes. "Isn't that Robert?"

Jeneva dropped her fork to the table. "Robert who?"

"Your Robert. Robert Douglas, your ex-husband."

Roshawn spun around quickly, rising up out of her seat slightly to see where it was that Bridget stared. She sat back down quickly. "That's Robert."

Jeneva shook her head. "He called me last night."

"He what?" both women asked, their voices melding into one loud whisper.

Jeneva nodded her head, wanting to sink down into her seat before the man could see her. "I can't believe this," she said, nervous tension filling the empty pit in her stomach where hunger had resided just moments before.

Bridget reached out to grab her hand. "Well, don't look now, but here he comes."

As if on cue, both Roshawn and Jeneva spun around to watch the man who was making his way over to where the three sat. Robert Douglas had aged well, Jeneva thought, her gaze racing from the top of his conservative haircut to the tips of his highly polished leather shoes. No longer as lean and lanky as he had been when they'd been married, his physique had filled out nicely.

"Brother's been hitting the gym," Roshawn said under her breath, voicing what Jeneva had just thought.

His face had slimmed some, his features more pronounced without the round fullness that had filled his cheeks in his youth. His eyes were still as dark as ever, seeming to penetrate right through everything they looked at. His complexion was a rich, deep, dark bronze, his soft skin looking like expensive silk. He'd acquired a mustache, the facial hair trimmed neatly above his thin lips. Robert wore an expensive black wool suit, pale gray dress shirt, and matching tie that fit him to a tee. The outfit was definitely tailored especially for him, and not off the rack, Jeneva thought. He looked good. Too good, she concluded, as he now stood directly in front of them, a shy grin gracing his face.

Robert nodded toward Bridget, then Roshawn, his gaze settling on the lines of Jeneva's face. "Bridget. Roshawn," he said to them, being polite but not really caring that they were there. "Hello, Jeneva. You look incredible." His eyes stayed locked on hers.

"My, my," Roshawn interjected. "First the rain, and

now the pestilence. God must be trying to tell us something."

"What are you doing here, Robert?" Jeneva asked.

"I called your office. That woman you work with said she thought you might be here tonight. Girls' night or something, she said."

Jeneva put it on her list to give the office secretary, an older woman named Beverly Hartley, a piece of her mind on Monday morning.

"Is your attorney aware that you're out stalking my client?" Bridget asked, her professional tone rising from some place deep in her midsection.

"I wasn't aware saying hello to the mother of my child was considered stalking," Robert quipped, not taking his eyes off Jeneva.

"Well, I sure hope you didn't come back for them tired clothes you left behind," Roshawn said, sipping on her drink. "We had us an exhale party the day after you left. Burned them bad boys up. It's been, what, thirteen, fourteen years now? You a little late for the festivities."

"I see you still have that great sense of humor, Roshawn. Nobody knocked it out of you yet?"

"No one stupid enough to try, either."

Silence swept across the table. Robert and Jeneva still stared at each other intently.

"I think we need to talk, Jeneva. Please. There's a lot that needs to be said."

"I don't have anything to say to you, Robert, and you don't have a thing to say that I'm interested in hearing."

Robert nodded his head slowly. He pursed his lips, his expression as if he'd bitten into something sour. "I think you and your attorney need to have a conversation then. She will advise you that I legally have a right to see my son, whether you agree or not. Now, I'm trying to do this peacefully. You can work with me, or you can choose not to. Personally, if you want to be ugly about it, then fine. I don't really give a damn. But I will see my son. In fact, I may arrange to take him back to Atlanta with me since I am entitled to visitation."

Jeneva bristled. "You won't be taking my son anywhere."

"No? You don't think so? I'll bet you that I'll not only take him, but I'll be able to keep him while you're still trying to get a judge to hear your case."

Robert finally broke the gaze between them. He looked from Roshawn to Bridget and back to Jeneva. "It's up to you how we do this, Jeneva. I'm staying at the Hyatt. If you want to be a child about this, you can have your attorney call me with your decision. Enjoy your dinner, ladies. The meal's on me tonight."

Robert turned and walked away, stopping to give the hostess his credit card for their charges. Jeneva felt as if she were about to explode. Reading her mind, Roshawn leaned to wrap her arms around her friend's shoulder, hugging her tightly. Jeneva could feel Bridget squeezing her hand. Neither of them said anything as Mindy placed their meals in front of them.

"Can he do that?" Jeneva asked as soon as the woman had retreated to another station, away from their conversation. "Can he take Quincy?" She turned to stare directly at Bridget.

"He has the right to see Quincy. Your divorce decree made no stipulations to restrict his visitation or prevent him from having the same physical custody that you have."

"But I don't understand. The judge gave me custody of Quincy."

"That's correct. He gave you physical custody, meaning that the child would reside in your home and you would be his primary caretaker. But he gave you both joint custody over Quincy's well being. And Robert has faithfully paid his child support and then some. If it goes to court, it's highly unlikely a judge would keep him from seeing his son."

"But can he take him?"

Bridget shrugged. "It's highly possible that a judge would allow him visitation without supervision for extended periods wherein he could take Quincy wherever he wanted."

"I think I'm going to be sick," Jeneva whispered, her body shaking in her seat. Without the support beneath her behind, she would have dropped straight to the floor.

"I can request a hearing first thing Monday morning to get us on the calendar. We can go before the judge and ask that all visitation be supervised, but I'll be honest, Jay, I don't think we'll win. Robert will easily show that he's capable of taking care of Quincy. He has a home. He's intelligent, well connected, and he's wealthy. He'll use his payment record to prove his interest in his son and, no doubt, use your unwillingness to work with him as proof of why he's not been active in the child's life sooner. He'll do everything to make you look bad and himself good. And the more you fight it, the more you'll just fall into the trap."

"What do I do, Bridget?"

"As your attorney, I'd advise you to do whatever you feel is best for Quincy. I'll support that. As your friend, I have to tell you that you need to talk with Robert. Find out exactly what he wants and take it from there. It won't hurt to talk to him."

"Please," Roshawn interjected. "She needs to tell the brother to go straight to—"

"That's not going to help, Roshawn," Bridget interrupted. "It won't make the problem go away."

The trio grew quiet, her friends giving her time to assess all that had happened. Pushing her food around on her plate, Jeneva had suddenly lost her appetite. She rose from her seat, reaching for her purse. "I'm sorry, but I have to go home."

Bridget clasped her hand. "Are you sure? Do you want us to go with you?"

Jeneva shook her head. "No. Finish your dinner. I'll be fine."

Roshawn rose from her seat. "I'll call you in the morning, okay?"

"I won't be there," Jeneva answered. "I'm going up early to see Quincy."

"Well, call me when you get home then," Roshawn said.

"Me, too," Bridget added. "We can talk about it more if you're still unsure about what to do."

Jeneva hugged Roshawn, then leaned down to kiss Bridget. "I love you guys," she said softly. "Thanks for being here for me."

"Just let us know what we can do, Jay," Roshawn said.

"Bye, Jeneva," Bridget called after her, watching as she crossed the room and headed out the door.

The Dynamic Divas looked from the door back to each other.

"Well, I know what we can do right now," Roshawn exclaimed, gesturing for the waitress.

"What?" Bridget asked.

"We can order another round of drinks, dessert, two meals to go, and make sure the waitress gets a nice hefty tip. It's all on Robert."

Bridget laughed as she waved her head from side to side.

Nine

It was fifty-six degrees and drizzling outside when Jeneva pulled out of her driveway and headed for Hewitt House. She felt cold, a deep chill shimmering through her body, and the heat inside the car wasn't rising fast enough. She'd not slept well for a second straight night and her body was feeling it, but she was excited at the prospect of seeing her son. She didn't know how to explain to anyone how much she missed her child. She didn't have the words to express how alone and empty she felt not having Quincy to take care of day in and day out.

The drive went quickly and she pulled into the gates of Hewitt House sooner than she had anticipated. As she put the car into park and set the brakes, the front door of the small home flew open and Mecan Tolliver stood in the entrance waving at her. At the sight of him, excitement filled Jeneva's face and she waved back, making her way out of the vehicle and across the lawn.

"Good morning," she said, a rise of energy flooding her face. "How are you this morning?"

"I'm doing well," Mecan answered, gesturing for her to come inside. "How about you? How was your drive?"

"Very pleasant, thank you."

"It's good to see you again."

Jeneva smiled. "It's good to be here. Where's Quincy?"

"He is actually at the pool this morning."

"Quincy doesn't swim," Jeneva said, nervous anxiety rising in her voice.

Across the room, Natalia waved at her excitedly, laughing as she made her way to Jeneva's side. "Good morning, Mama. How are you?"

"Fine, thank you, Natalia. I was just asking about Quincy. He doesn't swim."

"That one is going to surprise you," Natalia said. "He loves the water. He has physical therapy until ten-thirty," she said, looking at her watch. "Then he'll be back home. Come sit. Have you had breakfast?"

Jeneva shook her head as she made herself comfortable on the living room sofa. "No, I haven't," she said. "I left at six-thirty this morning and I didn't bother to stop."

"Well, how about a cup of coffee and something to eat?"

"Coffee would be wonderful, thank you."

"I don't know how wonderful it is." Natalia laughed. "Mac made it this morning."

"There's nothing wrong with my coffee," the man said, pretending to be offended as he laughed with her.

"So you say," Natalia teased, poking fun at him. "I'll be right back." She made her way out of the room.

Mecan came to take a seat beside Jeneva. "Natalia and I are enjoying the quiet this morning. All the boys are out of the house at the same time. It doesn't happen often so you try to take advantage of it."

Jeneva smiled, meeting Mecan's gaze, a wave of shyness washing over her. "Did all the boys have physical therapy this morning?" she asked, trying to ease her nervousness.

Mecan shook his head. "No. Joel and Michael went home with their parents for the weekend, and Billy went camping with his Boy Scout troop."

"Boy Scouts?" Jeneva asked, surprise filling her words.

"We try to give our kids everything they'd have outside of this facility. We've got a very active scouting troop. This is Billy's first year."

"Very nice," Jeneva said as Natalia returned, bearing a tray with two ceramic mugs filled with hot coffee, and a plate of warm cinnamon rolls. "That smells wonderful." She inhaled the rich aromas of freshly brewed coffee beans and warm cinnamon and sugar glaze.

"I can vouch for the rolls." Natalia smiled. "I made those."

Jeneva laughed as Mecan swatted his hand in Natalia's direction. "Aren't you going to join us?" he asked, gesturing toward the two cups.

Natalia glanced down at her watch for a second time. "No. I want to drop by Dr. Abernathy's office to pick up Joel's prescription refill before I go get Quincy."

Mecan nodded his head.

"You and Jeneva catch up. Quincy and I will be back shortly," she said as she grabbed her jacket and keys and headed to the door.

"Thank you, Natalia," Jeneva said, waving in the woman's direction. "Thank you so much."

Natalia winked at the two of them, said good-bye, then headed out the door.

Jeneva reached for her cup of coffee, blowing against the hot liquid before pulling it to her lips. She and Mecan both grabbed for a cinnamon roll at the same time, their hands bumping against each other. They laughed, the sound of each other's voices helping to ease the rise of tension that had fallen over the room.

"So, how is Quincy doing?" Jeneva asked. "Any more problems with his ears?"

"Not a one," Mecan answered, his head bobbing from side to side. "He's doing wonderfully. I think you're going to be very pleased with his progress so far. I've scheduled a number of activities for the two of you today. Once he gets home, we'll let you spend some time alone. I know how much you two have missed each other."

Jeneva smiled. "Thank you."

"A little later, if the sun comes out like they've promised, I thought we could head down to the pond. Quincy wants to go fishing and today's a good day for it with the other boys gone. We can have lunch down by the pond if it warms up enough. I'll pack a picnic basket to take with us."

"That sounds like fun."

"This afternoon I want you to meet Quincy's speech therapist, Dr. Simon Hull. He wants to train you on the new program we have to encourage Quincy's vocalization."

Jeneva nodded. "Wow."

"I know. It's a lot," Mecan said. "But I promise it's going to be a good day for the both of you."

Jeneva took a deep breath, filling her mouth with warm fluid. She swallowed, her eyes resting on Mecan's.

The man smiled nervously. "So," he said, "how's my coffee?"

Jeneva shrugged, rolling her eyes in jest. "It's okay, I guess."

Mecan laughed. "Go ahead. That's okay. You and Natalia both know that's some good coffee."

Jeneva laughed with him. "It's not bad."

"Not bad!" Mecan threw up his hands. "A man can't win around here."

Jeneva could feel herself grinning in his direction. There was a level of comfort developing between them and she was surprised by how tranquil and satisfying it felt. The observation took her by surprise.

"Can I get you something else?" Mecan asked, reaching for the empty dishes.

"No, thank you. That was good." She rose from her seat to go peer out the window.

Retreating into the kitchen, Mecan took a deep breath, inhaling oxygen as if he were starved for it. He'd been excited about seeing Jeneva again, so excited that the nervous energy had scared the wits out of him. He'd felt like an adolescent anticipating Christmas when she'd pulled her car into the driveway. At the door, it was as if he were meeting Santa Claus personally, a wealth of gifts embodied in the woman before him. Behind him, Natalia had laughed teasingly and he found himself fighting a barrage of emotions: excitement, nervousness, embarrassment, and anticipation. The flood of feelings felt new to him, like nothing he'd experienced before, and he felt as if he was fumbling in unknown territory, totally out of control.

As he made his way back into the living room, Jeneva was still standing in the window, her arms wrapped tightly around her upper body. He sensed that there was something on her mind and it suddenly worried him. Mecan found himself struggling not to stare, unable to take his eyes off her. As she turned, her gaze meeting his, a tremor of heat flooded his body. He could feel the flames rising in his cheeks and he was grateful she could not see the raging color that flushed his dark face. He smiled, not wanting to appear overly eager. When Jeneva returned the smile, her eyes still locked on his, it was almost too much for him and he could feel the tightening of muscle below his waist wanting to take control. Mecan inhaled sharply.

"Are you okay?" Jeneva asked.

Closing his eyes, Mecan pushed his hands deep into the pockets of his khaki pants. He nodded his head. "I'm sorry. I . . . I . . ." he stammered nervously. "I'm making a complete fool of myself," he finally said.

Jeneva shook her head. "No. You're not."

"It's just that," Mecan paused, "you are extremely beautiful," he said finally, blowing warm breath past his full lips. "I am very attracted to you, Jeneva."

Jeneva lowered her gaze for a split second, then looked back up at Mecan. Before she could respond, the front door flew open as Natalia ushered Quincy inside.

Shocked by the words that had just spilled out of his mouth, Mecan turned away, embarrassed that he would say something so unprofessional. Looking from one to the other, Natalia sensed the sudden rise of tension between the couple. Sexual energy had filled the small space and the woman smiled at them all-knowingly.

Stepping into the room, Quincy ran straight into Jeneva's arms, dropping his head against his mother's shoulder. Hugging him tightly, Jeneva could feel the tears spilling down over her cheeks and she fought the desire to cry, not wanting to do anything that might upset her son. She held him close, her eyes shut tightly, and when she opened them, looking past the boy's shoulder, Mecan stood smiling at the two of them.

As Jeneva let her son go, stepping back to stare up

at him, Quincy turned, walking to Mecan's side to hug him also. Jeneva watched curiously as Quincy looked up, raising his arm to press his hand against Mecan's throat.

"How was swimming, Quincy?" Mecan asked, his words slow and methodic. Quincy's fingers now rested against Mecan's lips. "How was swimming, Quincy?" Mecan asked again.

Quincy nodded his head, shaking it quickly up and down.

"Very good," Mecan said, the duo repeating the gestures. "Say hello to mommy." He repeated himself twice for Quincy.

Jeneva stared in awe as Quincy came back to her. She watched as he placed his hands on his own throat, and mouthed air in front of her. His fingers pressed against his own lips, then went back to his throat, as air blew past his lips. "Hel . . . lo, Ma . . . ma" filled the air.

Jeneva began to laugh and cry at the same time, tears flowing like floodwaters as she chuckled excitedly. Her son's fingers pressed anxiously against her neck.

"Just speak slowly," Mecan commanded, coming to stand beside them.

"Hello, baby boy," Jeneva said, still laughing. "Hello."

Quincy's head bobbed up and down as he clapped his hands together in front of him. Then he did something Jeneva had rarely seen him do in all his fourteen years. Her son smiled, looking directly at her as he fought to bend his lips upward.

The day flew by. Before Jeneva knew it, morning had given way to evening, and it was time for her and

Natalia to tuck Quincy into bed for the night. She had lain down beside him until he fell asleep, drifting off herself without realizing it. Some two hours later, as Quincy rolled against her, tossing a heavy arm across her face, Jeneva woke up startled. It was a few minutes before she realized where she was, and in the dim light coming from the hallway, she pulled her wrist to her face to see what time it was. Shaking her head, Jeneva eased herself out of the twin bed. Tucking the covers back around Quincy's body, she knelt down to kiss his forehead, smiling contentedly as she sat watching him sleep.

In the living room, Mecan sat reading, a new Walter Mosley novel having captured his attention. He looked up, startled, when Jeneva entered the room, surprised that she was awake. He had half expected her to sleep through the night, exhaustion having consumed both mother and son.

"Hi," Jeneva said, blushing brightly. "I didn't mean to disturb you."

"Not a problem," Mecan said, closing the hardcover book in his hand and setting it against the table. "You were resting so peacefully, we didn't want to bother you. Since the other boys aren't home, there was no reason."

"Thank you." Jeneva stretched her body upward, yawning widely. "Oh, excuse me," she said, a faint grin gracing her face. "I can't believe I was that tired."

"You're more than welcome to stay, if you like. I can make up Joel's bed for you. I don't want you driving if you're too tired."

"I think I'll be fine," Jeneva said with an uncertain shrug. "May I sit down?" She gestured toward the seat beside him.

"Please," Mecan answered, nodding his head.

Settling down against the sofa next to him, Jeneva

turned her body to face his. She inhaled deeply, searching for just the right words to express what she was feeling. The calm between them was warming and Jeneva felt comfortable sitting with him, silence spinning a faint web between them. She smiled, lifting her eyes to meet his.

As she reached out to take his hands into hers, his expression was one of mixed emotions, curiosity and pleasure melting together. Mecan could feel himself shaking ever so slightly and he hoped Jeneva didn't notice. He smiled back, the gesture manifested in his eyes.

"Thank you," Jeneva said, gratitude flooding her face. "I can't begin to tell you how much I appreciate everything you've done for my son. Natalia told me you've been working with Quincy every night to teach him how to say 'mama.'" Tears rose to Jeneva's eyes. "I didn't think I'd ever hear my child call me that. You'll never know how much that meant to me." Jeneva squeezed his flesh gently, brushing her palm against the back of his hand.

The emotion caught in Mecan's throat, the nearness of her causing his heart to beat rapidly. He nodded slowly, his gaze penetrating as he stared into her eyes. Both could feel the rise of heat that swept between them. Mecan pulled his hands away, sitting forward in his seat. He clasped his fingers together tightly, rocking slightly back and forth.

"I'd like to apologize if I was out of line earlier," Mecan said, taking a deep breath to calm his nerves. "I understand that our relationship is strictly professional and I would understand if you—"

Jeneva shook her head, pressing two fingers against his lips to stall his words. Her smile widened, her gaze caressing him softly. She twisted her hands nervously in her lap. "Mac, I would be lying if I said I wasn't feeling something. But I don't know what that something is. This is all very new for me." She blew warm air past her lips, then inhaled deeply. "I haven't given any man a second thought since Quincy's father and I were together. And I have to admit that I've been thinking about you a lot these past few weeks, and not all of it has been in relationship to my son. I've been enjoying our conversations over the telephone, and each week when I come, I'm excited at the prospect of seeing you."

Mecan nodded his head as Jeneva continued.

"But right now, all I can focus on is Quincy and what he needs. You've been a wonderful influence on him and I wouldn't want to do anything that might damage that."

"I understand," Mecan said, "and neither would I. I was just worried that you might have been insulted by what I said earlier."

"Mac, how could I be insulted? You were very sweet. I'm very flattered." She squeezed his hand again. "I just wanted you to understand where I'm at with this."

"I appreciate that," Mecan said. "I know that I overstepped my boundaries and I was so concerned that I had offended you."

Jeneva smiled again as she rose to her feet. She glanced down at her watch. "I should be leaving. If I leave now I can be home just after midnight."

"Are you sure? You're more than welcome to stay."

"I'm sure. I have some personal business I need to take care of tomorrow. But I'd like to come back again next week if that won't be a problem."

Mecan nodded his head. "Of course. Quincy enjoys when you come and I look forward to it, also." He followed as she headed to the front door, stopping to retrieve her jacket from the coat rack in the entranceway.

"Here, let me help you with that," Mecan said, moving to assist her into the warm outer garment. As his arms reached around her shoulders, both felt the rise of energy pass between them once again. Staring up at him, Jeneva could feel her breath slipping away, the wave of sensation overwhelming. Then, without a thought, she fell against him, wrapping her arms around his neck as she pressed her lips firmly against his. The kiss surprised them both and when Mecan rested his palms along the sides of her face, his fingers tangling in her hair, there was no denying the longing they had for each other. As his tongue caressed her mouth, eager to part her lips, Jeneva pulled away, inhaling air deeply. Pressing her lips against his cheek, she turned out the door, leaving him standing in the entrance, hungry for more.

Ten

Daylight saving time had given Jeneva an extra hour of sleep and she was thankful for it when the sound of the alarm clock rippled throughout the room. The female disc jockey at KZIZ 1560 had just transitioned from Mary Mary singing "In the Morning" to the a cappella quintet, the Golden Skylarks, vocalizing "Streets of Gold." The Sunday morning gospel was a welcome wake-up call and Jeneva lay listening to the melodies for some time before even thinking about rising from where she lay.

Jeneva rolled against the padded mattress top, her bedsheets in total disarray as she stretched the muscles in her body. A cramp threatened the back of her right calf and she pulled her toes upward, fighting the muscle that threatened to shoot pain down the length of her limb. As she willed her body awake, she lifted herself onto the wealth of pillows at the head of the bed, making herself comfortable. It was still early and she had some time to herself before her Sunday school class and morning services. With Quincy at school, all she had these days was time to herself. As she pondered the current events of her life, she toyed with the idea of skipping Sunday school altogether this week. She could always go to Wednesday night Bible study. She'd never been to church during the week before. There had never been time with the demands parenting a handicapped child had required of her.

The telephone ringing interrupted her thoughts. Reaching for the extension on the nightstand, Jeneva pulled the receiver to her ear. "Hello?"

"Jeneva, good morning."

She took a deep breath. "Good morning, Robert."

The man paused, anticipating harsh words following his name. When Jeneva didn't say anything else, he continued.

"I was hoping you'd given some thought to what I said."

"You threatened to take my son away. How could I not give that some thought?" she said, her tone controlled, just shy of being emotionless.

"I didn't mean it the way it came out. It was just . . ." He paused, searching for words that were slow in coming. "I'm sorry. I didn't mean it," he said instead. "I just wanted you to know how much I want to see Quincy."

Jeneva was focused on her breathing as she pondered his comments. With each intake of air, she filled her lungs to capacity, holding the oxygen tightly before allowing it to rush from her body. She could feel herself nodding as Robert attempted to convince her how much their child meant to him.

"Please, Jay," he said finally. "I don't want to fight. I just want to see my son."

"I'm going to church this morning and I have some things I need to do right after that. You can buy me an early dinner afterward."

"Didn't I buy you dinner Friday night?"

"You keeping track?"

Robert laughed. "No. Just trying to be funny."

"Well, you're never going to be a comedian so don't give up your day job."

The man chuckled again. "Would you like me to pick you up?"

"No. Just call and make reservations at Salty's for dinner. I'll meet you there at four."

"Will you be bringing Quincy?"

"No. Is that going to be an issue?"

The man shook his head. "I was just hoping," he said. "But we should probably talk alone first."

"I'll see you at four o'clock," Jeneva said, hanging up the telephone before Robert could say anything else.

She sighed. Bridget had been right. She needed to talk to her son's father. She knew that she could make no decisions about him and Quincy until she'd gotten the answers to questions that had haunted her since his departure, questions that she'd pretended were of no importance to her.

Lifting her body off the bed, Jeneva headed into the bathroom. The tiled floor was cold against her bare feet and she shivered from the chill. Reaching for the chrome handle, she turned on the bathtub faucet, willing the flow of hot water running from the spout to fill the room with heat. Within minutes, a rise of steam filled the small space, warm against her flesh.

Slipping out of her floral-printed, flannel pajamas, Jeneva dropped her naked body into the tub, relishing the warmth of wetness that wrapped around her. Laying back against the porcelain enclosure, she closed her eyes, appreciating the deep quiet that filled her home. With the exception of the last bit of rain that pattered against the bathroom window and a slow *drip drip drip* from the bathroom sink, the only other noise in the room was the rise and fall of her breathing.

She had kissed him. There had been no mistake

about who'd been the aggressor. She had leaned her body against Mecan's and kissed him, savoring the sensation of his lips pressed to hers. There had been no shame in her game, she thought, amused by the boldness that had consumed her. The memory of that moment caused her breathing to increase, heated desire rising to meet the warmth in the room. Any other time, any other place, and it might have been more than just one kiss, Jeneva thought, the prospect causing her to smile. Nearly fourteen years of bottled-up frustration was causing her to lose her mind.

Reaching for the bar of Ivory soap and a skin cloth, Jeneva bathed her body clean. As she did, she examined the faint growth of hair against her legs, noting that she should probably shave them when time allowed. She ran a finger against a rise of broken blood vessels that sat along the side of her kneecap. They had been her constant companions since forever, the dark, whisper-thin marks intricately adorning her legs. Her stomach was tight. Not that teenage tight she'd known before becoming pregnant, but a mature tight that allowed her slacks and skirts to hang nicely against her body. The type of tight that five extra pounds of weight could easily undo if she wasn't careful. Regular exercise had proven to be a faithful friend to her body, she mused, as her hands cupped the fullness of her breasts. Gravity was trying to claim them, Jeneva thought, wondering what she would need to do to fight the scientific flow of energy threatening to take control. She wondered how long it would be before she woke one morning to find her nipples reaching for her knees. She laughed out loud at the thought. Lifting herself out of the tub, Jeneva wrapped a plush, white towel around her body, then headed into the bedroom to get ready for morning service.

Jeneva had attended Mt. Zion Baptist Church since she'd been born. It had been her parents' church, and her grandparents' church, having served her family lineage since its inception at the close of the nineteenth century. As she pulled her car into the parking lot, she noted Roshawn's own vehicle parked four spaces away. She knew that if Bridget wasn't there already, she wouldn't be far behind.

Members of the congregation greeted her cheerfully, the elderly brethren stopping to squeeze her arm or hug her. Inside the vestibule, both of her friends were waiting to greet her.

"Good morning." Jeneva smiled, leaning to hug both Roshawn and Bridget.

"We were starting to worry," Bridget said. "You didn't call us last night."

"I didn't get in until after midnight."

"Everything go well with Quincy?" Roshawn asked, leading them to seats on a rear pew.

"He called me 'mama.'" Jeneva smiled, lifting her hand to wave at an elderly acquaintance of her mother's who'd called out to her.

"Jay, no!" Roshawn exclaimed excitedly. "They've got him talking already?"

Jeneva shook her head, chuckling softly. "Not really, but he is trying so hard. Mac spent the last few weeks teaching him how to say 'mama.' He still has a long way to go, but you should see him. He seemed so happy."

Bridget wrapped her arm around Jeneva's shoulders. "I think we need to go with you one weekend. I miss my godchild and we need to meet this Mr. Mac, Miracle Man."

Jeneva laughed, catching herself just as the organist started to play the processional. Bowing her head in prayer, Jeneva had a lot to give thanks for this morning. She also needed to pray for strength. She knew she would need it when she had to go meet Robert Douglas.

At the close of the service, the three women paid their respects to the church minister and his wife before heading toward their automobiles. Bridget led the way, Roshawn and Jeneva following close on her heels.

"You ladies want to go get something to eat?" Bridget asked.

"I can't," Roshawn responded. "I'm picking up Ming. She spent the weekend with her father."

"We haven't seen much of our girl lately. How's she doing?" Jeneva inquired.

Roshawn shrugged. "Girl turned thirteen and is starting to smell herself. Thinks she's grown. I told her father he needs to take some control before I hurt her. I caught her kissing some rusty-behind boy in my hallway Friday night when I got home. He had his hands all up under her shirt. You know I went off," she said.

"Oh, don't tell us that," Jeneva said, wincing. "Baby girl is too young for that nonsense. What happened to Barbie dolls?"

"Ken. A man will mess you up every time," Roshawn said. "Told that little pervert that if I ever caught him 'round my house or my child again, he'd have my foot so far up his little behind, it will take him and his family to pry it out. Be tasting my toes in the back of his throat and my knee would be knocking against his spleen. Then I told him Ming's daddy was head of the Chinese mafia and he was the first person I was going to call after I slapped the taste out of his mouth."

Bridget and Jeneva laughed.

"How is your ex?" Bridget asked.

"As sweet as ever with his little Oriental self. He had

my car fixed for me the other day. I told him I was going to have to give him some to say thank you."

Jeneva laughed. "You kill me. I don't know why you two didn't stay married. You have more sex now than you did when you were together."

"We could have stayed married if he hadn't been playing them Genghis Khan games with me," Roshawn said, leaning back against Jeneva's car. "If he hadn't been so busy trying to rule our home like it was his personal Asian empire, things with us could have been cool." She lifted her large, peacock-blue hat off her head, dropping it into the car's trunk. "You know I don't play with no control freaks. Men like that make me evil."

Her friends smiled, shaking their heads at her.

"Speaking of exes," Bridget started, "any decisions about yours, Jeneva?"

"I'm meeting him for dinner this afternoon."

"Is that a good thing?" Bridget asked.

"No," Roshawn interjected. "I told you what you need to do is—"

'We're still at church, Roshawn." Bridget laughed, waving her hand in the woman's face. "Don't you go there."

Roshawn sucked her teeth, rolling her eyes in jest.

Jeneva laughed. "I don't know if it's going to be good or bad," she said, after catching her breath. "I'm talking to him. That's all I've promised to do."

Bridget nodded her head. "Well, call us if you need us, okay?"

"Yeah, girl. I can get some of them Chinese herbs from Chen when I see him. We can work some roots on the brother."

The three women laughed again, mirth flooding the air around them.

"Let me go," Jeneva said finally, kissing both women on the cheek.

"Call me later, Jay," Bridget said, "or I will call you."

"I will," Jeneva promised, stepping into her car. "Have to tell you about my kiss."

"What kiss?" Roshawn said excitedly, reaching for the car door. "Who'd you kiss?"

Grinning at her friends, Jeneva started the engine, then shifted the car into reverse. "I'll call you two later," she shouted as she pulled the car out of the space. Roshawn shook a fist in her direction as Bridget stood laughing beside her.

Eleven

Jeneva felt good when she walked into Salty's on Alki Beach. The restaurant was one of her favorites and it had been some time since she'd last been there. Salty's had one of the most dynamic views of the Puget Sound and the Seattle skyscape in the city. A good meal always included a parade of ferries, barges, and fanciful sailboats. Jeneva loved it most in the early evening just as the sun was drifting away to nothingness, its flaming sphere reflected in the glass windows of the city's tall buildings. She had often fantasized that a romantic moment would be dinner at Salty's with a tall male companion by her side as they feasted on a decadent meal complete with cheesecake and the panorama of the city for dessert.

Glancing at her Timex, she realized she was a few minutes early. The hostess led her to their table, advising that Robert had not yet arrived. Jeneva was thankful for the time she had to herself. Reaching into her purse, she pulled out a silver compact, flipped open the lid, and gazed into the mirror at her reflection. Her makeup was meticulous.

After church she'd gone home and lain down for an hour to take a nap. She had wanted to be rested and clearheaded when she met with Robert. After a quick shower she'd changed from a conservative two-piece suit into a form-fitting cashmere dress cut low in the front and even lower in the back. The deep green fabric looked elegant against her light complexion and she had topped the look with the length of cultured pearls her mother had given her on her wedding day. The damp moisture in the air had accentuated the wealth of curls atop her head, and after spending an hour making up her face, she was pleased with her appearance. She looked good and she knew it. As Robert approached the table, it was obvious from his expression that he thought so also, his mouth dropping in obvious appreciation as he made his way over to her side.

"Jeneva, hello," he said, standing beside her, his hand extended in greeting.

"Robert." Jeneva smiled politely, ignoring his outstretched palm as she pulled a glass of ice water with a twist of lemon to her lips.

"Thank you for seeing me, Jay," he said, pulling out a chair to sit down.

A young waiter approached the table, slipping two menus in front of them as he introduced himself. "My name's Jerry and I'll be your waiter this afternoon. May I get you something to drink?" he said, glancing from Jeneva to Robert as he spoke.

Jeneva propped her chin against her hands, her elbows on the table. "I think a bottle of your most expensive Moët would be nice. Don't you, Robert? Since we are celebrating."

Robert smiled. "Is this what this is? A celebration?"

"Of sorts."

Robert nodded in the boy's direction. "A bottle of Moët, please."

"I think we're ready to order our appetizers also," Jeneva said, dropping her menu against the table. "At least I am."

"Please," Robert said, gesturing toward her.

"I'd like the French brie, please. And we'll share a plate of crab cakes."

"And you, sir?" Jerry asked.

"The crab cakes should be enough," Robert responded.

"I'll be right back then," Jerry said, turning and heading to the kitchen.

"So," Robert said, adjusting his napkin against his lap, "what are we celebrating?"

"Your dubious return, of course. How often does a man walk out on his family, stay gone for fourteen years, and then come back looking for absolution?"

Robert stared at her, the light in his eyes dimming. He dropped his gaze, inhaled deeply, then clasped his hands on the table in front of him. "I'm sorry, Jay."

"Please don't call me Jay. Only my friends call me Jay. You and I aren't friends."

He nodded his head. "I didn't mean to hurt you."

"Well, you did. You hurt me and you hurt Quincy and I can't forget that."

"I made a mistake, Jeneva, but I wasn't ready to be a father. I was barely ready to be a husband."

"And what? That was enough to absolve you of all your responsibilities?"

Robert took another deep breath. "I can't make you understand how I was feeling, and I surely don't expect you to forgive me, but I'm hoping you'll let me make it up to Quincy. At least let me try."

"Do you know anything about Quincy? Anything at all?"

The man looked away, embarrassed. His gaze focused on Jerry, who was headed toward their table with the bottle of champagne in his hands. He held his tongue until the bottle was uncorked and both their glasses were full. Jerry also set their appetizers down in front of them.

"Are you ready to order your meals?" the man asked.

Robert looked to Jeneva as she nodded her head. "What would you like to eat?" he asked.

"I'm having the lobster," Jeneva answered, directing her order to Jerry, "and give me a nice-sized one. I also want the spinach salad."

Jerry nodded as he jotted down her order. "And for you, sir?"

"Make that two lobsters, please."

The two watched as Jerry turned and left them stewing in the strained mood that had dropped over them.

When Jeneva looked over at him, tears had risen to his eyes, anguish painted across his face. His words were soft, barely audible as he spoke, staring intensely in her direction.

"I was a lousy father. I know it. I accept that you hate me for what I did, but you can't punish me nearly as much as I've spent the last fourteen years punishing myself. If a two hundred-dollar bottle of champagne and a damn lobster will help you feel better about me, then I'll buy them every day for the rest of my life if I have to.

"No. I don't know anything about my son. I know that he'll be fourteen on his next birthday. I know that I have only sent him one birthday card in all that time. I know that you have been a damn good mother, and that I probably don't deserve anything from you or Quincy, but I'm asking. I'm asking you to help me get to know my son. I'm begging for your forgiveness."

Silence followed. Time hung like a heavy veil against their shoulders, ticking past slowly. Both were oblivious to the chatter of the other patrons around them. Jeneva sat watching him, wondering from what place this Robert had risen. This Robert, who was so unlike the boy she'd loved and married, who seemed to have grown into a man she might have wanted to know. A man she could have liked, and maybe even have loved if given half an opportunity. She took a deep breath, breaking the gaze that had locked them to each other, if only for a brief moment.

Many minutes passed, and Jerry placed their dinners onto the table, wishing them a good meal before he departed. Jeneva stared down at the lobster, then looked back up to Robert.

"You're buying dessert, too," she said, bending her lips ever so slightly as she tried to smile, wanting to alleviate the rise of tension pressing against her heart.

Robert nodded. "Every day, for the rest of my life, if I have to."

"Tell me about your life, Robert," Jeneva asked, pulling a forkful of food to her mouth. "What happened to you when you left?"

"I spent the first few months with my brother Gerald. You remember him, don't you?"

She nodded. "He sends Quincy twenty dollars every Christmas. Did he ever get married?"

"No. Says he hasn't found the right woman yet."

"I always thought he and Bridget would have been nice together."

Robert shrugged. "Gerald and I didn't see eye to eye on things, so when I left him, I headed east. Ended up in Atlanta. Got a job working for a construction company. Best thing that ever happened to me. I went to school and got my degree, and a few years after that I was able to buy the company from the man who had mentored me. I'm very proud of it. We're doing quite well."

Jeneva laid her fork against her plate, lifting her glass to her lips as she took a sip of the bubbly drink. She set the flute back against the table, carefully adjusting it to the right side of her plate. Her palm ran across the fine crystal container.

"Did you ever remarry?" she asked, taking another bite of her food after she'd spoken.

Robert eyed her cautiously before responding, then nodded his head. "Yes. I met Fiona the year we got divorced. We were married six months later."

The food against Jeneva's tongue felt like sandpaper as she fought to swallow the shellfish down. "Where is she now?" she heard herself ask, not knowing from where the words had risen.

"Back home. In Atlanta."

"Does she know why you're here?"

"Yes."

"How does she feel about that?"

"She supports me. She knows how much I want to have a good relationship with all my children."

Jeneva lifted her eyebrows in surprise. "You have other children?"

"Another son, Robert, Jr., who's almost ten, and twin girls, Jennifer and Elizabeth. They just turned nine."

Jeneva could feel the hairs along the length of her arm and across the nape of her neck bristle. She had no doubt that color raged across her cheeks, visible acknowledgement of the anger that had just flooded through her.

She reached for her glass, knocking it over as she did. "Damn it," she hissed, grabbing for her napkin to catch the offending flow of fluid running across the table. "And damn you," she said to Robert, bitterness spewing past her long eyelashes. "You abandon me and Quincy and then you go build this whole new life with a new wife and new kids like we were trash you could just get rid of. Damn you, Robert."

Robert clinched his eyes closed, his breathing labored as he struggled to find the right words to explain what he had never had the courage to explain. When he opened them, Jeneva was reaching for her purse, rising from her seat. He reached out a hand and grabbed her arm.

"Please, Jeneva. We have to talk about this. I know how you must feel, but please don't leave."

Jeneva could feel herself shaking with rage, wanting to lash out and hurt him the same way she felt she'd been hurt. The plea in his eyes only fueled her ire. But she sat back down, not really knowing why, wanting instead to turn and leave him and the reminder of all his lies behind. Neither of them said anything. Both plates of food sat untouched as they stared around the room and out across the soft waves of water outside—stared everywhere but at each other. They inhaled, deep mournful breaths, almost simultaneously.

Jerry came to the table to check if all was well. "Is there anything wrong with your food?" he asked, genuine concern spilling from his voice.

Jeneva looked at Robert, who shook his head. "No. Everything is fine. We just weren't as hungry as we thought," he said, attempting a weak smile in the other man's direction.

"Would you like anything else?" Jerry asked.

"Just let us finish this," Robert said, his rising annoyance with the customer service spinning across his tongue. "We'll call you when we're ready. Thank you."

Jerry nodded, backing his way down the aisle and out of sight.

"What did you expect, Jeneva? Did you really think I wouldn't move on with my life?"

"I don't know what I expected. I had expected you to be a man and support your family the way a man should. You failed me. Then I expected you to be a father to your son. Your eldest son. And you failed him. So I don't know what I expected." She paused, the words catching in her throat, hurt painting a portrait over her body. "I do know I didn't expect to feel so betrayed," she said finally, the confession reaching out to slap him as the tears spilled out of her eyes.

Robert reached out for her hand. Jeneva pulled it away, almost knocking her glass off the table a second time. His own eyes misted over.

"I'm so sorry, Jeneva. God knows how sorry I am. If I could take it all back, I would, but I can't. All I can try to do is make it up to you and to Quincy."

She gestured for the waiter. Jerry came rushing to her side, curiosity gracing his face as he noted the tears streaming from eyes.

"Yes, ma'am," he said, "are you okay?"

She nodded. "Jerry, I'd like a very large slice of your Grand Marnier white chocolate cake and a shot of Jack Daniel's, please."

"That'll be two shots of Jack," Robert added, smiling weakly.

"Yes, sir. I'll be right back," Jerry said, rushing to appease them both.

Jeneva wiped at her eyes, brushing saline and mascara against the back of her hand. "Look what you made me do," she said, reaching for her purse and her compact. "You've got me drinking, swearing, and looking bad and it's Sunday."

"You look beautiful, Jay."

"Shut up, Robert. And don't call me Jay."

He smiled, then braved the moment. "Does Quincy know anything about me?" he asked.

Jeneva shot him a quick glance, then placed her

compact back into her bag. She sat back in her seat, choosing her words carefully.

"Let me give you the short version of your son's life," she said, staring her ex-husband in the face. "Quincy wouldn't understand if he did know anything about you, Robert. Quincy was diagnosed with development disorders that have left him with the emotional and intellectual capacity of a four-year-old. Before the age of five he endured surgery no less than nine times. He's had hydrocephalus, which is water on the brain, and had to have a shunt implanted in his head to divert the fluid to his abdominal cavity. There was the Wilms' tumor, which was a tumor on his kidney that had to be removed. That also required minor radiation treatment. He was almost six and a half when he learned to walk and he's still unsteady on his feet because his motor skills are lacking. He doesn't speak, at least not well, and definitely not without a lot of effort, but he's learning.

"Quincy is never going to be a star athlete, or a scientific genius, and he only learned how to say the word mama a few weeks ago. He is not the perfect child you wanted, Robert. He's flawed. He will never take over the family business, if that's what you were hoping for. He will more than likely have health issues and need specialized care until the day he dies. So what else do you want to know about your son?" she said in one deep breath, barely bothering to inhale until she'd finished speaking.

Robert looked at her hard, shock registered upon his face. "I didn't know," he said finally.

"No. You didn't. You were too busy being a father to Robert, Jr. to know what was going on in Quincy's life, and now you just want to walk in, and do what? Just what do you expect to accomplish?"

Robert hung his head. "I guess I hoped for a

chance to be the man I should have been from the start."

"Well, Quincy doesn't need you to use him to try and make yourself feel better about what you did, Robert. Go home. Go home to your family. Leave mine alone."

Robert lifted his heavy glance up from the table, his eyes racing across her face. "He's my son, Jeneva. Please." His tone was beseeching.

"No. He's my son. I'm the only one who's loved him unconditionally. I'm the one who's held his hand every time he's had to have a needle. I held him when he hurt and he cried or he was so sick that he couldn't keep anything down. When he threw up, he threw up on me. I'm the only one who's ever looked at him and seen what a beautiful, perfect little boy he is. I'm the one who's known from the moment that he was born that he was the greatest gift and the biggest blessing God could have ever bestowed upon me. You," she said, tears dripping out of her eyes, "you are nothing to him. Nothing more than a sperm donor, because you chose not to be there."

Robert looked at her, his ego sufficiently bruised, the flux of hurt spilling out of his eyes. "I still need to see my son," he repeated.

She took a deep breath, ignoring him as she pulled the shot glass to her lips and downed the bitter fluid in one quick gulp. She followed the drink with a bit of sweet cake. When she said nothing else, Robert finished his own drink, reaching with his fork to steal a bite of her cake.

Jeneva sat back against her seat, suddenly tired. She no longer felt pretty and wasn't feeling good about finally facing her ghosts. But more than anything, she was tired of being angry. Harboring a lifetime of bitterness had finally taken its toll and she was suddenly ready to let it go. The exhaustion from carrying so much hostility cloaked her face.

"I appreciate that you paid your support, Robert. I know it would have been harder for me if you hadn't. Thank you for that," she said finally.

Robert smiled. "Thank the state of Washington and child-support enforcement," he said.

This made Jeneva laugh and Robert laughed with her, the tension between them beginning to dissipate ever so slowly.

She sighed deeply. Her voice was once again monotone, devoid of feeling as she began to speak. "Eight weeks ago I enrolled Quincy in a special school upstate. Hewitt Hall is dedicated to teaching children like Quincy skills that will help them be able to take care of themselves." Emotion caused her voice to crack as she continued. "This is the first time since he was born that he and I have ever been separated."

"How's he doing?"

"He's making great progress, but this is all very new for him."

"How are you doing?" Robert asked, concern spreading over his expression.

She shrugged her shoulders, twisting the pearls around her neck between her manicured fingers.

Robert nodded his head. "I don't want to interfere, Jeneva. I just want the opportunity to get to know him. Maybe be able to spend more time with him."

She looked at him in earnest. "I need to speak with his doctors and the school's director. I don't want to do anything that might interfere with his progress."

"I understand."

"How long are you planning to be here?"

"Until I can see my son."

"Won't your new wife have something to say about that?"

Robert shrugged. "I don't care what it takes, Jeneva. I told you that."

Jeneva stared into his eyes, wanting to believe him. "I'll call you tomorrow," she said finally, rising from her seat.

Robert rose to his own feet, dropping his napkin against the tabletop. "Thank you," he said.

Jeneva looked back over her shoulder. She called out his name.

"Yes, Jay?"

"If I let you in, and you disappear when it gets too hard for you to deal with, I won't be as accommodating. Fourteen years ago I let it go because I didn't have any choice. Quincy didn't have to deal with it because he was too young and too sick to understand. But if you walk into his life now and then disappear, and he gets hurt, I will hurt you this time. I will hurt you with everything in me."

The man nodded his head. "I won't fail you, Jay. I swear I won't."

"Good night, Robert."

Twelve

There were four messages waiting for him when he returned to his hotel room. Robert read them quickly, then reached for the telephone and dialed. The phone barely rang before his wife picked up on the other end.

"Where have you been?" Fiona Douglas asked, not even bothering to say hello.

"What's wrong, Fiona?" Robert replied. "Are the children okay?"

"They're fine. We're just missing you is all. You haven't called since Thursday and I was beginning to worry."

"I'm sorry, baby. There's just been a lot going on."

"Have you seen him yet?"

"No. Not yet."

"Is his mother giving you a hard time?"

"Wouldn't you?"

"Probably."

"Jeneva and I actually just had dinner. I think we made a lot of progress. At least I hope we did."

"What's her problem? I mean, it's not like he's an infant. The boy is almost fourteen. Doesn't he have some say in whether or not he wants to see you?"

Robert dropped down on the side of the bed. He

fought to contain the anguish in his voice. "It's not that simple, Fiona."

"Then what is it?"

"Quincy has some medical issues. Things I never knew about."

"What things?"

"I don't want to go into it over the telephone."

"Robert, you have to tell me something."

"Not now, Fiona, please. How's Junior?" he asked, changing the subject.

"You missed his ball game. He was hoping you'd be back."

"Tell him I'm sorry. I'll make it up to him."

"The girls have a dance recital next week. Do you think you'll be back in time?"

"I don't know. I'll know better tomorrow."

His wife hesitated, not sure what to say or ask. "I love you," she finally said.

Robert nodded into the receiver. "I love you, too, Fiona."

"You know I'm here if you need me."

He smiled. "I love you, baby."

"Call me tomorrow. Please?"

Robert sighed. "Fiona, I need to know something."

"What?"

"How would you feel if I brought Quincy back home with me?"

The woman paused. "Is that a possibility?"

"I don't know. But if it is, how would you feel about it?"

"He's your son. I'd welcome him and love him like he was my own."

"I'll call you tomorrow," Robert said, heaving a deep sigh.

Fiona Douglas tightened her grip on the receiver in her hand. Something was tearing at her husband, and if she pushed, she knew he'd withdraw. Whatever it was had been building since before he left for Washington, wanting to go search out his son and ex-wife, family he'd rarely talked about in their twelve years together. And now something about his son had devastated him. She would have to wait until he was ready to find out what. "Bye, Robert."

When Jeneva pulled into her driveway, David sat on her front steps, bouncing his basketball against the concrete stoop. As she put her car into park, he came to his feet, watching her as she made her way to where he stood.

"Hi, David. How are you?"

"Fine. How are you, Miss Douglas?"

Jeneva smiled. "I'm hanging in here. Where's your mom?"

"Working."

Jeneva nodded. "Have you had dinner?"

David shrugged, shaking his blond head. "Mom left me some veggie casserole, but I wasn't hungry."

At the door, Jeneva inserted her key and unlocked the lock. "Would you like to come in for a while?"

David smiled. "I don't want to bother you."

"David, you are never a bother. Come on in."

Dropping her purse onto the table, Jeneva flipped on a lamp switch, flooding the living space with light. David took a seat on the living room sofa, dropping his basketball to his feet.

"I saw Quincy yesterday," Jeneva said, taking the seat beside him. "We went on a picnic and he caught a fish."

"I miss Quincy," David said.

"I know you do, honey. So, tell me. How's school?"

David shrugged, pushing his shoulders up toward his ears. "Okay, I guess."

"Just okay?"

David dropped her eyes. Jeneva sensed that there was something on the boy's mind. Something he desperately wanted to talk about.

"David, you know that if there's ever anything bothering you, you can always talk to me. Don't you?"

David nodded his head.

"Do you want to tell me what's wrong?" Maternal concern blessed Jeneva's face. Her expression was calming and David seemed to relax as he took a deep breath, glancing quickly in Jeneva's direction.

"There's something I need to tell my mom and I'm scared."

"Your mom loves you, David. There's nothing you can't tell her."

"She's just so busy all the time. All she ever does is work."

Jeneva nodded. "I know that's hard on you. But your mom has to do what she does to take care of you."

"You work, but you always had time for Quincy."

"But I didn't have to work two jobs like your mom does. Quincy's father helped with the money. Your mom has to do it all by herself."

"I hate my father for dying."

"No, you don't. You miss him. And you wish it hadn't happened. But you don't hate him."

The boy's eyes misted over, clouds peppering the sky-blue surface. Jeneva reached out to pull him into a hug, embracing him tightly as he started to sob. She held him for some time until his tears no longer fell against her shoulder. Reaching toward the coffee table, Jeneva pulled a tissue from the Kleenex box on the glass surface. She pressed it into the palm of his hand.

"Wipe your face," she commanded softly. "Now, tell me what's wrong."

David reached into the back pocket of his Fubu jeans, pulling out a white note card. He passed it to Jeneva, dropping his head against his chest as he did.

"What's this?" Jeneva asked, opening the tightly folded document.

"It's my report card."

Jeneva scanned the typed document, a row of Cs, Ds and an F in English staring back up at her. She laughed softly, reaching out a hand to tap David lightly against the back of his head.

"Ouch," he said, looking at her with surprise.

"Don't you 'ouch.' You deserved that." She smiled. "What in the world have you been doing in school? Because clearly you haven't been studying."

David shrugged. "I stopped doing my homework."

"Why?"

"I don't know."

"David, you know better. Is the work too hard? Do you need a tutor?"

"No, ma'am. I was just being lazy," he said, answering honestly. "My mother's going to kill me."

Jeneva laughed out loud. "No. She's going to be angry, but she won't kill you. I may kill you."

"I'm sorry," he said, smiling weakly.

"When's your mom getting home?"

"She said she'd be back before ten."

"I want you to show her this report card and I want you to tell her the truth like you told me. She may yell at you and I'm certain you'll probably lose your television and video-game privileges, but it won't be so bad. Okay?"

"My mom won't care."

"If you really believed that, you wouldn't be afraid of showing her these grades. You know your mom cares. You know how much she loves you. This is disappointing, but it's not the end of the world."

The boy shrugged again. "I guess."

"I want you to come see me tomorrow, okay? Bring your homework. Tell your mom I'm going to be checking on you. We've got to get those grades back up."

"Yes, ma'am." David stood up, pulling his ball up from the floor. "Quincy's lucky," he said, heading for the door.

"Why do you say that?" Jeneva asked.

"'Cause he's got you for a mom," David said, smiling sweetly.

"He's also got a pretty good friend, too," Jeneva added. "Now, get. Go do that homework."

"Bye, Miss Douglas."

"Bye, David."

Stepping out of her dress, Jeneva fell back across her bed. The day had been longer and harder than she had anticipated. She mulled over her meeting with Robert. Since Bridget had warned her that Robert might be able to see Quincy whether she agreed or not, she'd decided against doing battle with him. She didn't have the energy for it, and in her heart she knew that their son deserved much better from both of them. Maybe they could make it work, she thought, wondering what other changes this was going to cause in her life.

Closing her eyes, Jeneva smiled. She would call MaryAnne before she went to bed. David's presence allowed her to do mother things she would never do with Quincy. She would never have the opportunity to

scold Quincy about failing grades. Jeneva welcomed
the diversion, the brief reprieve that had allowed her
into the teenager's world. She had often envied
MaryAnne, knowing that she would never be able to
interact with her son the way David and his mother
did. David's tears made her realize that different
didn't necessarily mean better.

The telephone on the nightstand rang. Sliding up
to the headboard, Jeneva reached for the receiver.

"Hello?"

"How did it go?" Bridget asked.

"Did you tell that tired brother what he could do
for you?" Roshawn asked.

Jeneva laughed. "Who dialed the three-way?"

Roshawn laughed. "You know I did. We want to
know about this kiss, and please don't tell us you
kissed Robert."

"No, I did not kiss Robert."

Roshawn sighed. "Thank goodness. I was about to
have a heart attack."

"You kissed Mac, didn't you?" Bridget said.

"You two kill me," Jeneva exclaimed, the sound of
their laughter a welcome comfort.

"Oh, yes, she did." Roshawn giggled. "Miss Jeneva
don' broke that lifelong drought. Girl don' turned on
the faucets!"

"Well, I want details," Bridget said, giggling right
along with her.

Jeneva could feel herself blushing. "I'm actually embarrassed," she said to her friends. "He and I had this
conversation about how much we're attracted to one
another, and right before I left last night, I kissed him.
And I mean I kissed him."

"On-the-cheek kissed him, or slipped-him-a-little-
tongue kissed him?" Roshawn asked.

"Kissed-him-on-the-lips kissed him."

"You go, girl. Can he kiss?"

"Either it's been that long or the man is absolutely incredible. I almost wet my pants. Took me an hour to remember how to breathe again after I left."

"So what's up with you two?" Bridget asked.

"I don't know. There's something about him that I really like. And he's wonderful with my son, but I don't know. I have to think about what's good for Quincy."

"His mother thinking about herself for once in her life would be good for him," Bridget said. "Giving up your own happiness is not going to make you a better mother, Jay."

"She's right," Roshawn added. "We've been telling you for years now that you needed to think about yourself for once. Besides, a man in your son's life couldn't ever hurt, especially one who wants to be there."

Jeneva sighed. "Robert suddenly wants to play daddy."

"What did you tell him?" asked Bridget.

"Nothing definite. I want to talk to Mac first. See what he and Quincy's doctors think."

"That's a good idea."

"I told Robert I'd give him an answer tomorrow."

"You should have told him—"

"Don't say it, Roshawn. You are always trying to instigate something," Bridget said.

"Look, Miss Legal Eagle, just because you like to handle things nicely, doesn't mean it always works. Sometimes you need to throw a little commotion into the mix."

"I swear, Roshawn, you don't have any sense."

"Humph. Got more than you think I got."

"What I think is that you've been sniffing far too much hair dye in your off hours."

Jeneva laughed. "The two of you need to stop."

"By the way," Bridget said, "when can you give me a touch-up? My head is starting to look bad."

"Don't know if I can. Might sniff too much dye!"

The three of them broke out into laughter.

"Bridget, did you know Robert remarried and has three other kids?" Jeneva asked.

"Oh, no, he doesn't," Roshawn exclaimed. "Three kids?"

"No, I didn't know," Bridget said. "How old are these kids?"

"His son is ten, I think, and he's got twin girls who are nine. I think that's what he told me."

"Brother's been busy."

"Who'd he marry?" Bridget asked, ignoring Roshawn's commentary.

"I don't know. Some woman named Fiona. Said he met her when I filed for divorce."

"Fiona? Fiona Winslow?"

"I don't know. Do you know her?"

"Well, if it's who I think it is, she was an attorney at the law firm that handled his side of your divorce. But I only met her briefly."

Roshawn asked the question Jeneva was thinking. "So what's the sister look like, 'cause I've got to give Robert his props. He looks good for his age even though he does make me sick to my stomach."

When Bridget hesitated, clearing her voice as if she had a cold, Jeneva and Roshawn both knew instantly.

"Oh, no, he didn't," Roshawn exclaimed.

Jeneva shook her head and laughed. "Blond and blue-eyed?"

"No. She's Irish, I think, a redhead with green eyes. She's very pretty and very sweet. I can't believe she married Robert."

"Brother got some nerve," Roshawn interjected.

"Like you are one to talk," Bridget said. "You haven't dated a black man since you started dating, with that little half-and-half child of yours."

"That's different."

"Why?"

"Because I'm a woman who has devoted her entire life to challenging the system. It's past time we sisters starting testing the other side of the waters. Besides, it's not like there are a whole lot of cocoa-puff, Hershey-bar, chocolate-chip brothers in Washington for us women to choose from," Roshawn scoffed. "And don't be talking about my baby."

Laughter rang heavy across the telephone lines.

"Sounds like you're trying to find a pack of cookies," Bridget said, "not a man."

"Oh, I'm sorry, and the last time you had a man was when, Miss Thang?"

"I've had a date in the last five years."

"With your vibrator, maybe. I'm talking about a man with two legs, who's breathing on his own."

"Like you're an expert when it comes to romance, Miss Still Doing My Ex-Hubby Because I Can't Move On."

"I'm still doing him 'cause the sex is good."

"And he's breathing without batteries," Jeneva said with another chuckle.

Bridget and Roshawn laughed with her. "Oh, you can't say a word!" Bridget exclaimed. "Got some nerve, and you just getting a kiss after a hundred years."

"Well, all I'm saying is that as long as I don't limit my choices, there's more out there for me to choose from. Don't hate me 'cause I like my ice cream to come in different flavors and I have a sugar cone I get to lick every now and then," Roshawn said.

"I guess Robert thinks the same thing," Jeneva concluded.

"Does it bother you?" Bridget asked, turning serious.

"His being married didn't bother me. Not much. But when he told me he had three kids, I almost lost it. Spilled my glass of champagne."

"I hope it was expensive champagne," Roshawn said, "and that he was paying for it."

"It was and he did."

"That's what I'm talking about!"

The three women laughed and talked for another hour before Jeneva told them she had to get some rest. Promising to meet for lunch later in the week, they each hung up the telephone, still giggling over their tribulations with men.

Thirteen

The heavy smell of chlorine hung in the air, filling the large room with its pungent aroma. In the low end of the Olympic-sized swimming pool, Mecan, Quincy, and two physical therapists were doing a series of exercises in the three feet of ocean-blue water that filled the large cavity. Quincy was paddling as Dawn Summers held him afloat. He splashed water about excitedly.

Dawn's partner, Alex Treyburn, laughed. "I think we've created a monster. This one's a real fish."

Mecan chuckled. "Won't be too long before he's swimming laps on his own."

"Before the end of the year, if he keeps this up," Dawn said.

"Okay, Quincy," Alex commanded. "Time to float." The young man flipped the boy over onto his back, his hand supporting Quincy's head as he stared up toward the ceiling. Looking straight down at him, Alex repeated himself. "Float."

Almost instantly, Quincy relaxed his body, allowing the cushion of moisture to take control. He extended his arms against his sides, leaning his head back so that his ears were fully submerged. Looking on, Mecan smiled, pride shining on his face, as Quincy executed his breathing perfectly, inhaling and exhaling in quick full breaths. He remained perfectly still as Dawn and Alex backed away from him.

"He won't move until I tell him to. It's amazing," Dawn said. "He would stay like this all day if we let him."

"Fish," Alex said with a quick grin, bending his lips upward.

Mecan glanced up at the clock on the wall. "How much longer does he have?" he asked.

"I want to work with him for another thirty minutes," Dawn said. "I want to start teaching him how to scull. Then he has group play after that. Billy and Joel will be coming from your house and we should have about thirty others altogether."

"What's that?" Mecan asked. "What's sculling?"

"It's an arm-and-hand motion that propels you through the water in a back-float position," Alex said.

Mecan nodded his understanding.

"Will you be staying?" Dawn asked. "It's not often we get you down here in the pool with us, Mr. Tolliver."

Mecan shook his head. "I wish I could, but duty calls. I'm glad I was able to make it this time, though. But I need to go get dressed."

Dawn and Alex nodded, waving good-bye as Mecan pulled himself up and out of the pool of water. As he looked back over his shoulder, Quincy was still floating peacefully, lost safely in the warm blanket of wetness.

Thirty minutes later, after a hot shower, Mecan had changed into his requisite suit and tie. Pulling his jacket onto his shoulders, he took one last glance in the full-length mirror before stepping back out into the pool area. Natalia stood engaged in conversation with a group of house parents. The pool had filled quickly with students bobbing up and down playfully.

Mecan spotted Quincy splashing water, Billy and Joel having joined in the fun. At either end of the pool, two lifeguards had taken up residence, positioning themselves upon their high stools to oversee the student activities. From their seats, which towered over the water, allowing them full view from corner to corner, there was little they missed. Every so often, one would call a child by his or her name, admonish them for some wrongdoing, and send them in another direction to continue playing.

Joel spotted Mecan and began to wave excitedly. "Mac! Mac! Look! Me and Billy and Quincy are in the water! Look, Mac!

Mecan waved back, matching Joel's exuberance with his own. "Very good, son!" he called back. "That's very good!"

Natalia turned toward him, excusing herself from the dialogue she was having as she headed in his direction.

"Do you want me to pick up Michael from speech therapy?" he asked as she joined him, smiling widely.

"No, no, Juan is at the house. He arrived just after you and Quincy left. He took Michael and will bring him back. We will meet him for lunch, then Quincy has lessons with Talbot for a few hours. The other boys have classes also. Juan said he's going to stay to help out."

"Great!" Mecan exclaimed. "I look forward to seeing him. Glad that he's making his way back. I should be able to have lunch with everyone today, as long as it's not tuna fish. I have had my fill of tuna."

Natalia laughed. "It's not Joel's day to pick. I have the honors this afternoon."

"Thank goodness," Mecan said with a chuckle. "That boy is going to turn into the chicken of the sea if he doesn't learn to eat anything else."

"Well, it's beef stew today. I put the crock pot on before I left. It should be ready about one o'clock."

Mecan nodded his head, glancing down at the watch on his wrist. "I need to run. I have a ton of paperwork to get out of the way today. Anything else?"

Natalia nodded. "Yes. Ms. Douglas called this morning. She says she needs to speak with you when you have an opportunity."

Mecan, who'd been staring out at the children, dropped his gaze to Natalia's face, heat sweeping over his cheeks. His eyebrows were raised widely, excitement flooding his face. Natalia grinned.

"You are so funny," she said, giggling lightly.

"What?" Mecan asked, visibly embarrassed.

"Nothing. Go. Call Ms. Douglas."

The young woman seated outside his office greeted him cheerfully. "Mr. Tolliver, good morning. We weren't expecting you this morning."

"Good morning, Tanya. Figured if I didn't get in here to get some work done, I might not have a job next week."

"I don't think there's any possibility of that," Tanya Flynn, his secretary, responded. "Your messages are on your desk and I left the files for the new students there also. We have two coming in next month. Both girls."

Mecan nodded. "Thanks, Tanya."

"Can I get you a cup of coffee?"

"Thank you. That would be great right about now."

The young woman shook her head, smiling sweetly as she rose from her seat. Brushing past him, she said she'd be right back if there was anything else he needed. Mecan thanked her, then opened the large oak door that led into his personal space.

Much thought had gone into the interior decor of Mecan Tolliver's office. Feeling like an old, English library, the walls were paneled, the wood's grain a deep, dark mahogany. Floor-to-ceiling bookcases, filled with leather-bound books, occupied two side walls. Two large windows against the front wall allowed a wealth of natural light to enter, flooding the interior with brightness.

Mecan made his way over to his desk, an imposing structure, sitting in the room's center. Two upholstered chairs sat in front of the desk, one large, leather executive chair behind it. He flipped through the stack of mail and the pile of pink phone-message sheets Tanya had neatly left for his review. Just as he reached for his telephone, Tanya entered, bearing a large mug of steaming coffee in her hands.

"Just like you like it," she said, setting it down on the desk in front of where he stood. "Can I get you anything else?"

Mecan shook his head. "Not that I can think of," he said. "On second thought, take that back. We need to schedule a house parents meeting for the end of the month. I want all the parents to attend, so arrangements will need to be made for the students."

"Okay."

"Let's see if we can arrange it for a movie night. We should have enough staff to monitor the room while I meet with the parents. That should work. A Saturday night might help also since some of the kids will be away for the weekend. Let me know what you can do."

"And this meeting is for . . ."

"Fund-raising, what else? I'd like us to toss around some ideas that will help generate additional money for the houses. I was talking with Natalia and a few of the other mothers and they'd like to freshen up the homes. One wants to make each of her kids' bedrooms more personal. Natalia and Juan could use a new toaster. Just simple stuff, but those things that they don't want to wait till the beginning of the year for, and annual funding to acquire."

"Do you have some ideas already?"

"I think a community event might be nice."

Tanya nodded her head. "Some sort of carnival or fair?"

"Exactly. Each house could have its own booth. The parents could engage the kids in participating and helping run it. Something along that line."

"That sounds like it might be fun. I'll get the meeting on the calendar and make sure everyone knows where they need to be."

"Thanks, Tanya."

"By the way, are you going to be filling in at the house much longer? Juan stopped by to check in earlier. He said he hopes to be back full time by next week."

"I heard. Guess I'll have to give up my bed, huh?"

"I'm sure you'll be glad to get back to your own home and your own bed for a while."

Mecan shrugged. "Well, let me get to work. I'll buzz you if I need you."

"Yes, sir."

Tanya made her way out of the room, closing the door behind her. Dropping his jacket against the coat rack in the corner, Mecan sat down in his chair, making himself comfortable.

Reaching for the telephone, he dialed Jeneva's office number, fidgeting anxiously as he waited for the line to connect.

A pleasant voice answered the call. "Thank you for calling Northwest Marketing. How may I direct your call?" the voice sang into the receiver.

"Jeneva Douglas, please."

"Thank you. Please hold while I connect your call."
Elevator music filled the empty space as he was
transferred. A few seconds passed before Jeneva finally picked up.

"This is Jeneva Douglas."

"Jeneva. It's Mecan. I'm not disturbing you, am I?"

"Mac. No, not at all. How are you?"

He inhaled deeply. "I'm well. How about yourself?"

He could feel her smiling into the receiver. "I'm
good. How's Quincy?"

"Swimming. He was having a ball when I left him."

Jeneva shook her head. "I can't believe he's swimming. I have to see that the next time I come."

"We'll make sure of it. Natalia said you needed to
speak with me?"

Jeneva suddenly found herself searching for words,
almost anxious about explaining what her issues were.

"Yes. I have something that's come up and I could
use some advice."

"You know I'll help, any way I can. What's the problem?"

"Quincy's father is in town."

"Your ex-husband?"

"Yes. He's here in Seattle and he wants to see
Quincy. The problem I have with that is Robert hasn't
seen Quincy since he was an infant. He's never had
anything to do with our son and Quincy doesn't know
him. I'm concerned that this might not be a good
thing for Quincy."

"Is it safe to assume that you and Quincy's father
are not on the best of terms?"

"Very. Last night was the first time he and I have
spoken since he abandoned us. It was difficult. I still
harbor a lot of animosity. More than I realized."

"I'm sorry."

Jeneva smiled faintly across the phone line, welcoming Mecan's calming voice. "So how do you think this will affect Quincy?"

Mecan paused. "You may not want to hear this, but it will probably be good for him. Quincy needs as many people rooting for his success as he can get. Who better to help him do that than his father? That is, if he's willing to be supportive of the boy."

Jeneva sighed. "He says he is."

"Do you believe him?"

"I don't know. I would like to, for Quincy's sake, but he abandoned us before. I honestly don't know that I can trust him not to do it again."

"Can you hold on for a moment?" Mecan asked.

"Certainly."

"I'll be right back," the man said, before pushing the MUTE button on the telephone. He buzzed the intercom for Tanya. "Tanya, would you please bring me Quincy Douglas's file, specifically the copy of the parents' custody decree? Thank you."

"Yes, sir, Mr. Tolliver."

Within seconds, Tanya dropped the file onto his desk, opening the folder to expose the requested document on top.

"Thank you," Mecan said again, flipping quickly through the pages. He pulled the telephone back into his hand. "Jeneva?"

"I'm still here."

"Sorry about that. I'm looking at your custody order. I'm sure you know that Mr. Douglas has the legal right to see Quincy if he chooses. There isn't anything we could do to stop him."

"I do. But if you or his doctors thought it would be a problem, that it might hurt Quincy, then I'd fight not to allow it to happen."

Mecan sat back in his chair. "I want to have a conversation with Dr. Burton and Dr. Abernathy, but I think they'll both agree with me that Quincy would probably be well served to meet with his father."

Mecan could hear her sighing heavily into the telephone, almost sensing that she felt defeated. "We can make this very easy for Quincy. Obviously your ex-husband is going to require some training before the two can interact effectively. My staff and I can facilitate that. His initial meetings can easily be monitored to ensure Quincy has a positive reaction. Then we can take it from there, depending on what you and Mr. Douglas choose to do."

Jeneva nodded into the receiver. "Should I bring him with me next week?"

"I don't think that's a good idea. I think Quincy might be sensitive to your apprehensions and that may cause stress he doesn't need."

"I wouldn't do anything to upset my son," Jeneva said, slightly offended.

"Jeneva, I know that. Please don't misunderstand. All I'm saying is that Quincy is extremely perceptive when it comes to your moods. If he detects any anger or bitterness between you and his father, it may be more difficult for the two of them to bond," Mecan said, trying to soothe her ruffled feelings.

He could hear her breathing, but she didn't respond. Mecan continued. "Why don't you have Mr. Douglas call me? I'll make the necessary arrangements and keep you posted. When you come to visit Saturday, this may all be behind you, and the two of you can just enjoy your time together. Trust me, Jeneva. I promise I won't let anything happen to Quincy."

"Thank you, Mecan. "

After hanging up the telephone, Mecan felt as if all the air had been sucked out of him, his body deflated like a balloon without helium. He had heard some-

thing in Jeneva's voice when she'd talked about
Robert Douglas. Something that had more to do with
her than it would ever have to do with Quincy. He
couldn't put his finger on what the emotions were
that were fueling her, but he could sense the intensity.
Although her concern for her son was genuine, it ran
in tandem with something else.

Jeneva and Roshawn sat watching Roshawn's
daughter, Ming, and her two best friends, Kara and
Leslie, practicing their cheerleading routines. The afternoon was warmer than usual and the bright
sunlight flooded Roshawn's small backyard. The three
young girls were giggling and whispering as they attempted the kicks and jumps that would be required
of them at the school tryouts. Jeneva remembered
those days well and was grateful to have them behind
her. Roshawn expressed the same sentiments. "Do you
remember when we tried out for cheerleading?"

"Do I! I pulled a muscle in my thigh that first time.
Couldn't walk for a month!"

Roshawn laughed. "You were so pitiful!"

"Not nearly as pitiful as you were when Allison
Dunn fell out of that tripod, landed on top of your
head, and gave you a concussion."

The two women laughed at the memories. Roshawn
jumped to her feet. "Bet you don't remember that
cheer we used to do."

"Which one?"

Roshawn placed her hands on her hips, pulling her
torso straight. "Hey, now, we're here, everybody stay
clear, get your team right on back, the Seattle War-
riors are on the attack. Stay clear. We're here," she
chimed, her hands flapping in the wind as she ended
the chant with a high front kick.

Jeneva laughed as her friend grabbed the back of her leg, the expression across her face strained. "Yes, I do," she said, "but you're not supposed to look like you're in pain when you do it."

Across the yard, the three girls were chuckling loudly. Roshawn fanned a hand in their direction. "Mind your business," she called out to her daughter.

"That was so bad, Mom," Ming replied, still giggling. "You are so embarrassing!"

"I'll show you embarrassing," Roshawn said, returning to her seat. "She knows I still got it," she added, her comment directed at Jeneva.

"Please, you didn't have it back then," Jeneva said with a smile.

Roshawn rolled her eyes. Reaching for the pitcher of lemonade on the patio table, she refilled her glass and then Jeneva's, drawing the container to her mouth to sip on the tangy contents.

"So what's up with you and this man?" she asked.

"What man?"

Roshawn gave Jeneva one of her *you know what I'm talking about* looks.

Jeneva shrugged. "Oh, that man. Not much." She smiled at her friend, who shook her head knowingly.

"That's saying a lot for you. It's about time you found yourself a man."

"He's not my man."

"Not if you're not working on it. Need to throw some leg on him."

Jeneva shook her head. "Girl, please." She moved to change the subject. "Robert's going to see Quincy."

"Now you know you need to put your foot right up that brother's tight chocolate—"

"Mom, can we take our bikes over to Blockbuster and rent a video? Please?" Ming interrupted the conversation, cutting off her mother's words.

"Girl, did you see me talking to your aunt Jeneva? Don't you know how to say 'excuse me'?"

"Sorry. Excuse me. Can we, please?"

"What movie do you plan to rent?"

"We want to get a comedy. Something funny."

Roshawn nodded her head. "Nothing rated PG-thirteen or R, and you are all to come right back, is that understood?"

"Yes, ma'am."

"And make sure you each wear your helmets," Roshawn added before handing the girl a twenty-dollar bill from her pocket and shooing her off.

Ming skipped away excitedly, Leslie and Kara racing behind her.

Jeneva laughed. "She's growing up so fast."

"Too fast. That child is about to wear me down. My mother cursed me, you know. When I got pregnant, she told me she wished I had a child just like me. Now, what did she go and do that for? She knew what a torment I had been."

"That's why she did it. Payback for the misery you put her through."

Roshawn rolled her eyes. "Now, where were we? That's right, Robert. I can't believe that brother. He has some nerve."

"I know it. Does your ex-hubby have any Mafia connections? I could use a hit man!"

Roshawn laughed. "Don't I wish. All Chen would hit him with would be some Oriental tea."

The two women chuckled heartily. Roshawn stretched her body upward, still rubbing the muscle she'd strained in her leg.

"Back to Mr. Mac. Have you gotten another kiss yet?"

Jeneva blushed. "No, and I swear you have a one-track mind."

"What are you waiting for?"

"I'm not waiting for anything. We're just taking things slow."

"You can't go much slower, Jay. You haven't moved it along fast enough to get your engines warmed up yet."

"We're getting there. We spend a lot of time on the telephone. I love talking to him."

Roshawn lifted her leg up in the air, shaking her foot in Jeneva's direction. "Talk is cheap. You can't throw no leg on a man over the telephone. It doesn't work like that!" she exclaimed.

Jeneva giggled. "You are too crazy!"

"What you need to do," Roshawn said, dropping her foot back to the ground, "is drive up there in nothing but your birthday suit and your raincoat. Tell him your having some engine trouble and get him to meet you halfway. When he gets to you, ask him to give you a tune-up. Bet you when you drop that coat he'll know what buttons to push to warm you up."

Jeneva threw her hands up in the air. "It's time for me to go. You've lost your mind now."

Roshawn laughed. "Or invest in one of those video cameras for your computer. Since you spend so much time on the telephone, at least make it interesting. Give the brother a show he won't forget. You can shake those ta-tas at him in something tight and skimpy the next time you're having one of those wonderful conversations. Then when you see him in person, he'll be ready for you, girl!"

"Good-bye, Roshawn," Jeneva said, rising from her seat.

"Where are you going? I've got a million ideas to guarantee you catch this man. Just tell me what you're looking for," Roshawn said, still laughing.

Waving good-bye, Jeneva skipped across the yard

herself, thinking that if Ming was anything like her
mother, Roshawn definitely was going to have her
hands full.

Fourteen

As the knock on the door echoed around the room, Mecan knew Jeneva would be sitting on pins and needles waiting for him to report back to her. Since their conversation on Monday, he had arranged for Quincy and his father to meet for the first time. He closed the file of papers before him just as Tanya opened the door and escorted Robert Douglas inside. Mecan rose from his seat. He stood just a mere two inches taller than Robert, but had more bulk to his body, he thought, as he studied the other man quickly, noting his expensive suit and leather shoes. Robert Douglas wore his wealth nicely. Though he did not carry himself boastfully, it was obvious that Mr. Douglas had done well for himself. He extended his hand in greeting, the two shaking palm to palm as he said hello.

"Welcome to Hewitt House, Mr. Douglas."

Robert glanced quickly around the room as Mecan gestured for him to take a seat. "Please, call me Robert. I appreciate your help, Mr. Tolliver."

"Mecan. It rhymes with pecan. And that's what I'm here for."

"I'm sure Quincy's mother has filled you in."

"She has. She has some concerns, but she knows we support your involvement with your son as long as it's in his best interest."

Robert sat back in his seat. "How is my son doing?"

"I'm very pleased with Quincy. He's adjusted nicely. He's made marked progress and continues to surprise us."

Robert nodded. "When can I see him?"

Mecan smiled. "Quincy is in the middle of a lesson at the moment. We're going to allow you to sit and observe, but before you two meet, I want you to sit with one of our speech therapists. We're using a tactile therapy technique to teach Quincy how to talk. It's very simple to do and you will see his instructors doing it. Once you think you're comfortable, then I'll introduce you to your son."

"How do you think he'll react?"

"I honestly don't know. I've already explained who you are and that you were coming. He knows what a father is and he knows we all have one and how that parent should fit into his life. So, he's prepared. But as for how he'll react," Mecan shrugged, "we won't know until it happens."

"How long can I stay?"

"Well, if it goes well and Quincy seems comfortable, for as long as you like. Do you fish?"

Robert chuckled. "Haven't done that since I was a boy myself."

Mecan smiled with him. "Well, Quincy likes to fish. I've cleared my schedule and if you think you'd like to, we can take him fishing. That will give you some time to be together."

Robert nodded. "Thank you. I'd like to do that."

Minutes later the two men stood outside the educational classroom, peering through a large, two-way mirror that separated the main study area from a separate viewing room. Inside, Quincy sat at a table with Talbot, the two reading and viewing a series of black-and-white flash cards. Robert watched as Quincy placed his hands on the white man's neck each time the man spoke, repeating the gesture against his own throat when he tried to mimic what had just been said. A rush of tears clouded his vision. Even as the boy was sitting, he could see that his son stood almost as tall as he did. Quincy was his mother's child, Jeneva's features having clearly marked him. The boy's complexion was like hers; he had not inherited any of his father's dark hue. His round face, narrow nose, and thin lips were all her, and he saw Jeneva's beauty in his son's large eyes.

He could feel his emotion welling up in the back of his throat, threatening to cut off his air, and he inhaled deeply, fighting not to cry. Sensing his discomfort, Mecan dropped a heavy hand against the man's shoulder.

"Why don't you take some time, have a seat, and just observe? I'm going in to let Quincy know you're here."

Robert nodded, his gaze still locked on his child. He watched as Mecan entered the room and greeted the instructor and then Quincy. He watched as Quincy came to his feet, wrapping his arms warmly around Mecan, who returned the hug in earnest. The boy looked Mecan in the eyes as he pushed his fingers against Mecan's Adam's apple. The conversation passed quickly, then Quincy sat back down, pulling the flash cards back into his hands. The two men stood talking quietly, Mecan nodding his head as Talbot gave him an update on the young man's progress.

A few minutes later, Mecan returned to Robert's side, smiling politely. "Are you ready?" he asked. Robert's head bobbed up and down.

Mecan gestured for him to follow. As he entered the brightly decorated classroom, Talbot Lomas extended his hand and introduced himself. "Hello, Mr. Douglas. I'm Quincy's teacher."

"Very nice to meet you."

"He and I have had a good session today. He's doing well. He's recognizing the alphabet and he's starting to string words together. You should be very proud."

"Thank you," Robert responded, his gaze following Mecan, who'd gone to stand beside his son.

"Good luck," the man said as he tapped Robert encouragingly on the shoulder. Turning an about-face, Talbot smiled and made his way out of the room.

Quincy began to rock back and forth in his seat, his body moving in rapid succession. Mecan was speaking to him softly, running a hand against the boy's back to calm him down. He looked up and gestured for Robert to join them. Gripping Quincy by the elbow, Mecan pulled him to his feet as his father came to stand in front of him. He pulled Quincy's hand to his throat.

"Say hello to your father, Quincy. Say hello."

Quincy glanced quickly at Robert, then lifted his gaze to the ceiling. His hand fell back down to his side. Mecan took a deep breath. "Quincy, say hello," he repeated, hand to throat to lips and back again. This time Quincy turned to look directly at Robert. Taking two steps forward, he laid his head against his father's chest, his arms still hanging limply at his sides.

Tears spilled out of Robert's eyes. Mecan nodded his encouragement. Reaching out to hug his son, Robert wrapped his arms tightly around the boy's body, clasping him tightly against him. He held on, Quincy heavy against his chest, his arms like steel around the young man's lean frame. After a few minutes, Quincy lifted himself up and took a step back. He pressed his fingers against his father's neck.

"Hello, son," Robert said, communicating as he had been instructed. "Hello."

"Hel . . . lo," Quincy responded, his voice clear and strong. "Hel . . . lo, Da . . . dee."

Robert smiled brightly, glancing toward Mecan, who was watching them cautiously. The man smiled back.

The teenager put his hands to his lips and blew air. He turned to Mecan, who looked at him curiously. Looking back at his father, he reached for his throat and opened his mouth. "Name . . . Quin . . . cy," he said, stretching the syllables out of his mouth like saltwater taffy. "Quin . . . cy." Then, with a wide smile, he clapped his hands together excitedly.

Natalia greeted Robert politely as Quincy pulled him inside the house, leading him by the hand from room to room. Their dinners sat waiting on the stove-top, three plates set at the table.

"You must be hungry, Mr. Douglas," she said, after directing Quincy to go wash his hands so he could help with dinner.

"I hadn't even thought about it," Robert said. "I've been having such a good time."

Quincy returned and grabbed his father by his arm. He nodded when Natalia pried his fingers loose and pushed him toward the kitchen, following closely behind him as she directed him to the table.

Minutes later she called Mecan and Robert, ordering them to take a seat. The trio ate hungrily, feasting on the taco casserole Natalia had prepared. After two plates of food, Quincy sat back content, his stomach pleasantly full.

"These boys can eat." Natalia laughed as she offered

Quincy a slice of strawberry shortcake that he consumed with gusto.

The adults laughed comfortably as they sat watching Quincy. When the meal was complete, Natalia continued to give out commands.

"You two men get to do the dishes. Quincy, bath," she said.

Quincy stomped his foot.

Both she and Mecan looked at him in surprise. Mecan stood up, walking to stand beside Quincy. He shook his head from side to side. "Bath. Now," he commanded, pointing a finger toward the bathroom.

Quincy lifted his eyes to the ceiling, stomping his foot to the floor for a second time.

"Now, Quincy," Mecan repeated.

The moment of defiance passed and Quincy headed down the long hallway, humming loudly as Natalia trailed behind him.

"That's a first," Mecan said, lifting the dirty dishes from the table. "Our young man is starting to assert himself." He glanced at Robert, who stood, passing him the dishes from the sink.

"He's never been difficult before?"

"Not once. Quincy has been the model student since day one. Even when he was ill, he went out of his way to be mindful."

"She'll blame me."

"Who?"

"Jeneva."

Mecan laughed. "It's a good thing. It demonstrates that he's starting to think freely. He's making conscious decisions and communicating them. He is starting to do things and have experiences he didn't have when he was three and four years old. He's reacting just as he should. There's no blame in that. In fact, we celebrate that. It means we're making progress."

Robert heaved a deep sigh. Quiet filled the room, both men falling into his own thoughts. Before they knew it, Quincy bounded back down the hallway, Joel and Michael following closely on his heels.

"Yo! Slow those horses down," Mecan bellowed, wrapping each of them into a hug.

"Bedtime, Mac," Joel chimed. "Bedtime."

"Go to bed. Go to bed. Go to bed," Michael chanted as he marched in place.

Quincy waved his body from side to side, clapping his hands merrily together.

"Who's doing the story tonight?" Mecan asked.

"Nat, Nat, Nat," Michael sang, pointing at Natalia, who'd followed them into the living room.

"That's right," the woman said. "Say good night to Mac and Mr. Douglas, and as soon as you're all in bed, I'll read the story."

Joel reached out to hug Mecan and then Robert. "Good night, don't let the bed bugs bite." He giggled.

Michael followed, hesitating when he reached Robert, then smiling shyly as he turned and waved good-bye instead.

Quincy stood his ground, not moving from where he stood. Mecan tossed a look at Natalia, who shook her head.

"Quincy, would you like your father to put you to bed?" she asked.

Quincy's gaze rose to the corner of the ceiling, his eyes flitting back and forth.

"I'll take that as a yes," Natalia said, as she placed her hands against his cheeks and lowered his face until he was looking at her. "Bed, Quincy," she said. "Bed."

Robert went to his son's side. "Bed, Quincy," he

commanded, pulling his son's palm to his face as he mouthed the word against the boy's palm. "Bed. Now."

Leading the way, Quincy headed back down the hallway, his father following behind him. Mecan and Natalia watched them until they were out of sight.

"What do you make of that?" she asked him, lowering her voice as she spoke.

"I think we're going to have to reevaluate our approach," Mecan answered. "There's more going on in that young man's mind than we could ever have imagined."

She nodded her head in agreement. "I'm coming!" Natalia called out, hearing her name being called from the rear of the house. "I'm coming."

It was almost ten o'clock when Jeneva's telephone finally rang. She raced to answer the call.

"Hello."

"Jeneva, it's Mecan."

"How's Quincy? Did Robert come?" she asked, tossing questions at him with lightning speed.

"Quincy's fine and, yes, his father came. Robert spent the whole day with him."

Jeneva dropped down onto the sofa, pulling her legs up beneath her. "He didn't have any problems, did he?"

"Your son was excited to see his father. They formed quite a bond."

She could feel herself nodding. "That's good, I guess."

"It is good. Does it bother you?"

"I'd be lying if I said no. I've had Quincy all to myself since he was born. I don't know if I'm ready to share him with Robert."

Mecan chuckled softly. "Well, you may not have a choice, but I think it'll be good for both of you."

"Mac, don't take this personally, but sometimes your opinions irritate me."

Mecan laughed. "Do they, now?"

"Yes, they do. I haven't had a lot of experience with people telling me what they think is good for me and my son, but you've been doing it since I first spoke to you. Whether I've asked or not."

"I can be pushy like that," he said, smiling.

Silence floated between them before Jeneva spoke again. "I enjoyed our kiss the other night," she said softly. "I hope I wasn't being too bold."

Mecan grinned broadly. "Not at all. I'm glad you did. I wanted to, but I didn't have the nerve."

"Please don't think I make a habit of throwing myself at a man."

Mecan laughed. "Don't worry. I didn't."

Jeneva twisted the telephone cord around her finger. "Well, I guess I should say good night. Will I see you Saturday?"

"Definitely. In fact . . ." He paused, gathering his thoughts.

"Yes?" Jeneva asked.

"Will you have dinner with me Friday night? I would really like to see you."

"I would really like to do that," she said, not hesitating for a second.

"I'll call you tomorrow and we can make plans."

"Thank you, Mecan."

"Good night, Jeneva."

Jeneva dropped the telephone onto the hook, bobbing up and down excitedly in her seat. She had a date for Friday night. She hadn't had a date since high school. As she reached for the telephone to call

Bridget and Roshawn, the appliance rang, causing her to jump.

"Hello?" she said, pulling the receiver to her ear.

"Jeneva, it's Robert."

"Robert? Where are you?"

"I'm about two hours from Seattle. Finally got reception on my cell phone."

"Why are you calling?"

"I saw Quincy today. He's a beautiful boy, Jeneva."

Not knowing how to respond, Jeneva said nothing.

"You still there?" Robert asked.

"Yes."

"Well, I just called because I wanted to say thank you. That's all. Thank you, Jeneva."

"You're welcome."

"Good night, Jay."

"Drive safe, Robert."

Drawing the telephone to her chest, Jeneva took a deep breath, then wiped at the one tear that had managed to drip down her cheek.

Fifteen

Bridget and Roshawn were at her door before she'd even managed to crawl out of bed and brush her teeth. She wiped sleep from her eyes as she opened the front door to let them in.

"You're going to be late," Bridget said, setting a cardboard tray of coffee-filled cups and a bag of pastries onto her kitchen table.

"I'm not going to be late," Jeneva responded, yawning widely.

"Mmmm," Roshawn hummed. "Looking the way you look, you should have gotten up last night to get ready."

Jeneva laughed. "Leave me alone," she said as she headed into the bathroom.

"What are you wearing?" Roshawn asked, calling out from her bedroom closet.

Stepping back into the bedroom, brushing her teeth, Jeneva shrugged. "I don't know," she muttered, her mouth filled with toothpaste.

Bridget shook her head in disbelief. "You're going out with a man for the first time since your wedding and you don't know what you're wearing?"

Back in the bathroom, Jeneva rinsed her mouth. "This isn't a big deal."

"Oh, yes, it is," Roshawn exclaimed, pulling the

woman's clothes from the closet and dropping dresses on the bed.

"No dress," Bridget said, shaking her head. "She should do slacks. She needs to be comfortable. Where's that red pantsuit?"

"Not that one," Jeneva said, joining them. "It makes me look fat. The black one, I think." She pointed at a two-piece, cashmere sweater set that Bridget held in her hand.

"Yes," Roshawn exclaimed, rifling through her jewelry box for the right accessories. "Where's your Chanel scarf? Have to have the Chanel scarf."

"I can't believe you two." Jeneva chuckled as she dropped down onto the bed.

"What time are you leaving?" Bridget asked, sitting down next to her, passing her friend a cup of black coffee.

"More important," Roshawn asked, pulling her own cup to her lips, "where are you going?"

Bridget and Jeneva laughed.

"I'm meeting him on San Juan Island. Apparently he has a home there."

"You're kidding, right?"

Jeneva shook her head. "No. He has a home there and it's a good midway point between the school and Seattle. I'm meeting him there, we're going to spend the evening together, have dinner, and I'm staying the night."

"You go, girl!"

Bridget shook her head. "She's just spending the night on San Juan Island, not sleeping with the man, fool!"

"How do you know?" Roshawn asked.

"I'm not," Jeneva said, shaking her own head at Roshawn. "I don't know this man well enough to be sleeping with him."

"Uh-huh."

"I don't."

"Girl, you might throw them lips on him again and just lose your mind. Don't know what you might do if he touches just the right spot and makes you go crazy."

The other two women giggled as Roshawn fell across the bed, pretending to be lost in ecstasy.

"You're a fool," Bridget said, still laughing.

"No. I just got me some last night."

"The husband?" Jeneva asked.

"The ex-husband."

"You are so sick and twisted," Bridget added.

"And how was your vibrator?"

Bridget rolled her eyes, then turned her attention back to Jeneva. "So, do you know where you're staying?"

"He invited me to bunk in his guest room. I told him I'd think about it. But I made a reservation at the Harbor Lodge, just in case."

"Very nice."

"We'll go up to the school tomorrow so I can see Quincy, and then I'll come home tomorrow night."

"Did you call in sick to work?" Roshawn asked. "'Cause I can call for you if you want."

"No. I've got so much vacation time saved up, I could take the next six months off without it being an issue."

"What time's your ferry?" Bridget asked.

"I need to catch that ten forty-five into Seattle, I think. Then I'll drive up the coast to Anacortes Ferry and take it over to San Juan Island. It should be a nice day."

"I wouldn't worry about the day. Get you a nice night," Roshawn said. "Here," she reached into her large carry bag that sat at the foot of the bed, "I bought you something." She tossed a Victoria's Secret bag at Jeneva. "Have to have some pretty panties to be parading around in."

Jeneva burst out laughing when she pulled the sheer garments from the bag. The black lace teddy and matching thong fit neatly into the palm of her hand.

"Roshawn, I am not wearing this!"

"Not for long, anyway. Shouldn't take him but a few minutes to get you out of it, but you'll look good for the foreplay!"

Bridget pulled the garments out of Jeneva's hand, holding up the top against the front of her tailored blue blouse. "This is cute, Roshawn. Just the right touch of hoochie."

"I got taste, girl."

"You two have to go. I need to get ready," Jeneva said, still laughing.

The Dynamic Divas pulled themselves up, sipping the last of their coffee.

"Call us the minute you get back," Bridget said.

"With all the details," Roshawn chimed. "And girl, we know it's been a while. So please, don't hurt the brother!"

Nervous energy had been playing hide-and-seek with Jeneva since the Washington State ferry pulled into the Friday Harbor terminal, unloading her, her car, and its other passengers onto San Juan Island. Although Mecan's directions were precise, she stopped to ask a couple on matching mopeds to confirm that she was headed in the right direction. Glancing at the clock on the dashboard, she hoped she wasn't too early. She didn't want to appear too anxious when she reached her destination.

Maneuvering her way through town, Jeneva was captivated by the island's tranquil beauty. She gulped the fresh sea air through her opened window, invigorated by the cool breeze that rushed in to kiss her cheek and ruffle the curls in her hair. Turning onto a dead-end street, she pulled her car down the length of driveway that led to Mecan Tolliver's home. From behind a wealth of fir and pine trees, the sizable waterfront property loomed to the forefront. Stately evergreens graced the large lot, looming magnanimously over the postcard setting.

The house itself was classic, a luxurious one-story embodiment of structural detail and sophisticated design with sweeping views of the straits and the Olympic Mountains behind it, washing watercolored striations against the deep-blue sky. Jeneva stared dumbfounded toward the front door. Mecan was living large, Jeneva thought, as she parked her own vehicle behind an immaculate 2004 Chevy SSR.

Grabbing her purse, Jeneva walked the short distance to the front door and rang the bell, shivering ever so slightly as she waited for him to answer. She smiled brightly as the door opened, but the man holding the door open wasn't Mecan Tolliver.

"Hi. You must be Jeneva."

She nodded her head, speechless.

The man laughed. "Mac didn't tell you he had a twin brother, did he?"

"No," she said, finally finding her voice. "He didn't."

The man extended his hand. "I'm Darwin. Darwin Tolliver. The baby of the family.

Jeneva laughed lightly. "It's nice to meet you, Darwin."

"Please, come on in."

"Thank you."

"Mac called and he's on his way. I needed him to run to the market for me and he missed the ferry. Had to wait for the next one. He shouldn't be too long. I told him I'd take care of you until he got here."

Jeneva followed behind him as he guided her through the foyer into the open living space. The common areas wove from one into the other, and from where Jeneva stood in the family room, she could look into the dining area and kitchen. A large stone hearth filled the expanse of one wall. A spread of wood-clad, floor-to-ceiling windows ran from corner to corner, bringing the incredible views inside. Exposed beams ran the length of the mile-high ceilings. The decor was minimal, and decidedly masculine, Jeneva thought. She gazed out the rear of the house, taking in the view of an exterior garden room, in final bloom, which overlooked a fifty-foot lap pool and bluestone patio courtyard.

"So, Mac tells me your son is a student at Hewitt?"

"Yes," Jeneva responded, moving to the kitchen where Darwin was cutting fresh vegetables against a large cutting board on the center island. She took a seat on one of the cushioned stools at the counter.

"Mac talks about him all the time. He talks about you a good deal, too. I told Mama he was sweet on you."

Jeneva blushed, and Darwin seemed amused by her embarrassment. "Can I get you anything? Something to drink, maybe?"

"No, I'm fine, thank you." She watched as the man masterfully prepped the wealth of food sitting between them. Looking around the space, she noted the granite countertops, custom cabinets, and stainless-steel appliances. It was a true gourmet kitchen. "You must like to cook," she said, gesturing with her eyes at his adeptness with the slim blade in his hand.

"I do it for a living. I'm a professional chef."

Jeneva nodded. "Very nice."

"I hope so. Big brother asked me to prepare an incredible meal for the two of you this evening." The man looked up at her, smiling as his eyes met hers.

"The resemblance is uncanny. You do realize that?" Jeneva said, shaking the disbelief from her mind.

Darwin laughed. "We're identical. Side by side, though, you'll be able to tell us apart because Mecan is an inch shorter than I am. I'm also prettier than he is."

"Your voice is different," Jeneva commented. "I think Mecan's is deeper, and you have hair."

Darwin cleared his throat, pretending to drop his voice an octave. "Do you think so?" he asked, rubbing a hand against his head, brushing at the short growth of black locks.

Jeneva laughed. "So, is it just the two of you? Or do you have other siblings who look like you, too?"

Darwin turned his back, reaching for the faucet as he washed a spray of soap and water against his hands. "Just an older sister, Paris. And she's better-looking than both of us."

The two of them turned their heads as they heard the front door open and close. Mecan called out from the entrance. "Hello? Anybody home?"

Jeneva twisted her body toward the door as Mecan stepped from the foyer, grinning in her direction. Her smile was just as wide as she gave him a slight wave of her hand.

"Sorry I was late," he said, rushing to greet her, passing two canvas sacks to Darwin. Standing at her side, Mecan leaned and kissed her cheek, his hand brushing against her back. "I'm so glad you could come."

"Your brother has been keeping me company," Jeneva said, blushing. She could feel the warmth of color splashing her cheeks as he lightly squeezed her flesh beneath his palm.

"She thought I was you. I got me a kiss at the front door."

Jeneva laughed aloud. "I did not," she said, looking at Darwin in surprise.

"Couldn't keep her hands off me," he said, laughing as his brother shook his head.

"I know better," Mecan said, his arm wrapping around Jeneva's shoulder. "My brother plays a lot, Jeneva. Don't pay him a bit of attention."

"Fine!" Darwin exclaimed. "If a brother can't have any fun, then you two will need to get out of my kitchen. Out." He shooed his hands at the two of them.

Mecan reached for Jeneva's hand and pulled her to her feet. "What time's dinner?" he asked as he led her to the door of the enclosed garden room.

"I'll be ready to serve at six, unless you want to eat earlier."

Mecan shook his head. "No. Six is good with me if it's okay with Jeneva." He glanced down at her, her hand still clasped tightly beneath his.

"That's fine," she answered.

Warm air filled the glass space that smelled faintly of roses. Sunlight had beat a path of heat throughout the room. Mecan guided her to a cedar swing that hung in the rear corner. Both of them took a seat against the plush cushions that lined the frame.

"How was your trip?" Mecan asked, twisting his body to face her. He pulled his leg up against the seat so that his knee was pointed toward her while his ankle rested against the upper thigh of his other leg.

"It was very relaxing. I haven't been to this area since before my parents died. I'd forgotten how beautiful it is."

Mecan smiled. "I hope you don't mind eating in, but Darwin is an excellent cook and I thought this would give us an opportunity to just relax and talk."

"Oh, not at all. You have a beautiful home."

"Thank you. Darwin and I bought this house about five years ago. We had another not far from here, but we have a big family and just needed more space when we got together."

"He told me you had an older sister."

"Yes, Paris. Paris is thirty-seven, two years older than we are, but you would think she was older. She acts more like our mother than Mama does sometimes."

"Your folks are still alive?"

Mecan nodded. "Mama is. Our father died when we were seven years old. My father's brother, my uncle Jake, helped raise us after that. Uncle Jake had five kids of his own and we were always together. That's why we needed the bigger house. When one shows up, a dozen show up."

Jeneva laughed. "That sounds like fun. I was an only child and both my parents were also, so there was never a lot of family around."

Darwin, who'd entered the comfortable space bearing a bottle of wine, two glasses, and a tray of hors d'oeuvres, interrupted them.

"Thought you might like a little snack," he said, winking at her as he filled a glass and passed it to her.

"Thank you."

"Thanks, Darwin. This is some service, little brother."

"Not a problem, big brother," the man said, giving them a slight bow as he left.

Jeneva looked from one to the other, noting the remarkable similarities and the very minute differences. She shook her head and laughed.

"What's so funny?" Mecan asked.

"You two must have been something else growing up."

Mecan chuckled. "We gave Mama a run for her money, but Paris would always tell on us. The kicker is, not only were we twins, but Uncle Jake had a set of twins and a set of triplets. He and his wife had identical twin girls who are younger than we are and fraternal boys who are only six months older than us."

"Do you have any children of your own?" Jeneva asked.

"Just the ones I claim at Hewitt House. Those are my only kids."

Jeneva thought about Quincy. "When I first got married, I thought Robert and I would have at least three children. I wanted two boys and a girl."

"Do your regret not having more?"

She shook her head. "Not at all. Quincy has more than made up for it. Besides, having more would have required having a man, and that just never happened."

"Because you didn't want it to?"

"Because Quincy required so much of me. There just wasn't anything left to share with someone else, least of all a man."

Mecan's hand fell against her leg, gently stroking her knee. "Well, I'm glad that's changing," he said, his gaze so penetrating that it swept her breath away.

"So," Jeneva asked, wanting to change the subject, "how did you manage to get away from the house tonight?"

"Juan Santiago is back. He's returned to duty full time."

"So you won't be with the kids full time anymore?"

"Not in the house. But I'll still be with them during the day. And I'll help run them to their classes and activities. Can't leave my kids now."

She smiled. "That's good to hear. I know how much you mean to Quincy."

"You don't need to worry about Quincy. He and Juan have already made a strong connection. They are doing very well together," Mecan said, wanting to alleviate her obvious rise of concern. "And he will still see me every day."

She inhaled deeply, enjoying the fragrant air around her. They continued chatting easily, discovering things about each other that sometimes surprised them, and sometimes didn't. Two hours and a bottle of wine later, Darwin stuck his head out the door and called to Mecan.

"Would you please excuse me?" Mecan said, causing the swing to sway as he lifted himself onto his feet. He followed Darwin into the house. In the distance, Jeneva felt as if she could feel the vibration of the sun as it moved to settle down for the evening. The views were breathtaking and she was in awe to be in such a picture-perfect setting with a man like Mecan.

Mecan stood in the doorway, staring out at her as Darwin briefed him on what he needed to do to finish dinner. He could not help but notice the way the sun played on her skin, sending shimmering rays of gold against her red. A warm flush crept through him, causing him to shiver, and it was only when his brother yelled his name that he realized he'd been distracted. Minutes later, he and Darwin reentered the garden, seeming to have shared a secret Jeneva had not been privy to. She smiled, her gaze racing from one to the other.

"Jeneva, it was very nice to meet you," Darwin said, reaching out to embrace her.

"Are you leaving?"

He nodded his head. "I am. I have another engagement this evening."

"Well, it was nice to meet you, too. Maybe I'll see you before I leave?"

"Plan on it. You can tell me how boring my brother is over scones and strawberry preserves in the morning."

Jeneva smiled. "Homemade?"

"Is there any other kind?" Darwin winked again as he reached out to shake his brother's hand. "Enjoy. I will see you in the morning."

"Thanks, Darwin," Mecan responded.

"Any time," Darwin said, tapping him on the shoulder. "By the way, I'm taking your car. I think Jeneva's parked behind me."

Mecan nodded. "No problem."

They watched as he made his way through the house and out the front door.

"Have you decided whether or not you'll be staying or if you'd like me to get you a hotel room?" Mecan asked, turning his attention back to her.

Jeneva blushed, feeling her body grow warm and languid at the prospect of spending the night with Mecan.

"You are more than welcome to stay here," he continued. "As you can see, there is plenty of room. And I promise I'll be a gentleman."

"I don't know. . . ." Jeneva started.

"Please, Jeneva. There really isn't any reason why you can't."

Finally consenting, she nodded. "Thank you," she said. "I appreciate the offer."

Mecan beamed. "Good. Well, if you're hungry, we can eat anytime."

"If I can get my bag out of the car, I'd like to freshen up first."

"Of course. Let me show you where you'll be staying."

Leading her back into the house, Mecan walked with her to her car and then showed her back to the large guest room. The room had a more feminine touch, tastefully decorated in a pale floral motif. When she commented on it, Mecan told her his sister and mother had been instrumental in pulling the space together so that they felt comfortable whenever they came to stay. Promising not to be long, Jeneva lay across the bed after closing the door behind the man. She hugged herself, wrapping her arms tightly around her body, and questioned whether her agreeing to stay had been a mistake. She wished she could call the Dynamic Divas for their advice, she thought, suddenly feeling like an adolescent with her first crush.

Lifting herself upright, she headed into the adjoining bathroom to touch up her makeup and brush her hair into place. Deciding to change out of the cashmere pantsuit she'd arrived in, Jeneva put on a simple, button-up shirt and a pair of loose-fitting khaki slacks from her overnight bag. Kicking off her high heels, she slipped a pair of sandals onto her newly pedicured feet. The look was tasteful and elegant.

Minutes later when she entered the common living space, Mecan had transformed the room. Flames were blazing in the fireplace, casting intricate shadows around the dimly lit room. A low, black table had been set in front of the hearth, an assortment of brightly colored pillows spread on either end. Mecan sat waiting patiently for her as she approached. As she crossed over to his side, he was touched by her quiet beauty. Her presence filled the space between them, causing the rhythm of his heart to speed. He came to his feet.

"Very nice," he said, smiling his appreciation.

"Thank you."

Elegant silver bowls overflowed with food. Darwin had skillfully married curry and shrimp, saffron rice, and a sautéed vegetable mélange, the likes of which could have rivaled the most prestigious five-star restaurant. For dessert, the younger brother had capped the meal with a decadent chocolate mousse torte and Jeneva couldn't resist asking for a second serving.

"This is incredible," she said, enjoying the swirl of bittersweet chocolate melting like butter against her tongue.

"We eat well around here. My brother has some serious talent with a frying pan."

When they were finished, Mecan refused to let her help with the dishes. He rinsed and placed them into the dishwasher as they continued conversing, dialogue flowing easily between them.

"You can give me a hand with this table, if you want," Mecan said as he reached for one end of the low black structure. "I just want to move it out of the way so we can still enjoy the fire."

Reaching for the other end, Jeneva laughed when she lifted it, following him as he guided it to the corner and set it down. "I could have lifted that thing by myself," she said.

Mecan laughed with her. "I know, but I didn't want you to strain yourself after all that torte you ate."

"Make fun. I have a healthy appetite and I'm not ashamed to admit it."

"I like a woman with a healthy appetite," Mecan said, staring at her intently. The moment passed with Jeneva drowning in his large, brown eyes. She flinched ever so slightly when he touched her arm and she blushed, stammering foolishly. Mecan smiled again, and she could feel herself melt under his gaze.

Reaching for her hand, Mecan pressed his fingers between hers, guiding her back to the space in front of the fire. They both dropped to the floor, adjusting their bodies against the wealth of pillows.

"So, tell me, Mr. Tolliver," Jeneva said, breaking the quiet they had dropped into, "why haven't you married? How come there's no woman laying claim to you?"

Mecan shrugged, rolling onto his back. He pulled a large pillow beneath his head as he spoke. "I think the biggest reason is that I have just never slowed down long enough to let a woman catch up. After I got my master's degree, I worked in social services for a few years, dealing with the foster care system. Then I was offered a position at Hewitt House. They'd only been open for a short time and it was an opportunity to help build something special, to make a real difference. I haven't stopped since, nor have I met a woman who I was ready to slow down for."

"And now?"

His gaze locked with hers as he stared at her, the warmth from the fire melding with the heat rising between them. Sitting upright, he shifted his body closer to hers, wrapping an arm around her waist. Leaning in to kiss her cheek, he brushed his lips down the length of her face. "I'm ready to slow down," he whispered, his lips lightly grazing the line of her ear.

As the words filtered like fire through her bloodstream, Jeneva wrapped her arms around him, drawing him close. His mouth searched out hers as he pulled her into a deep kiss. They connected in a frenzy of passion and when she parted her lips, Mecan thrust his tongue into the recesses of her warm mouth.

A glow of anticipation covered them like a warm blanket. Butterflies danced in Jeneva's stomach as desire throbbed incessantly through Mecan's body. She could kiss this man forever, Jeneva thought, as his lips skimmed her face, fell against her neck, and caressed her closed eyelids. She could kiss him forever, and fall in love with the possibilities his kisses left burning in her heart.

Sixteen

They'd made out like two teenagers, Jeneva
thought, as she changed out of the wrinkled blouse
and slacks she'd slept in. Time had gotten lost somewhere between the kisses and the caresses, hands
blowing whispery passes against sensitive skin. She
knew it had been late when she'd finally drifted off to
sleep, the last of the embers in the fireplace fading
away quickly. When she woke again, Mecan had
wrapped a quilted blanket around them both, hugging her tightly as she lay pressed against his body.
She hadn't heard him rise, nor did she know when it
was he'd restarted the flames in the fireplace, but a
fire had blazed comfortably as he lay sleeping beside
her.

In the light of the flames, Jeneva had watched him,
noting every detail of his face. He was beautiful, she
thought, her gaze dancing over his ebony features.
His nose was broad, but fit nicely against the backdrop of his face. His eyes were set evenly, thick brows
arching almost delicately above his lids. His cheeks
were round and full; you could think him chubby if
they were all you ever saw of him. She loved his
mouth, the full, dark lips, like thick pillows perfectly
proportioned. She had searched his lips with her own,
discovering each line and crevice with her tongue. In

the dark, she'd pressed herself closer to him, sleep returning to consume her. Darwin's return with the
morning sunlight had moved them both from where
they lay, waking them earlier than either would have
liked.

Jeneva heaved a sigh as the memories flashed before her, causing her breath to become heavy and the
palpitations in her chest to beat in double time. Making her way into the kitchen, she could hear Mecan
and Darwin chatting animatedly. She could tell the
two brothers had an incredible relationship, sharing
identical bodies but with completely unique person-
alities. Mecan was the more serious of the two,
conservative, dependable, and structured. Darwin's
spirit was freer, his flights of fancy changing with the
weather.

She felt herself blushing as she entered the room,
the rise of color causing her even more embarrassment. "Good morning," she said cheerfully, wishing
away the crimson in her cheeks.

"Good morning, Jeneva," Darwin said, waving a
large wooden spoon in her direction.

Mecan met her as she headed toward the center island. "Good morning," he whispered as he wrapped
his arms around her and kissed her mouth, letting his
lips linger for a quick moment.

"You two didn't get enough of that last night?" Darwin said jokingly.

Mecan cut his eye toward his brother. "I think you
better remember who's the oldest here. Show some
respect."

"Like five minutes gives you some sort of advantage," Darwin retorted.

Jeneva laughed at their good-natured bantering.

"I hope you're hungry," Darwin said. "I made my famous breakfast casserole to go with these scones."

An Important Message From The ARABESQUE Publisher

Dear Arabesque Reader,

Arabesque is celebrating 10 years of award-winning African-American romance. This year look for our specially marked 10th Anniversary titles.

Why not be a part of the celebration and **let us send you four specially selected books FREE!** These exceptional romances will be sent right to your front door!

Please enjoy them with our compliments, and thank you for continuing to enjoy Arabesque.... the soul of romance bringing you ten years of love, passion and extraordinary romance.

Linda Gill
PUBLISHER, ARABESQUE ROMANCE NOVELS

P.S. Watch out for our upcoming Holiday titles including *Merry Little Christmas* by Melanie Schuster, *Making Promises* by Michelle Monkou, *Finding Love Again* by AlTonya Washington and the special release of *Winter Nights* by Francis Ray, Donna Hill and Shirley Hailstock—**Available wherever fine books are sold!**

New Holiday Titles

ARABESQUE

BET BOOKS

www.BET.co

SPECIAL OFFER!
4 BOOKS FREE!

A SPECIAL "THANK YOU" FROM ARABESQUE JUST FOR YOU!

Send this card back and you'll receive 4 FREE Arabesque Novels—a $25.96 value—absolutely FREE!

The introductory 4 Arabesque Romance books are yours FREE (plus $1.99 shipping & handling). If you wish to continue to receive 4 books every month, do nothing. Each month, we will send you 4 New Arabesque Romance Novels for your free examination. If you wish to keep them, pay just $18* (plus, $1.99 shipping & handling). If you decide not to continue, you owe nothing!

- Send no money now.
- Never an obligation.
- Books delivered to your door!

We hope that after receiving your FREE books you'll want to remain an Arabesque subscriber, but the choice is yours! So why not take advantage of this Arabesque offer, with no risk of any kind. You'll be glad you did!

In fact, we're so sure you will love your Arabesque novels, that we will send you an Arabesque Tote Bag FREE with your first paid shipment.

* PRICES SUBJECT TO CHANGE.

YOU'LL GET 4 SELECT ROMANCES PLUS THIS FABULOUS TOTE BAG!

ARABESQUE

Visit us at:
www.BET.com

THE "THANK YOU" GIFT INCLUDES:

- 4 books absolutely FREE (plus $1.99 for shipping and handling).
- A FREE newsletter, *Arabesque Romance News*, filled with author interviews, book previews, special offers, and more!
- No risks or obligations. You're free to cancel whenever you wish with no questions asked.

INTRODUCTORY OFFER CERTIFICATE

Yes! Please send me 4 FREE Arabesque novels (plus $1.99 for shipping & handling). I am under no obligation to purchase any books, as explained on the back of this card. Send my free tote bag after my first regular paid shipment.

NAME _____

ADDRESS _____ APT. _____

CITY _____ STATE _____ ZIP _____

TELEPHONE ( ) _____

E-MAIL _____

SIGNATURE _____

Offer limited to one per household and not valid to current subscribers. All orders subject to approval. Terms, offer, & price subject to change. Tote bags available while supplies last.

Thank You!

AN104A

ARABESQUE

Accepting the four introductory books for FREE (plus $1.99 to offset the cost of shipping & handling) places you under no obligation to buy anything. You may keep the books and return the shipping statement marked "cancelled". If you do not c   about a month later we will send 4 additional Arabesque novels, and you will be billed the preferred subscriber's price of just $4.50 per title. That's $18.00* for all 4 books for a savings of almost 30% off the cover price (Plus $1.99 for shipping and handling). You may cancel at any time, but if you choose to continue, every month we'll send you 4 more books, which you may either purchase at the preferred discount price. . . or return to us and cancel your subscription.

* PRICES SUBJECT TO CHANGE

THE ARABESQUE ROMANCE BOOK CLUB
P.O. BOX 5214
CLIFTON NJ 07015-5214

PLACE
STAMP
HERE

THE ARABESQUE ROMANCE CLUB: DEAL 3 IIOW IT WORKS

"If it's half as good as that dinner you made last night, I can't wait."

"Liked that, did you? Told you I was good."

"That chocolate torte was to die for."

Darwin danced a bad rendition of the Cabbage Patch, the spoon and a frying pan in his hands. "I'm bad, so bad, so very, very bad," he sang, looking as though he were trying to hurt himself.

Both Jeneva and Mecan laughed at his antics, shaking their heads at his silliness.

"Feed us," Mecan said. "My baby and I have someplace we need to be."

As Darwin continued to dance around the kitchen, Mecan leaned to kiss Jeneva one more time, and she smiled, suddenly comfortable with the idea of being his baby.

Jeneva was in a wonderful mood when she and Mecan arrived at Hewitt House. He'd convinced her to prolong her visit and spend one more night with him after their visit with Quincy. Since there was nothing, and no one, waiting for her in Seattle, she'd agreed. She was comfortable with the man, far more comfortable than she could have ever imagined being, and she welcomed the opportunity to discover more about him.

As they pulled up in front of the house, Natalia was standing in the yard, having a conversation with Dr. Abernathy. Their expressions were serious and as Jeneva's gaze flashed from them to Mecan and back again, she could sense from the change in his disposition that something wasn't quite right.

Natalia caught Mecan's eye as he stepped from the vehicle, giving him a quick shake of her head. Walking around the car, Mecan reached to open the passenger door, extending his hand as he helped Jeneva out.

"Good morning, Mac. Hello, Jeneva," Natalia said, reaching out to give them both a polite hug.

"Is there something wrong?" Mecan asked, looking from one woman to the other.

"Nothing major," Natalia responded, glancing at Jeneva. "Quincy's just having a difficult time this morning."

"What the matter with him?" Jeneva said, anxiety rising in her voice. "What's the matter with my son?"

Natalia reached out to caress her arm. "It's okay. It really is."

Rachel Abernathy nodded in agreement. "It's nothing physical. Quincy has just been a bit distraught since last night."

"Why? What happened?"

Natalia took a deep breath. "Both Joel and Billy have gone home for the weekend. When their parents arrived to pick them up, Quincy started asking for his father."

"His father?" Jeneva asked, shock on her face. Mecan placed a heavy hand against her lower back.

Natalia nodded. "Yes. He became upset and we just haven't been able to calm him. He was up and down all night. I called Rachel this morning and asked her to come over to check him. I wanted to make sure it wasn't anything else."

"There's absolutely nothing medically wrong with him," Rachel interjected. "But he's definitely experiencing some heavy anxiety. It comes in waves. He'll be fine for a while, then he'll get upset."

Jeneva shook her head. "He actually asked for his father?"

The two women looked at her, both understanding her obvious distress.

"Why don't we go inside so you can see him," Mecan said, gently guiding her to the front door. "Let's see if we can't calm him down."

"I'll be at the infirmary if you need me," Rachel said, clasping a tighter grip around the black medical bag in her hand. "If he doesn't calm down, we can discuss giving him something to help him sleep. I don't recommend it, though. I want Dr. Burton to spend some time with him. I think this may be a significant breakthrough for Quincy and I don't want to dull it with medication if there's another way around it."

Inside the home, they could hear Juan in the back room, trying to console Quincy. As Jeneva and Mecan entered the bedroom, the boy was pacing back and forth around the room, wearing a path along the carpeted floor.

"Quincy," Jeneva called out. "Hello, baby."

Seeing his mother, Quincy stopped short, then clapped his hands excitedly. His mother smiled as she reached to embrace him. The boy allowed himself to be held for only a brief moment before he pulled away. He struggled to speak. "My . . . da . . . dee . . ." he sputtered, forcing air from his midsection. "My . . . da . . . dee."

Jeneva heard herself gasp loudly. "You want your daddy?" she asked.

The young man clapped his hands excitedly. "Da . . . dee."

Jeneva looked from her son to Mecan. The man nodded his head.

"Can you reach him?" Mecan asked.

"I don't want to reach him," Jeneva replied curtly.

Quincy resumed his pacing, slapping his hands against his head as he pulled at his hair. "My . . . da . . . dee."

Natalia wrapped her arms around Jeneva. "He's

been doing this since yesterday," she said. "We can get him to stop for short periods, then he starts right back again."

"Who picked up Joel and Billy?" Mecan asked.

"Their fathers," Juan responded.

"Quincy, baby. Stop. Stop now," Jeneva said, going to stand in front of her son. "Stop, Quincy."

The boy ignored her, continuing to walk circles around the room. Jeneva suddenly felt her good mood evaporating. She looked toward Mecan.

"Okay, baby," she said finally. "Mommy will get your daddy."

At Mecan's insistence, they'd taken Quincy to the pool. Her child had dog-paddled until he was exhausted and now lay floating on his back, oblivious to everything except the water. She and Mecan sat poolside, watching him as he appeared to be dozing comfortably. Periodically, one of the physical therapists would move his arms and limbs and check his breathing. They had been right about him loving the water.

Jeneva looked down at her watch. "Why is this happening?" she said finally, turning to look at the man beside her.

Mecan wrapped her hand in his. "What we're learning about Quincy is that he has a very active mind that has been locked away. He's now learning how to unlock all that stuff he's been holding on to. Quincy understands he has a father. He is reacting like most little boys do when they want their dads."

She shook her head. "What's going to happen when he leaves? Robert's going back to Atlanta at some point. What then?"

"I honestly don't know. I do know that we're going

to have to make Quincy understand that, just like you, his father isn't going to always be here every day."

"Why didn't he act this way when I left him?"

"I think because he has always had you and he trusts that you will come and you will be here. Robert's new. He knows Robert belongs to him, but he's not quite sure how the two of them fit. But he wants to be like the other boys. He just wanted his daddy to come get him, too."

Conversation stopped as Quincy paddled to where Jeneva's legs dangled in the warm water. He pressed his cheek against her knees. Jeneva reached out to stroke her son's head, her fingers combing through his curly hair. He reached a hand to Mecan, who shifted his weight to help the boy up and out of the water.

"Are you tired, Quincy?" Mecan asked. "Tired?"

Quincy clapped his hands. Jeneva smiled, leaning to kiss her son's cheek. Wrapping a towel around his shoulders, she pulled his head down against her lap, her fingers gently rubbing the side of his face.

Before they could think about moving, Robert Douglas entered the room, strolling around the pool to join them. His concerned expression softened as he caught sight of them, sensing that Quincy had finally found some calm. Mecan rose from his seat to shake Robert's hand, then excused himself to give them some privacy with their son.

Quincy sat up excitedly, clapping his hands as if he'd just won a prize. Jeneva sighed.

"Dad . . . dy."

Robert smiled. "Hello, son," he said, grabbing Quincy's hand. "Hello." He smiled down at Jeneva. "Is everything okay?"

"He wanted you," she said, still kicking her bare feet

in the water as Quincy stood, hugging his father tightly.

The balance of their day went without further mishap. Quincy finally settled down, napping quietly as the adults discussed a course of action to guarantee the boy's comfort once his parents returned home. Dr. Burton facilitated an impromptu therapy session to help them explain to Quincy that Robert would leave like his mother and Robert would come back to visit when he could. Quincy seemed content to know his father would return.

As Robert helped Juan put Quincy to bed, Mecan and Jeneva waited patiently in the living room. Jeneva hadn't had much to say and Mecan could sense her displeasure with the turn of circumstances. He wrapped his arms around her, hugging her tightly, wanting to ease the quiver that shook her body as she fought back tears. He kissed the side of her face, neither of them saying anything. Rubbing his hands against her shoulders, he assured her that everything was going to be just fine and that he would be there for her no matter what.

"Jeneva," Robert called, interrupting them.

Pressing her lips quickly against Mecan's, Jeneva made her way to the bedroom, passing Juan in the hallway. The man smiled, tapping her on the shoulder as they crossed paths. Quincy lay sleeping peacefully, Robert at his side.

She stood at the foot of the bed, her arms crossed tightly across her upper body.

"Jeneva, I'm going back to Atlanta on Wednesday. I want to take Quincy with me," he said softly, reaching out to run his hand against his son's forehead.

Jeneva's expression was incredulous. "I know you've lost your mind now."

"Just for a couple of weeks. I know he has school

and I'll bring him back. It'll just be a short vacation and it'll give us a chance to spend some time with one another."

"No."

"Jeneva, please. You haven't even thought about it."

"I don't need to think about it. You haven't been Quincy's father for fourteen years and now you want to just take him and be a daddy. No. That's not happening."

Robert gave her a hard stare. "He needs me. You saw that today. It'll be good for him. It won't be permanent. Just for a few weeks."

Jeneva cast Robert a vile look, wanting to spew venom in his direction.

Natalia interrupted them. "Is everything okay? Quincy finally fell asleep?"

Jeneva forced herself to smile. "He's fine. Thank you so much, Natalia. I'm so sorry he gave you a difficult time last night."

"Oh, not to worry. The boys all have their bad days. Quincy will be fine."

Robert rose from his seat. "Well, I guess I'll be going."

"Yes. That sounds like a good idea," Jeneva said, not bothering to look in the man's direction.

Natalia glanced from one to the other, the tension between them obvious. Her gaze rested on Robert's face, the heaviness in his eyes drawing her attention.

"Good-bye, Natalia," Robert said, suddenly uncomfortable with her stare.

"You drive safe, Mr. Douglas," she answered, noting the drawn skin across his face and a sadness that seemed to linger around him.

The two women watched him exit the room. Jeneva took the seat Robert had just vacated.

"You and Mr. Douglas don't agree about something?"

Jeneva shrugged. "We don't agree about anything," she said, pressing her son's hand to her cheek.

In the living room, Mecan and Juan stood chatting quietly. When Robert entered, Juan politely excused himself.

"I appreciate everything you've done," Robert said, extending his hand to Mecan.

Mecan nodded as the two shook hands.

"We appreciate you driving up here. Quincy is adjusting to a lot. It's important that both of his parents support him."

"I would do anything for my son. I know Jeneva . . ." Robert started, then, thinking twice, said instead, "I'll call tomorrow to see how he's doing."

Mecan nodded again. "Natalia has your number, and she or Juan will call if he has any problems tonight. I'll come in myself tomorrow to check on him, but I'm sure he's going to be fine."

"Good night, Mecan."

"Good night, Robert."

Seventeen

The mood between them was somber as Mecan drove them back to his home. Even the ride on the ferry did nothing to lighten Jeneva's stress, the shimmer of moonlight against the ocean water barely catching her attention. As they stood looking over the rail of the seacraft, Mecan wrapped his arms around her, her back resting easily against his chest. His nuzzled his nose in her hair, inhaling the sweet aroma of her shampoo, a light citrus scent he found quite pleasing.

"Do you want to talk about it?" he finally asked.

"Robert wants to take Quincy back to Atlanta with him for a few weeks."

"What did you say?"

"I told him no. I'm not letting him take Quincy."

Mecan brushed his hands down the length of her arms. "I know you don't want to hear this, but—"

Jeneva spun around to face him. "You can't possibly think that would be a good thing for my son!"

"Why do you think it would be such a bad thing?"

Jeneva shook her head, throwing her hands up in exasperation. "Where do you want me to start?"

"Jeneva, he's your son's father. The man obviously cares about Quincy."

"Robert gave up his rights to being Quincy's father

the day he left. He doesn't care about anyone but himself."

"I don't think that's true and neither do you. I think we both know better."

Jeneva bristled, her body tensing as she moved herself away from Mecan. "This really isn't any of your business," she said, her tone chilled.

Mecan took a deep breath. "No. It isn't. But I care about you and Quincy. I only want what's best."

As their gaze connected, both knew the conversation could continue to flow badly. Mecan moved to change the subject. "You don't have to make any decisions about anything tonight, Jeneva. Let's just go have dinner and relax. If you want to talk more, fine. If not, that's okay also."

Jeneva lowered her eyes, pressing her lids shut as she searched the flood of emotions that filled her. She could feel him as he moved against her, pulling her back into his arms. Jeneva pressed her face into his chest. She didn't want to talk about it. She didn't want to think about it. All she wanted was for Robert to go away and leave them all alone.

The romance had flown out of the rest of her weekend on the same plane as her good mood, Jeneva thought, as she sorted through the miscellaneous documents piled on her desk. Mecan and Darwin had tried to make her comfortable, easing the tension with stories of their youth, and the twin antics that had gotten them into more than their fair share of trouble. Although she had laughed and lost herself in the moments, thoughts of Quincy and his father still weighed heavily on her spirit. Needing some time to herself, she had slept alone in the guest bedroom. Mecan had professed to understand, but she had seen the hurt in his eyes, and she had felt even worse for pushing him away.

Depression was working diligently to possess her spirit, wanting to consume her. She had no understanding of why she was feeling so lost. She only knew that for as long as she could remember, it had only been her and Quincy, and now there stood two men wanting to change that. Mecan offered an opportunity she'd thought lost to her, a chance at love. Robert, on the other hand, wanted nothing more than to tear her family apart for a second time. She sighed deeply as the telephone rang on her desk.

"Jeneva Douglas."

"Good morning."

Jeneva smiled into the telephone. "Mac. Good morning. How are you?"

"I am missing you. I missed waking up with you this morning. Breakfast wasn't the same without your smiling face."

"I miss you, too. Thank you for a wonderful time this weekend. I'm sorry I spoiled our last day together."

She could feel him shaking his head. "You didn't spoil anything," Mecan said. "I just loved being with you."

"Are you at the office already?"

"Yes. In fact, I just left Quincy. He was headed to physical therapy."

"Is he any better?"

"He was fine, Jeneva. He's going to have those moments when things seem difficult, and he's going to get past them."

"I know."

"Well, I just wanted to check that you were all right. I'll call you tonight, okay?"

"You better."

"Bye, baby."

"Bye, Mac."

Jeneva's second line was ringing before she could hang up from her call.

"Jeneva Douglas."

"You didn't come home so we know you got some. Was it good?"

"Hey, girl. It's me and your other freaky friend. How was it?"

Jeneva laughed. "I had a very nice time."

"Did you wear your lace?" Roshawn asked.

"No. I told you before I left I wasn't wearing that thing."

"Please don't tell me you stayed in a hotel," Bridget said.

"No, I didn't do that either."

"She got some. I told you. Girlfriend got her groove on. You hurt him, didn't you? All that pent-up frustration had the brother begging for mercy, I bet."

Jeneva laughed, rolling her eyes as she glanced over her shoulder to see if anyone was eavesdropping on her conversation. "We had a very nice time but we did not do that."

"Then what kind of nice time could you have?"

"Shut up, Roshawn. Just because you're easy doesn't mean the rest of us have to be."

"Ignore Bridget. It's either PMS or her vibrator don' broke."

"Look, cow. You need to stop inhaling those chemicals you keep playing with."

"Who are you calling a cow?"

"The two of you need to stop," Jeneva interjected. "I've got to run. Call me at home later."

"Call?! I'm bringing hot wings. Have something chilling in the fridge when we get there."

"Fine. See you both later."

"Bye."

"Bye."

Mecan had just completed a welcome call to a new parent when Natalia knocked on his door, peeking her head inside.

"Hola!" she said, sliding a plate of freshly baked cookies onto his desk.

"Mmmm," he said, smiling. "To what do I owe the honor?"

"I came to be nosey. Figured some hot cookies wouldn't get me thrown out."

Mecan laughed. "Should I ask?"

Natalia made herself comfortable on the office sofa as Mecan came from behind his desk to sit with her.

"You and Ms. Douglas looked very comfortable together this weekend."

"Did we?"

"Interesting that you rode over together and left together. Was it a weekend thing?"

He smiled, biting into a warm confection of oatmeal and raisins as he ignored her.

"I like Ms. Douglas," she said. "I like you two together."

"Thank you. So do I."

"Is this serious?"

Mecan shrugged, brushing crumbs from the front of his navy-blue suit. "I think it could be."

His friend nodded her head. "That's good. That's very good."

"I'm glad you approve."

"So what's your take on the ex-husband?" she asked.

"I'm not sure, yet. I do think his presence has been good for Quincy, though."

"But I'm sure you didn't say that to his mother, did you?"

"No. She's dealing with a lot of emotions right now. I don't think she's ready to hear that."

Natalia nodded. "Well, for what it's worth, I think there may be something not well with Mr. Douglas."

"What do you mean?"

"Nothing I can say specifically. Just my intuition. I just don't think the man is in the best of health."

Mecan placed the cookie he'd been ready to bite into back onto the plate. "Did he say anything?"

"No. It's just a feeling I get and you know my feelings are usually right."

Mecan nodded.

"So when are you and Jeneva going to see each other again?"

"Thanks for the cookies, Natalia. I appreciate you stopping by."

The woman laughed. She reached out to give him a warm hug. "I just wanted you to know how happy I am for you. If anyone deserves to find love, it's you, Mac."

Eighteen

Monday had come and gone with little fanfare. The Dynamic Divas had shown up on her doorstep minutes after she'd gotten home. By the end of the evening, the three of them and MaryAnne were playing poker at her kitchen table as David and Ming played video games in the living room. Jeneva had welcomed the company, realizing just how lonely she was in the house by herself. Minutes after lying down for the evening, Mecan had called and the two had talked until they were all talked out, wishing each other sweet dreams over the telephone.

On Tuesday, Jeneva glanced at her watch, grateful that another day had come to an end. She'd been stuck in a meeting for most of the afternoon and had had her fill of the Northwest Marketing Group. The daily doldrums of her job were starting to wear on her. As she pulled on her coat, the telephone rang. Jeneva ignored it, allowing the call to roll over to the answering service. She was done for the day and the office was closed. She'd retrieve the message in the morning.

Even the ride home seemed mundane. Jeneva was unable to find any pleasure in riding the ferry, a leg of her daily journey she usually enjoyed. She was half

tempted to call Roshawn to meet her in Pike Place
Market for a drink, but changed her mind.

There were two messages on her answering machine when she arrived home. The first call was from
Mecan. "Jeneva, call me when you get this. It's urgent
that I speak with you." The second message was from
Bridget. "Jay, I need to see you. I'm on my way over.
Don't leave." There was an urgency to both their
voices that Jeneva found alarming. Reaching for the
telephone, she dialed Mecan's number. His answering
machine picked up.

"Hi, Mac. It's me. I just got your message and was
returning your call. I'm home, so call me back."

Depressing the hook, she waited for a dial tone
then dialed Quincy's house number. The line rang
busy on the other end. As she moved to redial, her
doorbell rang.

Pulling the front door open, she greeted her best
friend. "Hey, Bridget. I just got your message. What's
up?"

"I tried to reach you at the office but you'd already
left," the woman said as she rushed inside.

"I was out the door the minute the clock struck
five," Jeneva said, following Bridget into the living
room. Her friend's expression was too serious for
comfort. "What's wrong? What's happened?" Jeneva
asked.

Bridget took a seat on the sofa. "Come sit down,"
she said.

"You're scaring me, Bridget."

Bridget reached into her leather portfolio and
pulled some papers from the interior pocket. "I was
about to leave the office when the clerk's office delivered this document. Robert went before the court this
afternoon and asked the judge to uphold a visitation
order for Quincy. He requested thirty days temporary

custody to be reviewed by the court at the end of that period and they gave it to him."

Jeneva's knees gave way as she dropped down to the sofa. She could feel the room spinning around her. She gasped for air. "How, Bridget? How could he do this?" she sputtered.

Bridget shook her head. "I don't know. He pulled some strings or called in some favors to get an emergency hearing. He listed extenuating circumstances that are to be provided to us by his attorney. I called their office, but of course no one was there who could tell me anything."

"I've got to call Mac."

"Jeneva, there's nothing Mac can do."

"He can make sure Quincy is okay until we can fix this."

Bridget grabbed her hand, pulling her back down to the sofa. "Pull yourself together. First thing tomorrow I will go to the judge and request an injunction and a hearing. Until then there's nothing we can do tonight. Besides, it's late. I doubt Robert will try to take Quincy before tomorrow. You would have heard already if he had."

"Mac tried to call me," she said as she reached for the telephone and hit redial. The phone at Hewitt House rang busy for a second time. "I think I'm going to be sick," Jeneva said as she raced into the bathroom.

Jeneva tried for two straight hours to reach Mecan. No one was answering at his home, his office, or the student house. She'd lost count of the number of messages she'd left on his cell phone. Roshawn had joined them, bringing dinner with her, and the three women sat side by side, trying to determine what had moved Robert to act so irrationally. As time ticked by, Jeneva felt as if the longer they sat doing nothing, the greater the chances she'd have of losing her son. She fought to keep her tears from falling and her stomach from again spewing its contents across the floor.

When the telephone rang, they all jumped, startled from where they sat.

"Hello?"

"Jeneva, it's Robert."

"It's not going to work, Robert. I won't let you do this!" Jeneva screamed into the receiver.

"Please, just listen, Jeneva," the man implored, his tone contained.

Jeneva could feel her grip tightening around the receiver. "I don't want to hear it, Robert."

"I have Quincy. Our flight leaves in ten minutes. I'll call you when we get to Atlanta."

Sobs racked her body as she felt herself falling to the floor. "Why? Why are you doing this?" she cried into the telephone.

"I have to do this, Jeneva. I'm so sorry."

The line went dead as Bridget pulled the receiver from Jeneva's hand. The dial tone was ringing loudly when she pulled it to her ear. Through all the commotion, Jeneva hadn't noticed when Roshawn raced to answer the front door, the doorbell chiming in the background. When the woman pulled it open, Mecan Tolliver stood waiting on the other side. As he raced to her side, dropping to the floor beside her, Jeneva's rage rushed to greet him.

"You promised!" she screamed, beating her fists against his chest. "You promised to take care of my baby! How could you let him take my son?"

Nineteen

She could hear them out in her kitchen and living room, sharing information, making telephone calls, whispering about everything so that they didn't disturb her. She could not will herself to move or do any of these things with them. Everything in her had gone numb. She didn't have a clue to the time, nor did she know how long she'd slept. She been lying there listening to them whisper outside her door since forever, and she hadn't given any thought to joining them.

She stretched her body against the bed, elongating her frame like a lazy cat with nothing to do. Someone had opened the bedroom window, and the sheer white curtains billowed with the light breeze that came inland from the ocean. In spite of the breeze, the weather was warm and Jeneva kicked the covers from around her body, wondering who had taken her clothes and dressed her in her nightgown.

There was a faint knock on the bedroom door before it was pushed open, and Bridget peeked her head in. The woman smiled, easing herself inside and closing the door when she saw that Jeneva was awake.

"Good morning. How do you feel?"

Jeneva shook her head. "Like roadkill."

Bridget laughed lightly. "Understandable."

"Why aren't you at work?"

"I am. You're my client and I'm working."

"Did he call?"

"Not yet, but I'm sure he will."

"You didn't think he'd take Quincy when he did."

Bridget winced. "You're right. I called that one wrong. I'm sorry. But with that order, we couldn't have stopped him anyway."

"How do I get my child back?"

Bridget reached out a hand to brush the hair from Jeneva's eyes. "I think you need to talk with Mecan first."

"I don't want to see him."

"Yes, you do. You can't blame him for what happened."

"It was his responsibility to take care of my son. He didn't do that and now Quincy's gone. I may never see my baby again and it's all Mac's fault," she said, her tone bitter.

"You don't believe that. You're angry, and you're hurt, and you're mad that Robert did this the way he did, especially when you were trying to be nice to him. You know that Mecan was caught in the middle of this mess just like everyone else."

Jeneva rolled her eyes. "Men make me sick. Liars, cheaters, and thieves. That's all any of them are. They don't do anything but make promises they don't keep. Mecan Tolliver is no exception."

Bridget laughed. "Girl, you're going from bad to worse. Get over yourself. You are not going to be of any use to Quincy with that attitude."

"I thought you were my friend."

"I am. Your best friend, which is why I can tell you crap you don't want to hear and get away with it. Now, I'm going to go fix you something to eat. Go wash your face and brush your teeth because I'm sending

Mecan in the minute I leave so that you two can talk. You can't be blowing that morning breath on a man as fine as he is."

Bridget's hand rested on the doorknob as she looked back over her shoulder toward Jeneva. "And for the record," she said, before making her exit, "Mecan Tolliver definitely has my approval. He's a pretty special man, Jeneva, so don't mess this up. Batteries start to get expensive after a while."

Mecan rested his elbows against Jeneva's kitchen counter. A pot of coffee sat percolating on the stovetop, the second pot Mecan had made that morning. The previous day's events still pressed ugly against his spirit and Jeneva's hurt had weighed heavy on his heart. He'd not been able to respond when she'd ranted in anger against him. He had understood her emotions all too well, furious himself with Robert Douglas, and how the man had chosen to handle things. But Mecan was privy to information Jeneva had yet to learn, and the impact these details would ultimately have on Jeneva and Quincy was far greater than she could even begin to imagine. Mecan understood that this turn of events was only the beginning of much more to follow, down what would inevitably be a very long road.

When Bridget had excused herself to go check on Jeneva, Mecan reflected on the day before, when Robert had shown up unannounced at his office door.

It had been a long morning and an even longer afternoon as Mecan had sifted through the pile of paperwork on top of his desk. The intercom buzzing had barely distracted him from the documents he'd been studying. "Yes, Tanya?" he muttered, his concentration focused on his work.

"Mr. Tolliver, Mr. Douglas is here to see you. He doesn't have an appointment."

Robert's name being spoken caused Mecan to lift his gaze from the grant application he had been reviewing. The clock on his desk read three-thirty. "Send him in, Tanya."

Mecan rose from his seat as Robert pushed the door open, finding his way inside.

"Thank you for seeing me, Mecan," Robert said, extending his hand.

"Not a problem. Is there something wrong?"

Robert appeared anxious as he struggled to look Mecan in the eye. "May I have a seat?" he asked, gesturing toward the sofa.

"Of course, I'm sorry. Please, sit down."

"I'm just going to be very direct, Mecan. When I was here Saturday, I got the impression that there was more to your relationship with Jeneva and with Quincy than you just being Quincy's adviser. Was I wrong?"

Mecan took the seat across from the man, looking him directly in the eye. "No, you aren't wrong. Jeneva and your son are very special to me, if that's what you want to know."

"It was pretty obvious that she feels the same way about you." Robert nodded, sighing softly before he continued. "I made a number of mistakes with Jeneva and Quincy. I'm sure she's shared the worst of it with you already. I can't take them back and I may never be able to make up for them. At least, I may never be able to make amends to Jeneva, but I have to try to do right by my son."

"I can understand that."

"But I don't think I can do that if I don't have a

chance to really get to know and understand my son and his needs. I can't be here for Quincy without knowing exactly what Jeneva has had to go through with him all these years. And she's not going to voluntarily give me a chance to do that."

"You don't know that. It's only been a week. It's going to take some time for the two of you to work through all your issues."

"I don't know that I have a lot of time, Mecan."

"I don't understand."

"Two years ago I was diagnosed with cancer. It was treated aggressively and, until last month, I was in remission. But it's back, and it's back with a vengeance. I don't know if I'm going to beat it this time, but I do know that I have to make things right in case I don't."

Mecan took a deep breath, resting his elbows against his upper thighs as he dropped his chin into his clasped hands. His gaze flickered from side to side as he took in what Robert had just told him.

Robert continued. "Saturday I asked Jeneva if she would let me take Quincy back to Atlanta with me. She said no. I have three kids with my second wife and I want them to know Quincy. I need for them to understand that he may need them some day and I have to know that they're going to be there for their brother. Jeneva's the only family Quincy's ever had, but if she's not here or I'm not here, then what? I want my kids to be there for each other and they have to start now."

"Robert, don't get me wrong. I understand where you're coming from, but that's a heavy burden to just throw on your children and your wife. Dealing with your being sick has to be devastating enough, but now you want them to deal with Quincy and his challenges, too? That may be a lot to ask."

"They don't know I'm sick and I don't plan to tell

them. At least not yet. Not until I absolutely have to. And I don't want Jeneva to know either."

Mecan sat back in his chair. He shook his head. "Why are you telling me this?" he asked finally.

"Because I'm taking Quincy." He reached into the inner pocket of his jacket and pulled a document from its confines. "This is a court order giving me temporary custody of my son. He and I are leaving for Atlanta tonight."

"Do you know what this is going to do to Jeneva?" Mecan asked as he took the paper from Robert's hand and read its contents.

"Yes, which is why I'm coming to you. She's going to need someone to help her through this. The way you two were looking at each other, I felt like you would be willing to do that."

The two men eyed each other for a quick moment.

"I have to do this," Robert said. "All I want is two weeks, maybe three, to be with Quincy, to have him be with his brother and his sisters. I need to get to know him and have him know me."

"Then what? How do you figure three weeks is going to help you?"

"I don't have all the answers. Hell, I don't have any answers. I just know that I have to do something."

"Does Jeneva know yet?"

Robert looked down at the Rolex watch on his wrist. "I doubt it, but she will soon."

"How do you plan to spend the next few weeks? Quincy is still going to require medical supervision."

"I was hoping you'd advise me."

Mecan rose from his seat, moving to the rear of his desk. He shook, his body quivering with anger, wanting nothing more than to grip Robert around the throat and shake him. The moment passed, the thought gone as quickly as it had risen. He turned and looked Robert in the eye, both men studying each other intensely.

"This order gives you thirty days with Quincy, but in three weeks I'm bringing Jeneva to Atlanta to pick up your son. Is that going to be a problem?"

Robert shook his head. "No, not at all. You have my word on that."

"She's also going to need to know that you're ill so that the two of you can work out a plan for Quincy that meets his needs."

"I understand, but I want to be the one to tell her. I don't want her to know yet, especially since I haven't even told my wife. I hope you'll respect that."

Mecan reached for the telephone and dialed. Natalia picked up the other end.

"Natalia, where is Quincy?" he asked, still staring at Robert.

"Juan took him for a session with James. They should be back in an hour."

"Quincy's father is here to pick him up. If you'll pack his belongings, we'll be over to pick them up."

"What's going on?"

"I'll explain later. Thank you, Natalia."

Mecan dropped the receiver back onto the hook. Displeasure graced his face. He returned to the seat across from Robert, sitting back down as he chose his words carefully.

"I don't have the authority to stop you from taking your son. If I did, I probably would. I don't know that I agree with what you're doing." Mecan heaved a deep sigh. "I do think that you and Quincy need to spend some time together. It's obvious to me, and to his doctors, that he's been starved for a male role model. Quincy's been yearning for a father, and now that he has one, he's not ready to let you go. I think right now he needs you just as much as you need him, maybe even more. So don't screw this up. Don't make me regret this.

"You'll need to call me when you get to Atlanta. I'll have the name and number of a physician who can assist you with Quincy while he's there. My staff will make sure they get any information that's needed."

"You love her, don't you?" Robert asked.

"We'll see you in three weeks," Mecan answered, ignoring the man's question. "Have Quincy ready to come home."

Bridget dropped a hand against his arm, shaking him from the memory.

"You still with us, Mr. Mac?" she said, eyeing him curiously.

Mecan smiled, nodding as he reached to turn off the pot of coffee. "Is Jeneva okay?"

"She's up. I told her you wanted to talk with her."

"Thank you."

Bridget looked over to the clock. "I'm going to head to the courthouse. Are you going to stay?"

"I don't plan to leave. I'll be here as long as it takes."

The woman gave him a deep smile. "I'm on her speed dial if you need me. I'll be back in a few hours," she said, heading for the front door. "Good luck. You're going to need it."

Mecan eased his way down the hallway, stopping in front of Jeneva's bedroom door. He filled his lungs with energy before knocking on the wooden frame, seeking permission to enter.

"What?" Jeneva asked brusquely.

Concern blessed his face as Mecan opened the door and came inside. "Still angry?"

"Shouldn't I be?"

He shrugged. "I know you're hurt."

"My child is gone. Don't I have a right to be hurt?"

"Are you going to answer all my questions with a question? Because if you are, you and I aren't going to get very far with this conversation."

"Why are you still here?" Jeneva asked, her hands resting on her hips as she stood in front of him. "I don't need you here."

"I think you do. And I think you want me here as much as I want to be here." Mecan's gaze caressed her face. Jeneva closed her eyes, not wanting to look at him.

"Stop telling me what I want. You don't have a clue what I need or don't need."

"Maybe not. But I do know that I love you. And I know that I want to be here for you," he said softly.

Jeneva took a step back, spinning around to stare at the wall. Mecan pressed his hands to her shoulders and turned her back around. He lifted her chin with the curve of his hand, pulling her face up to his. "I love you, Jeneva."

"No."

"Yes, I do. I love you."

"You let him take my son."

Mecan nodded, his head wafting up and down slowly. "Yes, I did. I believed Quincy needed to be with his father. You can't deny the bond between them. I don't care how much you want to try. I also think Robert needs to take some responsibility for Quincy so that you can finally start to let him go. I think it's the only way Quincy is ever going to be able to learn and grow into his full potential. Like it or not, the boy needs both of you."

"I may never see my son again because of you."

Mecan chuckled softly. "I promise that in three

weeks' time, not only will you see Quincy again, but you and I will be bringing him home."

"Like you promised to keep my son safe?"

"Your son is safe. He's with his father and his father loves him and will protect him."

"What's this? Some kind of male bonding thing? You're supporting Robert now?"

"Jeneva, I love you, and I love your son, and because I love you both so much, if I even thought Robert would do anything to hurt Quincy, I'd be the first one after him. You can believe that."

Before Jeneva could respond, the telephone rang. She stared anxiously toward the device, nervous about picking it up. Mecan strolled to the bedside and picked up the receiver.

"Hello, Douglas residence."

"Mecan? It's Robert."

"Is everything all right? How's Quincy?"

Jeneva rushed to Mecan's elbow. "Is that Robert?"

Mecan nodded his head. "Hold on, Robert. Jeneva wants to speak with you." He cupped his hand over the receiver. "Are you going to stay calm?"

"Yes," she said as she reached for the telephone. "Robert, is Quincy okay?"

"He's fine, Jeneva. It was a long flight and he's still asleep. But he's doing very well."

"Why did you do this, Robert?"

"I'm sorry, Jeneva. Honest to God, I didn't want to hurt you. I just didn't know what else to do. I didn't know how to make you understand how important this is."

"I want my son back, Robert."

Mecan wrapped his arms around her and Jeneva found herself staring up into his eyes. The sincerity of his gaze seemed to swell up and fill her, begging her to trust him. She passed the telephone back to him, leaning into his body, her cheek pressed against his chest.

"Robert, it's Mecan. Do you have a pen?"

"Yes."

"You need to contact Dr. Pamela Adler. She's affiliated with the Atlanta Children's Hospital. I've already spoken to her and she's expecting your call. Quincy has an appointment at ten o'clock tomorrow morning with her. My office has sent over his medical history. She's going to arrange for him to continue his therapy while he's there. No excuses."

"We'll be there."

"Do you have my cell-phone number?"

"Yes."

"If you have any problems with Quincy, you are to call me immediately. Jeneva and I will see you in three weeks."

"Thanks, Mecan."

After disconnecting the line, Mecan hung up the telephone. He tightened his hold around Jeneva, kissing her gently against the forehead.

"What am I going to do for three weeks?" she asked, her voice barely a whisper. "How am I going to get through this?"

"We'll get through this together," Mecan said as he lifted her face to his. "We're going to go get your son, that's what we're going to do." Then he kissed her, blowing his promise across her lips and deep into the essence of her soul.

Twenty

Robert looked in on Quincy, who lay sleeping in the twin bed in Robert, Jr.'s room. His youngest son waved in his direction, then pulled his index finger to his lips, and whispered, "Shhhh. He's asleep." The boy tiptoed out of the room. He looked like his father, possessing the man's chiseled features. His coloring was pale, cream with just a hint of chocolate syrup to warm his complexion. He was an interesting melding of both his parents, with his pale skin and thick, black, tightly curled hair, cut low against his head.

Robert leaned down to kiss the boy on his forehead. "Thank you for helping with your big brother."

"Can he play with me when he wakes up?"

"I think so. But we'll see, okay? It may take some time for him to get used to us."

"Okay."

"Where's Mom?"

"She's making breakfast. We're having pancakes!" the boy said excitedly.

"Mmmm. My favorite."

In the kitchen, Fiona Douglas was pouring warm maple syrup onto plates that sat in front of the girls. Robert wrapped an arm around his wife's waist as he leaned to kiss her ivory cheek. "Thank you."

Kissing him back, Fiona smiled. "Is he okay?"

"Still sleeping."

"Did you call his mother?"

The man nodded his head as he leaned down to hug his daughters. "Jenny-bean and Lizzie-Bitty! How are my princesses?" Fraternal twins, the two girls looked related but distinctly different. Jennifer was a miniature version of her mother with her ivory skin, deep green eyes and vivid red hair. Elizabeth's features reminded Robert of his mother. Her coloring was a deep café au lait, half white and half black. Her hair was black silk, falling down past her shoulders in a wealth of loose curls. Both had the same high-pitched giggle that adolescent girls had, and both whined annoyingly when it was least desired.

"Do we have to go to school today, Daddy? Can't we stay home with you and Quincy?" Jennifer asked, shaking two red ponytails from side to side.

"No. Not today. Quincy will be here when you get home."

"That's not fair," Elizabeth said, pouting profusely. "Why does he get to stay home?"

Fiona gave her daughter a hard stare. "We discussed this. Quincy will be going to school, but he goes to a special school and he doesn't have to go until tomorrow. Now, eat. The bus will be here in a few minutes and you cannot be late."

The little girl rolled her eyes, ignoring the look her parents gave her. Her sister giggled, poking her in the side with her elbow. It was obvious that Elizabeth was not amused. "Why do we have to have another brother?" she asked, dropping her fork to her plate as she turned to stare at her father. "Why did you have to go get him?"

"Because he's my son, just like Robbie is my son, just like you and your sister are my children. We are all family and I want him to get to know you."

"Well, I don't like him. He's retarded."

"That's enough, young lady. Don't you ever let me hear you say that again," her mother said. "I don't like your attitude at all. Finish your breakfast and get your things. It's time to leave."

As ordered, the young girl lifted her empty plate from the table and set it into the sink. Reaching for her book bag and her lunch, she headed out the door, not bothering to say anything else to her parents. Fiona and Robert exchanged a look as mother followed behind daughter, prepared to give the child a serious reprimand.

Jennifer reached up to hug her father's neck. "I love my brother, Daddy," she said, whispering in his ear, then kissed his cheek.

"Me, too," Robbie added.

Robert hugged her tightly, then swatted Robbie on the behind as he sent the two of them out the door. Staring out the window, he watched as the yellow school bus pulled up in front and all three of his kids got inside. Fiona stood waving as the bus pulled off and drove out of sight.

Back inside, Fiona poured the two of them a cup of coffee and took a seat beside him at the kitchen table. "She'll get better," she said. "You know Elizabeth has a difficult time when things change."

"I know."

"So are you going to tell me what's going on? And don't tell me it's nothing. I'm not stupid, Robert. I know when things aren't right with you."

The man met her gaze. "I took Quincy without his mother's consent. I didn't do anything illegal, but I probably should have handled it differently."

Fiona's expression was incredulous. "How could you? Why would you do that?"

He shrugged, not really wanting to hear a lecture,

but knowing one was coming. "It's only temporary. I know he needs to be close to his mother. Jeneva has him in a great school in Washington, but he and I needed some time together. When she comes to get him, I'm hoping we'll be able to work out a schedule where I can spend more time with him."

"When is she coming?"

"Three weeks. Her boyfriend is bringing her."

"I cannot believe you would do something like this, Robert."

He avoided her harsh stare, his eyes racing from one corner of the room to the other.

"You look tired," Fiona said, staring at him. "Are you feeling okay?"

Robert shrugged again, pushing his broad shoulders skyward. His eyes danced everywhere except on her face. "Jet lag. It'll pass." He took a sip of his coffee.

As Fiona opened her mouth to say something else, they were interrupted when Quincy came through the kitchen door, looking curiously around him.

"Da . . . dee."

"Good morning, son," Robert said, rising from his seat. "Are you okay?"

Quincy clapped his hands.

"Can you say hello to Fiona?" Robert asked, pointing at his wife as he mouthed the woman's name into the palm of Quincy's hand.

Fiona smiled warmly, coming to stand beside the two of them. "Hello, Quincy," she said nervously. "It's very nice to meet you."

Quincy clapped, his gaze shifting upward. Fiona looked at Robert, who smiled, nodding his head. Quincy clapped his hands again, then pressed his fingers to his lips.

"Hel . . . lo," he said finally. "Quin . . . cy . . . eat . . . food."

* * *

She'd distanced herself from him, choosing to disregard his presence in her home. Mecan moved about with relative ease, trying to make her comfortable, and Jeneva purposely ignored him, the last remnants of her anger still lingering in the air like some foul odor. Both Roshawn and Bridget chastised her for her behavior, but she would not be moved. As far as she was concerned, what Mecan Tolliver thought he knew couldn't fill a thimble despite his persistent efforts to tell her what he thought was best for her and her son. Where did he get off? she questioned. He didn't know her well enough to tell her what she did or did not need.

As she entered the living room, he sat comfortably on the sofa, surveying a pile of road maps spread across her coffee table. He smiled as she dropped down onto the oversize recliner across from him.

"Feeling any better?" Mecan asked.

Jeneva shrugged, pushing her shoulders up to the ceiling.

Mecan sat back against the sofa, eyeing her curiously. "You really like to hold a grudge, don't you?"

The look she returned bordered on hostile. "Look, I know what you're trying to do and I appreciate it, but how I choose to deal with you giving my son away is my business."

"I did not give your son away," he said with a slight laugh.

"That's your opinion," Jeneva responded, pulling her legs up beneath her buttocks into the chair. "What are you doing?"

Mecan stared at her briefly before responding. "I had an idea. I thought that you and I might take a road trip to go get Quincy. If we leave at the end of the week we can drive cross-country, go to Atlanta, and come back. Bridget says you have plenty of vacation time coming and I've taken a short leave of absence from Hewitt House. We could do this."

Jeneva rolled her eyes. "Oh, please. That's just crazy."

Mecan laced his fingers together in front of him, resting his hands against his abdomen. He stared at her intently, studying the lines of her face. "Why is it crazy?"

"Because it is. Why would I want to spend the next three weeks in a car with you?"

"Because I'm a great conversationalist. Some people think I'm charming, and what better way for us to get to know one another better?"

"I know all I want to know about you."

He smiled. "Well, I don't know nearly enough about you. I want to know more, because what I do know already, I'm completely enamored with."

"You don't know anything about me."

The man leaned forward, his grin widening. "I know that you're hard-headed and stubborn. "

She cut her eyes in his direction, then shifted her body to stare at the wall.

Mecan continued. "I know that you're an avid collector with quite an incredible glass collection. You have great taste in music. You eat far too much junk food, and your wine selections leave much to be desired. You're a meticulous housekeeper. You had a great relationship with your parents. You like the color blue. You have an affinity for great books, especially classic literature. You—"

Jeneva turned back to him, cutting him off. "The books were my father's. I haven't read them."

Mecan looked at her questioningly.

"Well, not all of them," she said. "Why are you going through my things?"

"I wasn't. All I had to do was look around."

"Okay, so you're observant. You still don't know me."

Rising from his seat, Mecan crossed over to where she sat, sitting down against the arm of the recliner. He cupped his palm beneath her chin and lifted her eyes to meet his. "Yes, I do," he said, "and I want to know you better. So stop fighting me."

Jeneva stared up at him. "Stop telling me what to do," she said, wrapping her hand around his forearm, gently caressing his flesh against her palm.

Mecan smiled down at her. "So what do you say about that trip?"

"As long as we don't stay in any flea-trap motels along the way, I guess I can deal with it."

Mecan leaned over to kiss her forehead. "Thank you. I promise you'll have a great time."

"You sure like to make me a lot of promises."

"I'm not making any I can't keep."

Rolling her eyes, Jeneva shifted her body away from his. "And for the record," she said, "my favorite color is green, not blue."

Mecan laughed. "I stand corrected. Mine is red."

"And I like sunsets, too," she quipped.

"I like sunrises."

"The ocean in the summertime."

"The mountains in the winter."

"Jazz."

"Blues."

"What's your favorite holiday?" Jeneva asked quickly.

"Christmas."

"Mine, too."

"Where's the craziest place you ever made love?"

Mecan shrugged. "Don't think I've ever made love in any place crazy. You?"

She shook her head. "Robert's the only man I've ever been with. My love life's been boring."

"We'll have to do something about that."

They stared at each other, energy shifting between them like an electrical current out of control. "I'm still mad at you," Jeneva said finally, crossing to the other side of the room, putting some distance between the rising heat.

Mecan laughed. "That's okay," he said. "You'll get over it."

"When's Mecan coming back?" Roshawn asked as she and Bridget helped Jeneva pack her suitcase.

"He said he'd get back before midnight. We're leaving in the morning."

"Why don't you just hang around here and fly out in three weeks? Doesn't make much sense to me," Roshawn said, dropping down onto the bed.

"Me, either," Jeneva said, "but he asked me to trust him."

"Do you?" Bridget asked.

She looked at her two friends. "I don't know. But I want to. I really want to."

Bridget smiled. "You haven't had a vacation since forever. Try to enjoy it. I think it'll be fun."

"Please," Roshawn interjected, "two weeks in Hawaii is fun. Two weeks hotel-moteling it on a road trip is crazy."

"It'll give them some time together. What can be wrong with that?"

"It sounds about as exciting as your vibrator."

Bridget rolled her eyes as Jeneva chuckled lightly. "Will you two ever quit?" she asked.

Roshawn leaned to kiss Bridget's cheek. "Wouldn't be any fun if we did."

"You tell her, girl."

Darwin Tolliver dropped the telephone receiver back onto the hook. Rising from his seat on the bed, he reached across the dresser, pulling at the toiletries that sat waiting to be packed. Mecan was tossing his clothing into a leather suitcase, his mind lost on the task at hand.

"Mama said to tell you she'll see you soon, and that she'll take care of everything."

"Thanks, Darwin. I appreciate that."

His brother nodded. "I can't believe you're actually going to do this."

Mecan turned to look at him, smiling as his hands dropped to his side, a cotton sweater swinging from his hands. "Me, either. But I have to."

"Anything else you need me to do for you?"

"Yes. I took care of things at the office, but I didn't get a chance to speak to Natalia. Would you call her for me? Tell her what's happened and let her know I'll give her a call in a few days to check on the kids."

"Yeah. I can do that." Darwin laughed.

"What's so funny?"

"You. In love. You look like a little puppy with those sad eyes."

Mecan tossed his brother a dirty look.

"I'm serious, big brother. Since you met Jeneva, you haven't been the same. You've been all goggle-eyed and mushy. I was beginning to think you were sick."

"I have not been that bad."

"Yes, you have. But it's cool. I'm happy for you."

Mecan smiled. "I love her, Darwin. Never thought I'd feel this way. But I do. I love her."

"You must. I can't think of any other reason why you'd pull that car out of the garage."

"It looks good, doesn't it?"

"It's a beauty. You had everything checked, right? Brakes, oil, water?"

"She's ready. I filled it up this morning and she's ready to go."

Mecan dropped the last of his items into the suitcase and closed the top. Picking up his luggage, he headed into the living room, toward the front door.

"Call me," Darwin commanded. "Let me know where you are. Keep me up to date with what's going on."

"I will."

"And give Jeneva a kiss for me. Tell her we're all saying a prayer." Darwin smiled, then spun around and went to the kitchen. "Shoot. I almost forgot." He reached for a large plastic cooler and wicker picnic basket. "Got you some sodas and ice and I packed some food for the road. Tell Jeneva there are a couple of slices of torte in there for her."

Mecan laughed as they carried the items to the car, packing the trunk and the backseat. As he closed the trunk, Mecan met his brother's gaze. The two men lightly punched fists, pressing the back of their knuckles against each other. Mecan pulled his younger sibling into a warm embrace.

"If you need me, call!" Darwin called after him, tapping a fist against his heart. "You know I'll be there."

Mecan started the engine, shifting the car into drive. "Ditto, little brother. You can take that to the bank."

Twenty-one

Both Roshawn and Bridget were waving excitedly as Jeneva and Mecan pulled out of her driveway in a classic 1976 Cadillac Eldorado convertible. In pristine condition, the cherry-red vehicle with its white leather seats was polished to a high shine. When Mecan had pulled up out front, riding with the top down, the three women had tossed each other a look. Jeneva could only shake her head.

"Oh, you're cooking now," Roshawn had exclaimed, breaking out into laughter. "Why didn't you just go get a ticket on the pony express? That might get you two there faster than this pimp mobile will."

"Do people still drive these things?" Jeneva asked, the expression on her face causing Mecan to laugh himself.

"Baby, this car is a work of art," he said. "I'm willing to wager that this is going to be one of the best rides you're ever going to have."

Jeneva cut her eyes at him. "I hope your triple A is paid up."

Mecan had laughed, lifting her off her feet as he hugged her close. "Have faith, woman. Have faith."

Their drive started out quietly as Mecan settled the car on interstate 90 and Jeneva settled herself against the leather seats. The radio played in the background, and every so often Mecan would join in, singing along with the music. At the first rest stop, he pulled off the road and parked.

"Do you want to stretch your legs?" he asked.

"I need to use the restroom," Jeneva said, lifting herself out of the vehicle. "I'll be right back."

Mecan watched as she made her way into the service center, and smiled. She looked comfortable in her terry cotton pull-on pants and hooded jacket. She'd finally relaxed, allowing herself to enjoy the views as they traversed the highways. When she finally made her way back, two bottles of chilled soda and a large bag of barbecued potato chips in hand, his smile widened, breaking out into a full-fledged grin.

"Thought we could use a snack," she said, setting her purchases on the seat. Mecan winked. "You were reading my mind."

"So, tell me about this car," Jeneva said, coming to stand beside him as he looked under the hood, checking the engine.

"This was my father's car."

"You're kidding me, right?"

"No. This was my dad's. It was the first car he ever bought. I was six years old. I thought it was the coolest thing in the world, my dad having a red Cadillac. Thought we were rich. He died a year later. Mom parked it in the garage and left it. After college, she let me have it. I had to have some minor work done to her, but she's in mint condition."

"How often do you drive it?"

"Not often. This is really the first time she's been on the road for a long trip."

Jeneva nodded her head.

Mecan closed the hood. "Are you ready?" he asked.

"I am. Do you want me to drive?"

"Not yet. I'm good for a while. But we have a lot of

road to cover today. We've got about seven hundred miles to go before I want to stop tonight."

"You're kidding, right?"

"No. If we don't make too many stops, we should get there about nine or ten."

"Get where?"

"It's a surprise."

Jeneva rolled her eyes. "I hate surprises."

"I don't. Let's go."

Mecan drove for another three hours before they stopped for lunch and he turned the wheel over to her. As she got comfortable, Mecan eased himself down in the seat, closed his eyes, and dozed off. Every so often, Jeneva would cast a glance over, noting how his mouth fell open just so, or his eyes twitched, laughing softly when he snored.

When he woke, they talked about nothing. Nothing important, nothing specific, just easy conversation that helped pass the time away. After refilling the gas tank twice, stopping for only one full meal and an additional bathroom break, Mecan pulled the car over the Wyoming border, picking up US-89 south. Jeneva stretched her body awake just as he turned onto Norris Canyon Road, heading into Yellowstone National Park.

"Where are we?" she asked, looking anxiously around her.

"Almost there," he answered, turning toward a line of log cabins that sat nestled in a thick growth of forest. The sun had set hours ago, a sliver of moon lighting the sky. Pulling up in front of a large lodge, Mecan put the car into park and shut the engine down.

"I'll be right back," he said, "I just have to check us in."

Minutes later, he guided them a little farther down the road, stopping in front of a small log cabin.

"At least we're not camping," Jeneva mumbled.

"We can if you want," Mecan said.

Jeneva shot a look in his direction. "So what is this place?"

"Hibernation Cabins. We're in the park."

"What park?"

"Yellowstone."

Jeneva laughed. "You mean the Yogi Bear, 'Hey, Boo Boo' Yellowstone park?" she asked, doing an impressive imitation of the old Saturday morning cartoon character.

"Yes," Mecan said, laughing with her. "That's the one."

Inside, Mecan flipped on the lights. The small enclosure was warm and inviting, bearing an incredible Southern decor. Quilted blankets were tossed against the sofa and chairs. There was a large living room, dining room, kitchenette combination in the front of the cabin and a king-size bedroom suite with a fireplace in full burn and a very modern bathroom with a large soaking tub in the rear. The whole place made her smile and Jeneva could hear that bathtub calling her name.

"What time do we have to leave in the morning?" Jeneva asked.

"We don't. I thought we'd spend the day in the park exploring. We'll get some rest and another good night's sleep and we'll take off after that."

Jeneva smiled, shaking her head. "Why are you doing this?"

"Doing what?"

"This whole trip. It's like Roshawn said: we could

have gotten on a plane three weeks from now, flown down to get Quincy, and come back. Why this road trip?"

Mecan took a deep breath, dropping down against the arm of the sofa. For a brief moment he stared off into the distance, his eyes focused someplace other than in that room as he gathered memories and collected thoughts that would explain why this was so important to him.

"My father always talked about driving cross-country in that car. He had this incredible trip all mapped out. The places he was going to take my mother to see, the things they were going to do. He never got the chance to share that dream with her. When he died, it became my dream. It was just something I wanted to do with the woman I loved. So I'm doing it."

Jeneva stared into his eyes, his gaze like a comfortable security blanket falling down over her. Mecan leaned forward in his seat and kissed her, brushing his lips lightly across hers. His arms stayed crossed against his chest.

"You look tired," he said softly. "Why don't I run you a bath."

Jeneva licked her lips, her tongue brushing lightly against her mouth. She nodded as Mecan pressed his palm against her cheek and headed into the bathroom. In the distance, she could hear the rush of water fall from the faucet. Leaving the water still running, Mecan came back into the room.

"I'll sleep here on the sofa. You take the bed," he said as he lifted her suitcase and headed into the bedroom. Jeneva followed behind him. She watched as he lowered her bag against a cedar chest that sat at the foot of the bed and headed back inside the bathroom.

A few minutes later, the water shut off and he came back, wiping his hands against a pale-blue towel.

"Take all the time you want," he said. "I think I'm going to go take a short walk."

"In the dark?"

"I'll be all right. You just relax and enjoy yourself," he said, heading for the door.

"Mecan?" Jeneva said, her voice rising ever so slightly as she called after him.

"Yes?" He turned back toward her.

"Don't leave," she said. "I don't want you to go."

Jeneva slipped the terry jacket off her shoulders, exposing a matching laced tank top beneath. Mecan stared as she pushed the straps off her shoulders, slowing easing the garment down to her waist. He stood riveted to the spot as he watched inch after inch of brown flesh being revealed to him. Jeneva pushed the top past her hips, pulling her pants along as she did so until all her clothing lay puddled on the floor at her feet. Mecan could feel his breath slipping away, the rise of his manhood pressing anxiously at the front of his pants. He swallowed hard, gulping for oxygen, as the dampness of perspiration tinted the palms of his hands. Jeneva's gaze remained locked with his as she walked naked past him and into the bathroom. Her beauty warmed him like the warmth of sunlight on a cool spring day.

A wealth of bubbles filled the porcelain container of warm water. Jeneva tested the temperature with her big toe before submerging her whole foot and then her legs and her body. The water felt like balm against her skin and she closed her eyes, sinking into the wetness. She was barely aware of her surroundings as she focused on her breathing, slowly inhaling and exhaling her nervousness away. Movement above her caused her to open her eyes.

Mecan stood in the doorway, staring down at her. Desire was carved in the curvature of his face, filling the hollow of his eyes. They stared, neither of them saying anything, until Jeneva sat up straight and reached her hand out to him.

Closing the door behind him, Mecan stood in the center of the room, still staring. His hands slowly unbuttoned his shirt and he pulled the casual cotton top from around his chest. Solid as stone, Jeneva thought, her lips parting as a chill shot into the pit of her stomach. As Mecan unsnapped his jeans and pulled at the zipper, Jeneva pulled her legs to her chest, pressing her breasts tightly against her thighs. She rested her cheek against her knees, still staring as Mecan stepped out of his pants and stood naked before her. He was perfection, she thought, and he took her breath away.

Stepping into the water behind her, Mecan lowered himself around her body so that Jeneva sat between his legs, her back pressed against his chest. He leaned to kiss her shoulder, his hands moving up and down the length of her arms. The thick of his erection pressed eagerly against her lower back.

Pulling her head back, Mecan kissed her, his mouth dancing against hers. His hands walked slowly across her body, strolling over each breast, her stomach, and the back of her thighs. His caresses were slow and easy and burned like fire against her skin. She hugged his calves with the palms of her hands, then traced her fingers along the back of his thighs. She drew small circles with her shoulders against his nipples, pulling his arms up and around to hug her body. As they explored each other, bubbles played around them and between them and the warmth of the water washed any nervousness straight down the drain.

* * *

When Jeneva awoke the next morning, her body lay sprawled atop Mecan's, naked pressed against naked. She smiled at the sweet memories the previous night had left her with. She stirred ever so slowly, not wanting to disturb him from his rest. His arm came around to hug her waist and a smile crept slowly across his face.

"Good morning, baby," he said, pulling a large paw through her hair.

"Good morning." Jeneva lifted herself off the bed and headed into the bathroom. After emptying her bladder and rinsing her mouth, she returned to bed, crawling up under the covers to lay her head against his chest. Mecan dozed for a few more minutes, then retreated to the lavatory to do the same thing. Back in bed, he pulled her against him and kissed her. The back of his hand brushed against her nipple and she smiled when her body reacted on its own accord, her breasts rising to meet his mouth. His tongue felt like silk against her skin.

Mecan played with her, teasing her sweetly with his soft touch. When she could no longer stand the waiting, she opened herself and invited him in, wanting all of what he had to offer. He loved her slowly, taking his time as he tested the waters of each nerve, introducing himself to every inch of her body. He loved her completely, and he loved her like no one had ever loved her before.

Twenty-two

Jeneva had never been on a horse before and Mecan had taken her horseback riding. His instructions had been slow and methodic as he guided her and the large animal supporting her bottom through the trails of Yellowstone National Park. The weather was spectacular, warm even breezes blowing gently, sunshine raining down from overhead. It took them back to another time and another era, and Jeneva imagined that a big black cowboy on a big black horse could have caused many a woman to breathe heavy with wanting back in the day.

Losing herself in the fantasy, she almost slid off the back of the beast, which neighed his annoyance at her. "Okay," she said firmly. "I've had enough."

"What happened?" Mecan asked as he led her to a clearing and helped her to unsaddle.

"I was daydreaming. The horse didn't like it."

"Must have been something good."

"It was. The animal spoiled the moment."

Mecan grinned. "You were supposed to be concentrating on riding him."

"I was, but my thighs are sore and I don't want to do this anymore."

"What's wrong with your thighs?"

Jeneva smiled. "Nothing a massage won't cure."

Mecan laughed as he guided both animals back to the stables and returned them to their owners. He looped his arm through Jeneva's as they walked back to the car and climbed inside. Leaning across the seat, he kissed her, pressing his closed mouth to hers.

"So, tell me what you were daydreaming about?" he asked.

Jeneva giggled. "I was fantasizing about something naughty and I'm not going to tell you."

"I'd tell you."

"No, you wouldn't."

"Yes, I would. I'd tell you my fantasies."

"Go ahead. Tell me one."

This time Mecan giggled, which made Jeneva laugh even harder.

"No fair. I asked first," Mecan said.

Jeneva shrugged as if it didn't matter to her one way or the other. "Suit yourself."

Mecan started the car and pulled it out of the parking space, heading back down toward their cabin.

"You ever make love in this car?" Jeneva asked, breaking the silence.

The man laughed, shaking his head. "No. But I admit I've thought about it. That's a pretty big backseat there."

"Did you think about being naked when you did it?"

"No. Clothes on, somewhere public where you might get caught. It would add to the thrill."

"So you're a freak!"

"No, baby. I just have a creative imagination."

Jeneva smiled as they stepped out of the car and up the stairs into the cabin. "Well, come be creative on my thighs," she said, pulling him along by the hand. "Let's see what kind of imagination you have, Mr. Tolliver."

* * *

They got an early start the next morning, pulling out of Yellowstone shortly before seven o'clock in the morning. Mecan had planned another long day of driving, mapping out their trail before they'd lain down for bed the night before. Jeneva was actually excited as she perused the maps he'd marked and highlighted for them to follow.

"Have you done a lot of traveling?" Jeneva asked.

Mecan shook his head. "No. Not really. But I've always wanted to travel the United States. Darwin lived in Europe for a few years and he was always crossing the borders from one country to another. I used to wonder why people here don't do more of that, go exploring the country since it's so much easier for us to cross from one state to another."

"I like your brother."

Mecan smiled. "I'm glad. Darwin's my best friend."

Jeneva adjusted the seat belt across her chest, pulling at the strap until it felt more comfortable against her breasts. Mecan's eyes flickered from the road to the rearview mirror and back again.

"How about you? What exotic places have you been to?"

"Never really had a chance to travel. I was always afraid to leave Quincy alone with anybody. When my parents were alive, I did take a cruise to the Bahamas one year with Roshawn and Bridget, but that's about it."

Mecan pursed his lips, pushing his mouth out and then back in again. "Why do you think you were so overprotective of Quincy?" he asked, his eyes focused on the road.

Jeneva stared at him, the question catching her off guard. "I had to be," she said finally. "There wasn't anyone else there to take care of him. I had to protect him."

Mecan nodded. "I understand that, but why were

you so overprotective? Both you and he have missed out on a lot of things that you could have been doing. There's a lot Quincy should have been doing that he didn't because you wouldn't let him. Why?"

"Are you saying I held my son back?"

"No. I'm saying that he missed out on a lot of living because you were afraid. I want to know what it was you were afraid of. I'm asking because I feel like you're still afraid. If I can understand it, I can help change it."

The statement slapped her, pushing her back against the seat. Her first reaction was to become angry, but when she glanced back at Mecan, his eyes piercing hers, she fought it. She stared out the passenger window, counting the cars around them. Mecan let her fall down in the silence, waiting for her answer.

"When Robert left, that hurt. It hurt more than I was willing to admit to anyone, most especially myself. Quincy was all I had left of him and he embodied all the love I thought Robert and I had for each other. Every time my baby was sick, I was petrified that I'd lose him and then all that was left of Robert's love would be gone from me, too. I didn't want to take any chances on that happening because Robert had stopped loving me and I didn't trust that anyone else would. I figured if Robert could love me once and then leave like he did, how could I trust that any other man would love me and stay. If I lost Quincy, then I was sure I'd never have any love at all."

Mecan nodded his head, appreciating her honesty. The car sped down the road as Mecan maneuvered from one lane to another.

"I hurt my son, didn't I?" Jeneva asked, her voice low.

Mecan shook his head. "Not at all. You loved him. You did what you had to do. Quincy will come into his own. Every time you made a decision about his care, you did it with his best interests at heart. Not being willing to take risks surely didn't make you a bad parent.

"I honestly think you hurt yourself more. You've missed out on a lot of living, Jeneva. There's this whole big world out here just waiting for you and you've been letting it slip right on by. When you did that to yourself, you also did it to your son."

Six hundred miles later, they pulled into Denver, Colorado. Mecan checked his directions and headed for downtown and the Loews Denver Hotel. The Tuscany-inspired luxury hotel welcomed them both warmly and when Jeneva dropped her tired body across the magnificent king-size bed, she thought it had to have been touched by heaven-inspired hands. Mecan laughed as she rolled from side to side.

Dropping his clothes along the way, he headed into the expansive bathroom and right for the shower. Jeneva watched from the door as he soaped himself, his hands kneading suds against the muscles of his arms and chest, down to his stomach, the length of his manhood, his thighs, and his buttocks. As Mecan watched her watching him, he slowed the pace of his hands, suds coating his dark flesh a sheer, milky white. Jeneva smiled, slowly unfastening the buttons of her cotton blouse. The floral-printed top fell off her shoulders, hooked in the crevice of her elbows as she unsnapped her denim jeans and pulled at the zipper. As her clothing fell to the floor, Mecan beckoned her to him, desire gracing his face.

Taking two steps toward him, she unsnapped her lace bra and let it fall to the floor as she stepped out of the matching panties. Mecan inhaled sharply, his gaze stroking the length of her body. Jeneva stepped into the water behind him, replacing his hands with her own. Her fingers tiptoed down his torso as she gently kneaded his flesh. Following her fingers with her warm mouth, she planted kisses behind her caresses. He shuddered as she pressed her lips against the center of his back and then the base of his spine. Stretching up on her toes, she glided her hands across his bald head, then kissed his mouth, her tongue probing. The crush of his mouth against her own was as soft as silk, and he tasted sweet. At the same time, the kiss was filled with passion strong enough to warm her right down to her toes. The sheer magnitude of how much she hungered for him flooded her senses. Tears ran the length of her face, dripping into the mist of water that poured forth from the shower.

"Here, let me wash your back," Mecan whispered as he spun her into the water and ran his fingers from her neck down to her knees. Working the tired out of her flesh, Mecan's touch was soothing, almost healing, and she marveled at the heat that raced from his touch.

Later, they lay sprawled across the massive bed, limbs entangled until their bodies seemed more one than two. Mecan had flipped on the television and they lay dozing lightly as CNN played in the background. Stretching, Jeneva pulled her body up and around and laid her head in his lap, curling up against him. Mecan rubbed her back, his hand pressing nicely into her side. He flipped the channels on the remote control, pausing periodically to study one show or another, nothing capturing either of their attentions.

"What's this?" Mecan asked as he stopped to view the action across the screen.

"That reality show, *The Bachelor*."

"Don't know it."

"They put this man with twenty-five women who are trying to become his wife or at least outlast all the others to capture his attention. In the end they're supposed to find true love."

Mecan laughed. "So he's dating all these women at one time?"

"Each week he kicks a few of them off as he narrows down the field."

Mecan nodded his head as he turned up the volume. They watched, both shaking their heads when two blondes and a brunette were professing to have so much love for the millionaire catch of the day.

"Could you do that?" Jeneva asked, leaning up to look at Mecan.

"What? Date all those women to find true love?"

She nodded.

"No. It's not possible."

"Why not?"

"Because at some point you have to realize that you're either lying to one of the women, all of the women, or yourself. If it's true love, you don't want to be with another woman. I mean, look at this guy. He's taking three different women to three different romantic spots. All three of them joined him in some overnight suite. Of course we will never know what, if anything, happened, but if he was feeling an ounce of love for either one of them, he wouldn't have even wanted to take the other two to some hotel room, and then to bed. But then, that's just how I would feel. I couldn't do it and wouldn't want to."

Jeneva smiled, nodding slowly. "Are you tired yet?" she asked, brushing her palm against his chest.

Mecan stifled a yawn, stretching his arms over his head. "I am tired."

Jeneva pulled herself up off the bed.

"What's wrong?" Mecan asked as she dropped down to her knees.

"Nothing. I just haven't said my prayers yet."

Mecan tossed the covers from his legs. "May I join you?"

Jeneva clasped his hand beneath hers as he fell to her side, bowing his head against the mattress. Together they both sent a silent message to God's ears, both in need of and asking for the same things. Whispering an amen, Mecan lifted himself back into bed first, then waited for Jeneva to join him.

Pulling the blankets back up and over their bodies, Jeneva snuggled against him and smiled. "Do you think Quincy's okay?" she asked softly, her eyes fluttering open and then closed.

"Quincy's just fine," Mecan said as he switched off the light and closed his eyes. "Good night, baby."

"Good night, my love."

Twenty-three

The day in Denver was a whirlwind. Jeneva and Mecan ran from one tourist attraction to another, inhaling the vibe of the big city like needed oxygen. The morning had been spent racing to museums, muddling through the daily congestion of traffic as they explored the sprawling city. Jeneva loved the Denver Art Museum with its vast collection of Native American art. Both she and Mecan had been enthralled with the history at the Black American West Museum.

Housed in the home of Dr. Justina Ford, Denver's first black doctor, the museum was a wealth of information about the African-American cowboys who helped mold the American West. The two were fascinated to learn that one-third of cowboys in history had been black and that there had been numerous self-sufficient, all-black towns back in the day.

Though she could have done without the insect center and its exhibitions, Jeneva had also enjoyed the Denver Butterfly Pavilion, the lush, tropical forest with its multitude of free-flying butterflies feeling like a whole other world.

At the Cherry Creek shopping center, they stocked up on trinkets to take back home with them and Jeneva had to laugh as the two of them struggled to pack the added weight into their luggage. The purchase of an additional suitcase helped ease that dilemma. That night, after an incredible Italian dinner, Mecan surprised her with tickets to a Denver Broncos game. The team was playing the New England Patriots, and, though she never considered herself a football fan, Jeneva was surprised to discover just how much she enjoyed the sport as Mecan explained the action, play by play. Sleep came quickly and both of them marveled at how comfortable sleeping side by side had become.

The next day, they slept in, lounging the day away in bed, the *Do Not Disturb* sign front and center on the room's door. Both enjoyed having no place to go and nothing to do, as they slept, ate, made love, slept, and made love. Checking out of the hotel the following day, Jeneva almost wished they could stay for another week. But once she was behind the wheel of the car, tooling down the road with the wind blowing in her hair, she was glad to be moving, excited about the next leg of their exploration.

Night was fast approaching as they exited I-135 south into Wichita, Kansas. As Mecan pulled into the parking lot of the Best Western hotel, Jeneva suddenly felt hungry, the yearning coming from somewhere low in her midsection.

"You check us in," Jeneva said. "I'll grab our bags."

"You sure?" Mecan asked, looking at her strangely.

She nodded. "I just want to stay out here and get some air for a minute.

"Well, just bring my toiletry bag and the small sports bag. I won't need anything else."

"I'll be right behind you," Jeneva said as Mecan headed across the parking lot toward the entrance door.

The check-in went quickly and Mecan became nervous when Jeneva didn't come inside. He headed back out to find her. Across the way, the car appeared locked, no sign of her anywhere. Nervous energy filled Mecan's stomach as he rushed to the car.

When he pulled on the vehicle's door handle, leaning down to peer inside, he found Jeneva seated comfortably in the backseat.

"What's wrong?" Mecan asked.

Jeneva smiled seductively. Her head swayed from side to side. "Come here," she said, her voice low.

Mecan glanced over his shoulder and across the half-full parking lot. A row of exterior lights lined the black pavement, illuminating the lot, the walkway, and the hotel's door. "What's going on?" he asked, looking back at her.

"Come here," she said again, crooking her index finger in his direction.

Mecan smiled, crawling into the backseat with her. Pulling the door closed, he reached for the lock, depressing first the driver's door and then the passenger's. Pulling him toward her, Jeneva pressed her mouth to his, kissing him hungrily. Her tongue danced alongside his, performing an erotic tango inside his mouth.

Lifting herself up, Jeneva straddled his body, the length of her skirt rising high above her knees. She settled herself against his lap, rotating her hips as she closed the gap between them. Mecan's breathing intensified as Jeneva's hands reached under his shirt, her fingers slowly stroking his chest. Reaching around her, Mecan cupped the round of her bottom and pulled her closer. His eyes widened in astonishment when his palms touched bare flesh, Jeneva's panties lost somewhere on the car's floor.

Noting his surprise, Jeneva broke the kiss. She

laughed, a low, wicked laugh that vibrated every nerve ending in Mecan's body. He felt himself shiver, heat rushing from his head to his toes. She nipped the flesh against his lower lip, her tongue tracing a line along his chin, his neck, the orbs of his ears. Blood surged through his crotch, filling what little space he had in his jeans.

"What are we doing?" Mecan managed to whisper, his hands groping her now fully exposed breasts.

"Making your fantasy come true," Jeneva whispered, her breath hot against his ear.

As Jeneva pulled at the buttons across his crotch, opening his fly, Mecan scanned the parking lot for a second time. Another car had pulled into a space two rows in front of them, the occupants still sitting inside.

"Someone might see us," he said, lifting Jeneva and his hips off the seat as she pulled urgently at his pants.

"Then we better hurry," she replied, plunging her mouth and her body back against his.

Lounging by the hotel's indoor pool, Jeneva welcomed the opportunity to sit back and relax. Mecan lay on the lounge chair beside her, his face buried in the pages of the morning newspaper. In the clear blue water, a woman splashed about with her young daughter, the duo spiriting liquid all around them and anyone else who happened to be within distance of their playful spray. Jeneva smiled at the little girl, who giggled with abandonment, relishing the impromptu playtime.

Reaching for a glass of orange juice that sat on the table between her and Mecan, Jeneva pulled the cool beverage to her mouth, sipping it slowly.

"Mac?"

"Yes, ma'am?"

"What do you aspire to be when you grow up?" she asked, staring over the top of her sunshades toward him.

Mecan lowered the newspaper to his lap as he turned to stare in her direction. "That's an interesting question."

"Do you have an interesting answer?" she prompted.

He pondered the query for a moment before responding. "I aspire to have my own school one day. Maybe a dozen of them, but all dedicated to bringing back the basics to our young people."

"Tell me more."

"I've always known I'd be in education in some capacity. I love kids. I love giving them the skills to do whatever it is they want to do. The problem I have with public education today is that teachers have to spend so much time being parents and counselors, they don't have time to teach. And when they teach, too often they have to teach to ensure their respective school system passes some standardized government exam. Kids nowadays don't know the pure joy of learning for the sake of learning. We've taken the excitement out of education."

Jeneva nodded her head. "I'll tell you a secret, but you have to promise not to laugh at me."

Mecan smiled. "I would never laugh at you."

"I always wanted to be a professional gospel singer."

Mecan chuckled.

"You're laughing at me."

"I'm not. Do you sing?"

"I can hold my own. When I got married, obviously I couldn't do that, but it's what I aspired to do when I grew up. Sing gospel."

"Do you sing in your church choir?"

She shook her head. "I wanted to, but I could never find the time."

"So why don't you do it now?'

Jeneva shrugged. "I hadn't thought about it. Maybe I will. When I get Quincy back, maybe I will."

Jeneva lay back against her chair, adjusting her shades against her face. Mecan reached a hand and brushed his palms against her upper thigh. He squeezed her leg gently.

"Darling, when you grow up, you can be anything you want to be," he said, caressing her with the warmth of his smile.

Twenty-four

When Mecan's cell phone rang, neither he nor Jeneva was prepared, the catchy jingle surprising them. With the state of Kansas some two hours behind them, they had stopped at a rest area to fill the engine with oil, and to add ice and soda to the plastic cooler that sat on the backseat. Both stared as the phone rang, then Mecan pulled it from the front console and answered the call.

"Hello?"

A woman's frantic voice spilled from the other end. "Umm, yes. Is this Mecan Tolliver?"

"Yes, it is. May I help you?"

"My name's Fiona Douglas. My husband, Robert, asked me to call."

"Is something wrong, Mrs. Douglas?"

"Y—yes. Quincy's not well," she stammered into the receiver. "He's, he's . . ."

Mecan could hear the panic in the woman's voice and her anxiety caused his own to rise. "Please calm down, Mrs. Douglas, and tell me what's wrong."

Jeneva pressed at his elbow, looking at him anxiously.

"Here. Please talk to my husband."

"Mecan, it's Robert."

"What's going on?"

"Quincy's throwing a fit, or having a seizure. I don't know what to do. I tried to call Dr. Adler, but she's away from her office and can't be reached."

"Okay, tell me what he's doing."

Mecan cupped the receiver and turned toward Jeneva. "Quincy is having a fit of some sort. Has this happened before?"

"What's he doing?" Jeneva asked.

On the other end, Robert was yelling at his wife, who was yelling at one of her own children, who was crying as if the world had come to an abrupt end. Chaos rang over the telephone line.

"Robert!" Mecan yelled. "Talk to me."

"I'm sorry. Something upset him and now he's screaming, throwing his body against the floor and walls. When I tried to stop him, he just got worse. He's hitting his head and tearing at his hair. I don't know what to do. What do I do?"

As Mecan relayed the information to Jeneva, she pulled the phone from his hand.

"Robert, it's Jeneva. Listen to me carefully."

"Okay. I'm listening."

"Are you in the room with Quincy?"

"In the doorway. He's right here in my bedroom. I'm afraid he's going to hurt himself."

"Give your wife the telephone. I'm going to talk you through this. Grab Quincy and pull him down to the floor between your legs. Do it. Now."

Robert threw the phone at his wife. "Talk to Jeneva," he commanded, rushing to his son's side.

"Hello?"

"Tell Robert to grab Quincy and pull him down to the floor."

"Okay, he's got him."

"Tell him to wrap his legs and arms around

Quincy's body so that he can't move. Tell him he has to hold tight because Quincy's strong."

Fiona relayed the instructions.

"Now tell him to just hum. He can hum anything. Put his mouth right against Quincy's ear and just hum. Tell him don't let go and don't stop humming."

As Fiona passed on the message, Jeneva took a deep breath. Her eyes met Mecan's and she smiled, nodding her head calmly. In the background, she could hear Robert humming an old Luther Vandross tune. Within minutes, she could hear Quincy humming with him.

Fiona returned to the telephone. "He's stopped. He seems to be calm."

"He was angry. Someone did something to make him angry."

"He was playing with his brother and sister. I don't know what happened."

"That's okay. It was just a temper tantrum, but he doesn't know how to stop them when he starts. I guess we're going to have to get him some anger management classes."

There was brief silence as the two women each stood holding the phone, one watching her husband rock his son against his chest, the other staring deeply into the eyes of the man she loved.

"Thank you," Fiona said softly. "I'm sorry if we frightened you, but we didn't know what to do."

Jeneva smiled. "Tell Robert he's okay now. He can let Quincy go. If he needs us, tell him to call. Goodbye." She disconnected the line and placed the phone onto the dashboard. She took a deep breath, held it, then let the flow of oxygen spill back out into the air.

Mecan clasped her fingers between his and leaned to kiss her forehead. "I'm very proud of you," he said, smiling down at her. "You handled that beautifully."

Jeneva smiled back. "I'm learning from a pro."

* * *

As Mecan pulled back on the highway, Jeneva thought about Robert and their child. Before, she would have been frantic to get to the child's side, concerned that no one could care for him as well as she could. Now there was understanding that everyone who loved Quincy would fight to do right by him and keep him safe. Maybe not in the way that she would, but in their own way, and just as well.

She pulled the cell phone into her hands and dialed. It rang once, twice, three times before being picked up on the other end.

"Hello!"

"Roshawn, it's me."

"Girl, where are you? Is everything okay?"

"Everything is fine. I'm having a wonderful time."

"You're kidding, right?"

"No, girl. Trust me when I tell you this is the only way to travel."

Jeneva could just see Roshawn shaking her head on the other end.

"Guess what!" Roshawn said excitedly. "Ming made the cheerleading squad and got her first period, all on the same day!"

Jeneva laughed with her friend. "Baby girl is growing up, Roshawn."

"How's Quincy? Have you heard from them?"

"Well, Robert is still hanging in there, so I guess that counts for something."

"Still need to tell the son of a—"

"Be nice, Roshawn. He's growing up, too."

"I guess we all have to do it sooner or later."

"I hear you. Kiss my girl for me and tell Bridget I'll call her over the weekend."

"Hey, you wear that lace yet?"

Jeneva grinned. "Right through the foreplay!"

"That's what I'm talking about! You are so nasty!"

"I love you, too, Roshawn."

"Tell Mr. Mac we all said hello."

"I will. Bye, Roshawn!"

"Bye."

As she settled back in her seat, Mecan glanced over her. "Everything okay?" he asked.

She smiled. "Things couldn't be more perfect."

Mecan stared over at Jeneva, who lay sleeping soundly beside him. Traffic had slowed, a few miles of road construction ahead of them. If perfection could be personified, it would be Jeneva, he thought, reaching out his hand to brush his fingers gently against her face. She shifted slightly, making herself comfortable against the reclined seat.

He liked that they could talk about everything. With each mile, her levels of comfort increased and she wasn't afraid to express her emotions, telling him things he'd already known, but needed to hear her say. She'd harbored much resentment toward her ex-husband, her faith in men severely ravaged. His taking Quincy had only served to bring those feelings front and center, forcing her to deal with the issues that had ended the marriage. Mecan recognized that she wanted to be angry and she wanted to stay angry. He also recognized that the spirit of her heart was finally letting that anger go, swallowing it whole each and every time she focused on being honest with herself.

Mecan smiled, the warmth of it filling his face. She had wanted to know about him. His past, his present, his dreams and hopes for his future. She'd asked questions and had listened to the answers. She'd validated his experiences, had believed as he believed, and had made him feel special. She had wanted him as much as he'd wanted her, and she hadn't stopped herself from showing him. She let him know that she welcomed what was happening between them. She hadn't yet called it love, but she had claimed it, had labeled it theirs, and had ensured that Mecan knew how much she valued it.

He loved her. It showed on his face, in his eyes, with every breath he took. A blind man could have seen it, would have felt it like warm breath against his skin. He loved her, and every ounce of sense he possessed told him that she loved him right back.

Twenty-five

There are moments when every twist and turn in
life serves to remind a person of how blessed they are.
This was one of those moments, Jeneva thought, as
Mecan reached for her hand, pressing his fingers between hers. The day's drive had been pleasant, the
duo stopping and starting as the desire moved them.
The weather had been God-sent, the sun shining
brightly against the bluest of blue skies. The temperature had peaked at eighty-two degrees with minimal
humidity, and the subtlest breeze blew sweetly. Traffic
had moved as if timed to a tee, and on this leg of their
excursion, they were spared the drama of any acci-
dents or congestion. After crossing over the Louisiana
border, Mecan had taken the wheel, picking up the
drive where she'd left off.

"So, where are we bunking tonight?" Jeneva asked
as she pulled his hand to her mouth and kissed the
center of his palm.

Mecan smiled. "Shreveport."

"You've selected some unusual places for us to visit,
Mac. Why Shreveport?"

"We're visiting family," he said, giving her a sly wink.

"Whose family?"

"Mine, and hopefully yours some day very soon."

Jeneva's hands flew to her hair, which blew wildly in

every direction. "What family is this that we're going to visit, Mac?"

"It's Uncle Jake's birthday today. I thought we'd stop by and say hello. Maybe spend a day or two. My sister and my mother should both be here and I want them to meet you."

Jeneva's eyes grew wide. "Your mother? I can't meet your mother. I look bad."

Mecan laughed. "No, you don't. You look beautiful."

Jeneva covered her face with her hands, shaking her head. "Why didn't you warn me?" she said, pulling at the sum visor to check her makeup.

Mecan smiled. "Are you going to panic? Because if you're going to panic, I should probably pull over."

She shook her head, cutting her eyes toward him. "I'm going to get you for this. I cannot believe you! Didn't anyone ever tell you that meeting a man's mother for the first time is a very big deal? One that requires at least half a day, not half an hour, to prepare for?"

Mecan laughed. As he pulled off the highway, she could see his mind racing while he focused on remembering the lefts and rights that would bring him to his family's front door. Jeneva sat back, trying to admire the expansive views, nervous tension knotting the muscles across her abdomen.

Shreveport was steamed in Southern tradition. Jeneva could feel the history seeping into her spirit as they passed a row of old historic homes. Mecan pointed out the sites, slowing the car at one point as they rolled past an old plantation, the antebellum home with its Georgian architecture sitting piously off in the distance. Jeneva imagined she heard the black bodies who'd given their lives working the vast fields still chanting an old hymn. It blew like mist through the massive old oak trees that lined streets and formed intricate canopies over the ancient land.

Two quick turns and Mecan drove through the gates of a newer subdivision of contemporary homes. Two more turns and he pulled into the driveway of a two-story brick structure situated on the ninth green of a residential golf community. The afternoon sun had begun its western decline and Jeneva thought the air suddenly seemed warmer. Mecan squeezed her hand, leaning to kiss her cheek.

As he moved to step out of the car, Jeneva grabbed his arm, her fingernails pressing into his flesh.

"What's wrong?" Mecan said, sitting back down.

"I just need to tell you something before we go inside."

"Are you all right?"

She nodded. "I love you, Mecan Tolliver." Joy shone in her eyes. "I love you and I just wanted you to know how much I want to be a part of you and your life. I just wanted you to know that before I met your family because you've been telling me you love me since before we left Washington and I've never said it back. But I do. I love you very much. And I had to tell you first before I met your mother and told her."

Mecan grinned, pressing his lips to hers.

"That's enough," Jeneva said, pulling away. "I'm about to meet your mother. I don't want her to think I'm a tramp or anything. Making out in your car won't look good."

The man laughed, a deep vibrato that flew from his midsection. "My mother is going to love you as much as I do. And what she doesn't know about what you and I do in this car won't hurt any one of us."

Lifting his large body out of the car, Mecan walked around to Jeneva's door to help her out. He gave her another quick kiss before grabbing her hand and pulling her along behind him as he headed up the front walk to the door, ringing the doorbell excitedly.

Jake Tolliver pulled the door open, his imposing frame filling the entranceway. Jeneva suddenly thought of the actor Michael Clarke Duncan in the movie *The Green Mile*. Jeneva saw instantly that the gene pool ran deep with the Tolliver males, and she felt as if she were staring at Mecan some thirty years down the road. Taller than Mecan and with considerably more bulk to his massive frame, there was no mistaking the fact that the two men were related. Mecan must have taken after his father, Jeneva thought, the notion instantly confirmed when she caught a glimpse of the silver-haired woman coming from the rear of the home.

The two men stood staring at each other, Mecan grinning from ear to ear. "Happy birthday, old man," he said, wrapping his uncle in a heavy bear hug.

Uncle Jake said nothing, tears starting to rain down his dark face, his bottom lip quivering with happiness. Jake kissed his nephew on the cheek, tapping him heavily on the back. When the man opened his mouth to speak, the thick Southern drawl that pulled at his tongue was as large as he was.

"Lord, have mercy. Looky here, looky here," the man said, his hands clasped against Mecan's shoulders. He hugged him again, peering over Mecan's shoulder down at Jeneva.

She smiled, her eyes brimming with happiness.

"Boy, why ain't you call nobody? Ain't this some surprise! Who's this pretty little thing you got here wit you?" he said in one big breath.

"Uncle Jake, this is Jeneva. Jeneva, this is Uncle Jake."

"It's very nice to meet you, Mr. Tolliver, and happy birthday to you."

Jake hugged her tightly, lifting her off her feet. "You best call me Uncle Jake. Ain't you a pretty little sight!"

Jeneva laughed as the man dropped her back to the ground.

"How you two get here?" he asked, stepping out the door to stare at the driveway. When he saw the car, he spun back around, the old man's tears falling for a second time. He grabbed Jeneva's hand and kissed the back of it, his whole body shaking with glee.

"Doesn't your mama get a hug and kiss?" a soft voice asked, stepping up behind Mecan.

The man turned and beamed, leaning to kiss and hug the elegant black woman who laughed excitedly to see him.

"I missed you, lady," Mecan said, holding as tightly to his mother as she held to him.

Jeneva brushed a wisp of hair out of her face, running her hand against her damp eyes as she did. Mecan reached out for her hand and pulled her close. Frances Tolliver stood as tall as Jeneva, her five-foot, one-inch framed lifted by two inches of heel. Snow-white hair pulled back into a French chignon framed her rich, chocolate face. Her crystal clear complexion, accented by just a faint touch of makeup, belied her age and Jeneva found her beautiful. She smiled shyly as Mecan's mother extended her hand.

"And you must be Jeneva," she said sweetly, reaching to pull Jeneva into a warm embrace.

"Yes, ma'am. It's very nice to meet you, Mrs. Tolliver."

Frances laughed. "Please, everyone 'round here calls me Mama Frances. Even my children, so you call me that, too." Her own accent was as lyrical. "I've heard so much about you, baby. I was waiting to hear when this child of mine was going to make sure I met you. Darwin told me weeks ago how sweet Mecan was on you and Mecan couldn't stop calling your name when I spoke to him the other week."

Jeneva blushed, her cheeks turning a flaming red.

"How's that baby boy of yours doing?" Frances asked as she pulled Jeneva along by the hand, leading her to the rear of the house and the family room.

"He's well, thank you."

"I look forward to meeting him when you two come back from Georgia," she said.

Jeneva smiled, glancing at Mecan, who nodded his head.

"Sit, baby," Frances said, her tone commanding. "Are you hungry? Dinner's almost finished but I can make you a snack if you like."

"I'm fine, thank you."

"How about you, Mecan? Are you hungry, honey?"

Mecan dropped onto the sofa beside Jeneva, wrapping his arms around her as he pulled her against his chest. His mother smiled. "Not just yet," Mecan replied. "So what have you been up to since I last talked to you?"

Uncle Jake interrupted. "You knew Mac was coming, Frances, and ain't say nothing to nobody?"

"It was a surprise, Jake. He said he wanted to surprise you for your birthday."

"He sure 'nuf did. Did just that," Jake said, sitting down in an oversize recliner.

Frances jumped to her feet. "I'm about to burn my cornbread," she exclaimed, racing into the kitchen.

"What else did you cook?" Mecan asked.

His mother didn't answer, her head deep in the oven as she pulled out her food.

"What's for dinner, Uncle Jake?" he asked.

"Did some of my ribs on the grill, and we got some shrimp and crabs we'll throw in the pot when everyone gets here, and yo' mama made some greens, some slaw, cornbread, and just a whole mess a stuff."

Jeneva smiled. She rose from the seat. "I'll see if your mother needs any help," she said, squeezing Mecan's hand.

In the kitchen, Frances was cutting the warm bread into squares and transferring the cakelike substance to a serving plate.

"Can I give you a hand?" Jeneva asked politely as she entered the room.

The older woman looked up, smiling. "You can come sit and talk with me. Let me get to know you better."

Jeneva took a seat on a cushioned stool Frances pointed her to. "I can help if you want me."

"No, I'm finished. Once the other children get here, we're going to toss them shrimp and crabs into the water pot. We'll be ready to eat, then." Frances took the seat beside her. She stared intently at Jeneva, nodding her head slowly, then pressed her palm against Jeneva's cheek.

"You've made my son very happy. I hear it in his voice every time he talks about you."

"Your son is a very special man and he's made me very happy. Happier than I thought I ever could be."

"You have a son, so you know how we mothers worry about them. How much we want our babies to be happy."

"Yes, ma'am. I do."

"Well, it's long past time one of my children thought about giving me some grandbabies. I can't get no grayer than this waiting on them."

Jeneva laughed, never having given any thought to there being any more babies in her life until just that moment when the words eased out of his mother's mouth. And when she said so, Frances laughed with her.

The two women sat together for some time, getting to know one another, laughing, and sharing stories. It wasn't too long before Mecan came looking for them, amused to see them having such a good time together.

"What's going on back here?" he said, leaning to kiss his mother's cheek, then wrapping his arms around Jeneva as he dropped his lips against hers. "What are you telling my mother?"

"She told me she loves you, but for the life of me I can't figure out why, with that rusty behind of yours. You've been trouble since the day I birthed you," his mother said jokingly.

"I think it's my car. Women love a Cadillac!"

"Your daddy sure would have loved to see that. That man loved that car." She directed her next comment at Jeneva. "When my husband, Darryl, bought that car, I told him it didn't make any kind of sense to be buying a red car. He'd toss on this big old hat and go out of the house looking like Superfly. It was just too flashy for my tastes, but he sure loved it."

Jeneva laughed, the last bit of nervousness fading into oblivion. When the doorbell chimed, she jumped, almost having forgotten that other family was coming. The tension resurfaced as she worried once again about Mecan's family liking her. Paris Tolliver led the way, pulling a tall blond man behind her. The woman squealed loudly when she laid eyes on her younger brother.

"Mac!" she cheered, rushing to hug him around the neck. "So you did make it!"

"You knew, too?" Uncle Jake exclaimed. "Everybody knew but me?"

"How was it supposed to be a surprise if we told

you?" Frances laughed. "Stop whining and go turn on
the seafood pot!"

Frances leaned up to kiss her daughter's cheek.
Paris was as tall as her brothers, her pencil-thin frame
long and lean. Her complexion fell somewhere between Mecan's blue-black and her mother's Hershey
brown, a deep, dark brown that looked like winter
satin. Like her mother, she was exquisite, her features
like that of an African queen. She extended a hand to
Jeneva.

"Hi, you must be Jeneva. I'm Paris."

"It's nice to meet you, Paris."

"And this is my friend Taylor. Taylor Mills." Taylor
Mills shook hands with everyone in the room, Frances
eyeing him from the top of his dirty-blond hair to the
soles of his leather loafers.

"Where do you know Paris from, Mr. Mills?" she
asked politely.

"We work together, Mrs. Tolliver. I didn't have anything to do this afternoon so she was kind enough to
invite me along. I hope you don't mind?"

"Oh, heavens, no, child. The more the merrier."

Mecan pressed his hands against Jeneva's shoulder.
"This is why Darwin and I bought the bigger house.
You just wait," he whispered in her ear.

Before Jeneva knew it, the room had actually become crowded. Within minutes of Paris and Taylor's
arrival, Uncle Jake's daughters, Belinda and Melanie,
arrived with husbands and children in tow. Then his
son Jessie and Jessie's girlfriend blew in, followed by
Jessie's brother George, with his wife and family. A
host of cousins and friends were also filing in, and before she knew it, there was a full-fledged party going
on.

Everyone stopped long enough to feast on the
abundance of food that had been prepared. The ribs

THE RIGHT SIDE OF LOVE

melted like butter in their mouths and by the time
Frances was ready to serve the three cakes and two
pies she'd baked, Jeneva was stuffed. After cake and
ice cream, the activities really kicked off. Children ran
from one end of the backyard to the other. Uncle Jake
and a host of his friends were playing horseshoes in
one corner of the property. There was a bid whist
game being played at the kitchen table, and some
people were dancing to K.C. and the Sunshine Band's
"Boogie Shoes" in the living room. Laughter rained
from room to room and Jeneva was amazed at how
comfortable everyone tried to make her feel. Paris
grabbed her hand as George, a tire salesman, was
picking her brain about marketing strategies. Mecan's
sister pulled her through the house and up the stairs,
closing the door to an upper bedroom to shut the
noise out behind them.

"Whew. I didn't think I was ever going to get a
chance to welcome you properly," she said, dropping
down onto the edge of the bed and patting the mattress for Jeneva to join her.

Jeneva laughed. "Your family's great. I'm an only
child so this is very new to me."

"I hope we don't scare you off. We can get a little
wild and crazy at times."

"Not at all. I'm loving every minute of it."

"I just wanted to tell you how happy I am for you
and that bald-headed brother of mine. He's been
telling Mama and me about you for weeks now. He
was so excited to be able to bring you out here to
meet us."

Jeneva shook her head. "Your brother's had more
faith in us than I did. I had no idea we were going to
be coming, most especially by car."

"He tell you about that car?"

"He said it was your father's."

Paris nodded. "That was Daddy's baby! When Mecan took that car he told all of us that the day he drove it back here would be the day he found the woman he wanted to marry and that we would all know because he was going to bring her home in that car."

Jeneva blushed.

"My brother must have a lot of love for you, girl."

"Your brother is an incredible man."

"Do you love him?"

"I do. Very much."

"That's good, 'cause I wouldn't want to have to hurt you. He's my little brother and I've got to keep my eye on him."

"I think he's in good hands."

Paris smiled. "So do I. If nothing, Mac's got great instincts. Darwin's the one who would worry me. I've seen some of the hoochies he's dated."

The two women giggled as Paris continued. "If you two don't have plans for tomorrow, I'd love to take you shopping. Just us girls. I'm sure if you've been with Mecan in that car for the last week, you're about ready for some girl time."

"I'd like that. I'd like that a lot."

Paris leaned in and hugged her warmly. "Welcome to the Tolliver family!"

The two women were interrupted by a knock on the door as Mecan opened it a crack to peek in. "Am I interrupting something?"

"Just some female bonding," Paris replied, gesturing for him to join them. "What's up, little brother?"

"You need to go save your friend."

"What are they doing to poor Taylor now?"

"Belinda is trying to braid the poor fool's hair. He's got about three rows of cornrows already and it doesn't look like she's going to stop."

Paris and Jeneva laughed as Paris came to her feet. She winked at Jeneva. "If he can hold his own with this group, he might be husband material yet."

"Whose husband?" Mecan asked, his eyebrows arched high.

"Just kidding," Paris said, kissing his cheek. "Knew that would get a rise out of you. See you two downstairs." She exited the room, closing the door behind her.

"So, how's my baby doing?" Mecan asked, taking the seat his sister had just vacated.

"I'm doing just fine."

"They're not too much for you, now, are they?"

She smiled, wrapping her arms around his neck as she pulled him down against the bed to lay beside her. "They're all wonderful."

Mecan kissed her, a long, deep kiss that made her toes twitch and that spot just below her navel shiver with anticipation. "I love you," he said, pulling away to stare down at her.

"I love you, too," Jeneva answered, reaching back up to meet his lips again.

Twenty-six

Exhaustion finally caught up with Jeneva and when she laid her head down on the pillows in the home's guest bedroom, she'd not expected to fall so deeply into sleep. The morning sun woke Mecan as he lay in his cousin's old twin bed down the hall, and he couldn't help taking a peek to check on her as he headed down the stairs. The inviting smell of fresh coffee brewing drew him into the kitchen as he followed the aroma and the sounds of his mother bustling about.

Frances stood in front of the refrigerator, a plush terry robe wrapped around her, and Mecan couldn't help but smile as he stood in the doorway watching her.

"Good morning," he said, sneaking up behind her to give her a hug.

"Oh, boy! You scared me!" she exclaimed, smacking him lightly against the arm. "How are you this morning?"

"I feel good, Mama. How about yourself?"

"I can't complain. Come have some coffee with me." After pulling a can of Pet milk from the refrigerator, she poured a second cup of coffee for Mecan, added two spoonfuls of sugar, and then a splash of the canned milk to both mugs. She used one spoon to stir them both, then carried the cups to the kitchen table, Mecan trailing behind her.

"Is Jeneva up yet?"

Mecan shook his head as he took a cup of the hot fluid, blowing gently across its surface. "No. She's out like a light."

"I like her. She's a good woman and she really cares about you."

Mecan smiled, reaching for his mother's hand. "The last two weeks with her have been incredible. She's opened up so much, and to see her blossom like she has feels really good, Mama."

"So what is going on with her son? Is he still with his father?"

Mecan nodded. "We're going to pick him up next week. You're going to love Quincy. He's done a lot of blossoming also, but he still has a good ways to go."

"When do you go back to work?" Frances asked. "Them other kids must miss you."

"I'm not sure yet. I took an extended leave of absence, and once we get Quincy and decide what happens next, I'll know better. Jeneva and I have a lot of decisions to make and we've not really talked about what we want to do. We've just been spending the time learning how to enjoy each other."

"And do you like everything you know about this woman?"

"I love most of it, and I like the rest, and if there is anything I don't like, it hasn't been important because it hasn't bothered me in the least."

His mother smiled. "That's good. If you'd told me you loved everything about her, then I'd be worried. I don't care how much you love somebody, there's always going to be something that's going to irritate you. None of us are perfect, so our flaws have got to get on somebody's nerves. Lord knows I loved your daddy to death, but the man had some funny ways."

Mecan chuckled, taking another sip of his coffee.

Frances continued. "I only have one thing to say about you and Jeneva. If you love her, then make the commitment. Don't play these games you young people like to play. Don't be sharing a bed and your bills and the same home if you're not willing to share your name. If you love her, then love her like you mean it, not like you trying to figure it out along the way, or just for the moment on the chance you might change your mind. If you truly love her, then give her what your daddy gave me."

"You have my word on that, Mama. And I can tell you that I love Jeneva so much, I can't imagine my life without her."

Frances smiled, leaning to give her son a kiss.

Shortly after lunch, the women had left Mecan and Jake dozing in front of the television while Kobe and Shaq dueled it out with the New York Knicks. Awakened by his own snores, Jake shifted his large body against the sofa, disturbing Mecan as he woke up and sprang up out of his seat, cheering a quick pass, a jump shot, and the Lakers winning the game.

"You know dem boys gon' take the championship again this year. Yes, sir, they keep playing like that and they gon' sure nuff get themselves another ring."

"You never know, Uncle Jake," Mecan said, stretching the sleep out of his body. "They might get surprised this year."

"They might be giving some surprises, but that's about it."

"How much you want to wager on that, old man?"

"Who you calling old? I'm in my prime."

Mecan rose to his feet. "How's your game? Can you still handle a ball? Because if you can't, I'm calling you old."

"Looks like I need to teach you a thing or two," the man said, joining his nephew as he headed out the front door, grabbing the basketball out of the hall closet as he passed. "Need to show you how good my game is."

Mecan laughed as the two squared off under the basketball hoop in the driveway. After a check and a dribble, Mecan scored the first basket.

"All right now." Mecan laughed, teasing his uncle.

"Oh, it's like that!" Uncle Jake responded, stealing the ball and blowing past Mecan to drop two into the hoop.

Mecan laughed again. "Not bad. Not bad at all," he said as the two men continued to battle back and forth. Within minutes, both were sweating profusely. Jake grabbed the ball for the final shot, giving Mecan a high five as he fell back against a pearl-white Cadillac Escalade parked in the driveway.

"Nice car," Mecan said, walking the distance around the vehicle. "When did you buy this one?"

"Last month. Traded in the old one. I tell you, boy, them Caddy people keep making 'em better and better every year."

"I have to agree with you there, Uncle Jake."

"How'd that baby ride?" Jake asked, pointing to the red Eldorado Mecan had spent the morning washing clean and polishing to a high shine.

"She's sweet, Uncle Jake. Daddy knew what he was doing when her bought her."

Jake smiled. "That brother of mine knew his cars, now."

A pregnant pause swelled between them as both fell into his own memories of Darryl Tolliver, father and

brother. Mecan leaned back against the Escalade with
his uncle, propping one foot on the basketball he'd
dropped to the ground. Jake finally broke the silence.

"That's a sweet little thing you don' brought home
for us to meet. Sweet as sugar, she is."

Mecan smiled. "She's my baby, Uncle Jake."

"Your mama likes her, too. I can tell."

The man nodded. "I knew she would. Jeneva's one
of a kind."

"Hard to get past your mama. She just don't let anybody in. Paris can tell you that. Paris sho nuff don'
seen a hard time with the men she be dating. Frances
let her know real quick when some boy ain't right,
though. And Miss Paris listens. Dem hardheads of
mine don't pay an ounce of attention. That's why
George on his second wife and Jessie can't get nobody
to marry him."

Mecan laughed. "They're not that bad, Uncle Jake.
Melanie and Belinda both married great guys."

Jake rolled his eyes. "So when you gon' marry this
girl, 'cause I know if you don' brought her home in
your daddy's car, then it's serious."

"Soon, Uncle Jake. I'm hoping she'll marry me very
soon."

"You ask her yet?"

"Not officially, but I'm planning on it."

The older man nodded. "Well, you gon' need this,"
he said, reaching into the pocket of his sweat pants
and pulling out a small jewelry box. He passed the
container to Mecan.

"What's this, Uncle Jake?"

"This was yo' grandmama's wedding band and her
mama's. When she died, my daddy gave it to Darryl
'cause he was the oldest. Gave it to him so he could
give it to his wife. This is the ring he gave Frances
when he proposed to her. Your mama been wearing

this ring ever since. She gave it to me this morning so that I could give it to you. You the oldest boy and it's only right that yo' wife be the next one to wear it. If yo' daddy was still here, he'd be the one giving it to you. Since he's not, Frances wanted me to."

Lifting the lid, Mecan stared down at the gold band that had adorned his mother's finger since forever. Jake reached out a hand and patted him against the back. "I don't have to tell you how to do right by that woman, Mecan. You know that already. You saw how your daddy loved your mama. Darryl use to say if you gon' love a woman, then love her hard and love her completely, or don't waste your time with loving her at all. You've grown into a fine man, so I don't have to give you no other advice. I'm proud of you, Mac. Your daddy would be proud of you, too, and he'd be happy that you found a sweet woman like Jeneva." The man paused, wiping at a tear in his eye. "Well, I'm hungry now. Don' worked me up an appetite. Let's go find us some leftovers. Must be some ribs somewhere in that house."

Twenty-seven

Robert and Fiona sat poolside watching as their children played in the water. The physical therapist Robert had hired was working with Quincy in one end of the pool while Jennifer and Robbie played on the other. Elizabeth sat with her feet dangling in the water, her customary pout pulling at her face. Her mother gestured toward Robert, then her, then back to her husband.

"Your child is really trying to test my patience," Fiona said.

"What's wrong with her now?"

"I don't have a clue. But she's been disagreeable ever since . . ." The woman stopped.

"Since Quincy arrived?"

"Since you left, Robert."

Robert nodded his head. "I'll talk to her."

"Thank you. Then you and I need to talk."

"What about?" he asked, glancing at his wife.

"Your daughter first," Fiona said, rising from her seat. She called to her other children. "Jen! Robbie! Would you two come give me a hand, please?"

Robert watched as his family entered the house. His attention focused on Quincy briefly, studying the young boy who was learning how to do a crawl stroke, and the instructor who was teaching him. Elizabeth

Douglas still sat at the edge of the pool, her expression angry. Robert moved to her side, sitting down against the edge of the pool as he tossed his legs into the water. Neither said a word as they warmed to each other's close company.

"Do you want to talk about it?" Robert finally asked.

"What?"

"What's bothering you so much that you've been acting so ugly toward everybody. That's what."

The little girl shrugged, her pout deepening.

"I can't help if you don't let me, Elizabeth," Robert said, shifting his body to look directly at his daughter. "You have to talk to me."

"You love Quincy more than you love us."

"That's not true. I love Quincy as much as I love all of you. Not more and not less. Just the same."

"But you went away for weeks to go get him and bring him here and now you spend all your time with him. You don't love us."

Robert took a deep breath, the chore more difficult than it should have been. He closed his eyes briefly before opening them to stare back at the young girl looking intently at him. "That's not true and it's not fair for you to say so. Right now Quincy needs me more than you do because he can't do a lot of the things you and your sister and brother can do. He needs our help. I had to go away when I did because I needed to check on Quincy and bring him here so he could see what a great family he had."

"Why couldn't he just stay with his own mommy?"

"Because he has a daddy, too, and I live here with you. I haven't always been a good daddy to him. Not like I was to you. In fact, I was a really bad father to Quincy. I never called him, and I never went to see him, and he didn't know how much I loved him. But you had me every day, telling you how special you are and how much I love you. Quincy didn't have that and I have to make that up to him."

The little girl's eyes flickered across his face. "Didn't you like Quincy? Is that why you treated him bad?"

"I love Quincy, but when he was born he was very sick and I was scared. I didn't think I could be a good daddy and I was afraid to try."

"Did that hurt his feelings?"

"I think it did and I'm trying really hard to show him how sorry I am for what I did. I want him to love me like you do and like Jennifer does."

"He loves you, Daddy."

Robert could feel the threat of tears washing over him.

"Is he always going to be like that, Daddy?"

"Quincy will always do things slower than you will. He will always have to try harder to get things done. One day he will need you, Jennifer, and Robbie to help him. You're his family, too."

The little girl leaned her head against her father's arm as she stared over the water toward her brother. "When you left, I thought you weren't coming back. I heard Mommy talking to Grandma Jean and she told Grandma that you'd left your son a long time ago. Grandma said that was really bad and that you were bad for doing it and she said you might leave us one day because that's how you men are. She called you some really bad names."

Robert bristled, making a mental note to deal with his mother-in-law for talking out of turn. He nodded his head slowly.

"Grandma Jean was wrong. That's not how all men are. Sometimes people make mistakes. If they can fix them, then they should. Sometimes they can't, and there are some people who do things wrong who don't want to change. But everybody is different and every man should try to do what he knows he should do. I made a mistake and I knew I had to fix it. That's what I'm doing."

"So you're not going to leave us?"

"Elizabeth, I will be here for as long as I can."

"Is Quincy going to stay with us for good?"

"No. Quincy has to go back home to his mommy soon, but I hope he'll come back and stay with us when he can. We can also go to see him when we want. We'll just have to wait and see, though."

"I haven't been very nice to Quincy."

Her father nodded. "I hope that will change."

She nodded, her hair blowing all over her head. "I love you, Daddy, and I promise I'll try to be really nice to Quincy and help him when I can."

"I love you too, Lizzie-Bitty."

The little girl jumped up from her seat, gave him a quick hug, then raced into the house to find her sister. A few minutes later Fiona sat down beside him. He reached for the woman's hand and pulled it to his lips. She shifted her body closer to him, brushing her thigh against his.

"When were you going to tell me that the cancer was back, Robert?"

He turned to look the woman in the eye, heaving a deep sigh. "I don't know. How did you find out?"

"Your doctor called earlier. He wanted to know if you'd made a decision about your treatment."

"I haven't."

"Why not? Why are you avoiding this, Robert?"

"Because I'm scared, Fiona. I'm scared. Suddenly my whole life seems out of control and I don't know how to handle it."

"You can't run from this, Robert. You can't disappear until you feel better and come back in a few years to deal with it. This could kill you and then we would all be without you. Me, the kids, and Quincy. What then? What would we do then?"

Robert's tears finally fell, dripping over his cheek and into his lap.

"Does Jeneva know?"

"I don't think so. I told Mecan, but he promised not to tell her until I was ready."

"This impacts her and Quincy also. If you're sick it will affect what you can do for him."

"I know that."

Silence flew through the air. Neither of them said anything.

Fiona rose to her feet. "I love you, Robert, but you have got to stop shutting me out. If we're going to fight this together, then you have to let me in."

He looked up at her, the sun shining in his wife's face. She reached out a hand to help him up on his feet. When he was standing, he wrapped his arms around her and hugged her tightly.

"I'm sorry," he said, his voice a whisper in her ear.

She nodded, kissing his cheek. "Quincy should be finished in a few minutes. I thought it would be nice to take all the kids out for a pizza dinner."

"Okay."

"Tomorrow we're going to go see Dr. Fisher and discuss your options. We'll drop Quincy off for his sessions with Dr. Adler. I made an appointment for ten-thirty."

"Thank you."

"And Mr. Tolliver called. He said they'll be here next week and that if you had any questions, you should call him."

Twenty-eight

Jeneva and Mecan lay side by side on the white, nylon hammock that sat in the center of the yard. They lay watching the parade of golfers who were making the most of the early morning weather before the sun rose to sky's center, burning rays of heat down upon them.

"We should pull out early in the morning," Mecan said, brushing his fingers down the length of her arm.

"How far are we from Atlanta?"

"About seven hundred miles, give or take. We'll drive to Alabama tomorrow, spend some time there, then head on into Atlanta."

"Mac, do you ever think about coming back here to live? To be close to your family?"

"I have. But Hewitt House has always been very important to me and I like the life I've built for myself in Washington. Having Darwin close has helped also. Besides, Mama, Jake, and Paris travel up to visit all the time so it's not like I never get to see them. Why?"

"I was just curious. Your family has been so good to me. I'm going to miss them all when we leave."

"We're coming right back and we can stay for a while, if you'd like. You and Quincy can decide."

"You were very sure of yourself, weren't you? Sure

that I'd come on this trip with you and things would work out between us."

"I had faith that you were feeling the same love I was and that we could grow that between us. That's what I was certain of." He leaned to kiss her, pressing his mouth to hers. Jeneva parted her lips slightly, tasting him with her tongue. She inhaled deeply when they parted, nestling her head against his chest.

"I love you, Mecan," she said, smiling up at him. "I love you so much."

"Enough to marry me?"

"Are you asking?"

"I'm asking if it's something you'd consider and have an answer for when I do ask you."

Jeneva studied the lines of his face, searching his eyes.

"You haven't answered. Do you love me enough to marry me?"

"In a heartbeat," Jeneva said, brushing her hand against his chest.

Mecan smiled back. "Good

She changed the subject. "What's going to happen if Robert gives us a hard time about Quincy? What will we do then?"

"He won't."

"How can you be so sure?"

"He gave me his word."

"And you trust him?"

"I trust that, come next week, you and I will be back here, with our son, and when that happens, I'm going to ask you to be my wife and you're going to say yes. That's what I trust."

"Our son?"

Mecan nodded. "I'm in this for the long haul, Jeneva. If I wasn't willing to love Quincy like he was my own son, then I wouldn't even think about the two of us getting married. This is an all-or-nothing proposition for both of us."

Jeneva leaned to kiss that spot just under his chin. She inhaled his scent, wallowing in the light aroma of his cologne.

"Do you want to know what I trust?" Jeneva asked, pressing herself against him, the hammock swaying slightly in the breeze.

"What's that?"

"I trust that for the first time in my life, I'm standing on the right side of love, and I have to tell you, it feels really good."

The house was quiet when Jeneva and Mecan finally entered through the back door, calling out for his mother and Jake. Peering through the living room windows, Mecan noted that Jake's car was gone. A note on the kitchen countertop confirmed that the duo had gone to the supermarket for groceries.

From where he stood in the center of the room, Mecan stared at Jeneva anxiously. Sunlight filtered through the sheer curtains behind him, casting a warm glow around his body. Jeneva smiled, exchanging the same look of wanting that filled his dark eyes.

"You are so bad," she said, as if able to read his thoughts. There was an air of seduction to her voice.

Mecan laughed, a low, sensuous laugh that filtered like electricity through Jeneva's body. The effect was magnetic, causing her knees to wobble, and her desire to throb steadily. He glanced down at his watch. "We don't have much time," he said, beckoning her to his side.

As Jeneva walked into his outstretched arms, he hugged her tightly, wrapping the length of his limbs around her body. Jeneva welcomed the embrace and when she finally pulled back, the two stood staring at each other, their connection undeniable. Mecan leaned in to kiss her lips, his touch soft and tender. Their kisses became more passionate and insistent as Mecan's hands explored the curves of her body, reacquainting himself with the woman's figure. Jeneva felt her breath slip away when his palms brushed lightly against the round of her breasts, his fingers dancing against the full tissue. The silence in the room was broken by their moans of pleasure.

Falling back against the sofa, Jeneva wrapped her legs around him, sitting on his lap. She pulled at his T-shirt, pushing the cotton fabric up over his head, welcoming the strength of his naked chest pressed tightly to hers. Mecan teased her, slipping a hand beneath her skirt as his fingers traced the length of her thighs.

Jeneva used her tongue to draw a fine line down the side of his face, around the curve of his ear, to the length of his neck. She occupied herself with kissing the soft flesh just beneath his chin. Sweat beaded across Mecan's brow, his body reflecting the rise of temperature between them. As Jeneva pressed her pelvis against his, Mecan found it harder to breathe, intense pleasure sweeping over him.

The sounds of a car door slamming and Uncle Jake's robust voice floated through the window, and they both jumped, startled from the moment. They stared at each other for a quick second and then burst into laughter.

Jeneva giggled as she leaned her forehead against Mecan's, the man's head waving from side to side.

"I guess we'll have to finish this later," she said, sliding onto the cushioned seat beside him. She adjusted her skirt and blouse as Mecan pulled his T-shirt back over his head.

As his mother pushed the front door open and stepped inside, Mecan kissed Jeneva quickly, her laughter reflected in his eyes. "I'm going to hold you to that," he said, rising from his seat to help the older woman with her bags. "You owe me."

Jeneva dialed the Seattle number by heart. It rang twice before the woman on the other end picked up.

"Hello?"

"Bridget, it's me. How are you?"

"Jeneva, girl, I was just about to send the troops out after you. How are you? Is everything going okay?"

"Things are really good. We're in Louisiana. In Shreveport, with Mecan's family."

"The family? My, my, my, this sounds serious."

"It's like a dozen dreams come true. His mother is so sweet."

"I am so happy for you, I can't tell you. Have you spoken to Robert or Quincy?" Bridget asked.

"Yes. I spoke to Robert the other day. Quincy was having a tantrum."

Bridget laughed. "I bet that shook him up a bit."

Jeneva laughed with her. "Did his attorney ever get back to you?"

"Just to say that Robert had no intentions of pursuing an extension of the thirty-day order and that he indicated the two of you would be negotiating a visitation settlement yourselves."

Jeneva nodded into the telephone.

"Are you prepared to do that, Jay? I don't want you to be pressured into anything you don't want to do."

"I won't. I'll hear him out, but all I want is to bring Quincy back home."

"What does Mecan think?"

"He is just so supportive, Bridget. The man has been my rock."

"Well, if you are the least bit uncomfortable with anything, you call me. Immediately. Don't wait."

"I promise."

"When are you coming home?"

"Well, once we get Quincy, we plan to come back to his mother's for a few days. Then we'll head back. I'd say at least another week, maybe two."

"Well, keep in touch and remember me and Roshawn are here if you need us."

"Love you guys."

"Bye, Jeneva."

Saying good-bye to Frances, Jake, and Paris was much harder than Jeneva would have ever imagined. She actually got teary when Frances pulled her into a warm embrace, holding the hug as she patted Jeneva against the back.

"You take care of my baby boy, Jeneva. I'm counting on you."

"I will. I promise to keep my eye on him."

Paris kissed her on the cheek, making plans for a girls' night out when she returned. Uncle Jake, with his soft heart, was the one who made her tears fall, telling her how much they loved knowing she was going to be a part of the family. The big man had wrapped her in an even bigger hug that reminded her of her father, and she suddenly missed her parents, wishing they were there to share in her happiness.

Mecan pulled his mother aside as Paris stood talking with Jeneva, who was dropping the last of her belongings into the trunk of the car. He hugged the older woman tightly, leaning to kiss her cheek. Reaching for her left hand, he fingered her ring finger, spinning the diamond cocktail ring she now wore against her skin.

"Thank you," he said, kissing her cheek for a second time.

Frances nodded. "I wanted you to have it because I believe that you and Jeneva are good for one another. I can see the love between you. It's what your daddy and I wanted for you. I honestly believe that a union blessed with that ring is destined to last forever."

"I hope so, Mama. I want that with Jeneva more than I can tell you."

His mother smiled. "Keep telling her that. Make sure she always knows how much you love her."

"I will."

"When will you be back?"

"In a week, I think. We've got some business to resolve in Atlanta, and depending on how long that takes will decide how soon we're going to be able to get back here."

His mother nodded. She called out to Jake and Jeneva. "Jake, come say a prayer. Can't let these children leave without saying a prayer over them."

Standing beside the car, Frances took Jeneva's hand and then Mecan's. Jake and Paris completed the circle as they dropped their heads.

Jake cleared his throat and then took a deep breath. "Heavenly Father, hear our prayer as we come before you this morning, first and foremost, dear Lord, to give you thanks for the blessings of this new day. Thank you God for allowing us to rise again this morning to witness the wealth of your love, Lord. We ask you to bless our children this morning, Lord, bless each of them, and give strength to the family, Father. We come before you and ask that you bid Mecan and Jeneva safe passage down the highways. Let your hand be with them, Father, as they find their way and do your bidding. We ask this in the name of your son, Jesus Christ. Amen."

"Amen," the group said in unison.

"Very nice, Jake." Frances smiled. She squeezed Jeneva and Mecan's hands between her own. "Keep God close and you two will be just fine," she said, reaching to give them both a kiss. "Mecan, you drive safe. Don't let that flashy automobile get you in any trouble."

"I love you, Mama."

"I love you, too, baby."

Sporadic thunder showers and rain-soaked roads turned their eight-hour drive to Montgomery, Alabama, into a fourteen-hour nightmare. Both Mecan and Jeneva were tired and on the edge of irritability when they finally pulled into the parking lot of the Wingate Inn. Inside the suite Mecan had reserved, they both collapsed across the king-size bed, falling asleep still wearing the clothes they'd arrived in. It was close to three in the morning when Jeneva woke, not quite sure where she was. Mecan snoring beside her, his back pressed against hers, eased the sudden rise of anxiety that had snatched her from sleep.

Slipping off the edge of the bed, Jeneva tiptoed into the bathroom and the shower, the rush of water over her skin a welcome retreat. She was pleasantly surprised when Mecan slipped into the water beside her.

"I'm sorry. I didn't mean to wake you."

"You didn't. The empty bed woke me up."

"I just had to get a bath," she said. "I had no intentions of falling asleep like that."

Mecan smiled. "Me, either. I guess we were exhausted."

Jeneva yawned. "I think I still am."

Mecan soaped her slowly, allowing his hands to rest gently against her skin. Jeneva welcomed his touch, having missed their intimacy when they'd been at his mother's, his room down the hall from hers. When he finished, Jeneva returned the favor, running her fingers against his body with much pleasure. Back in bed, they fell back to sleep, his body wrapped around hers, the radio playing quietly in the background.

"Dress comfortably," Mecan said the next morning, "and wear your sneakers."

"What are we doing?"

"I want to do the Black Heritage Trail. Darwin did it a few years ago and he said we shouldn't miss it. The entire tour actually runs through Selma, Montgomery, and Tuskegee, but we're only going to do the Montgomery leg today."

"I forgot how much of history is in this area."

"The whole civil rights movement was born right here. There are some hard memories here."

The day passed quickly, with Mecan and Jeneva touring a host of cultural and historic sites. Observing their reflections in the waters of the Civil Rights Memorial had been especially touching for Jeneva. The Nat King Cole House, Cole's birthplace and childhood home, also gave her a chill, the memory of her parents dancing to "Mona Lisa" a fresh impression from her past. Tears had risen to Mecan's eyes when they stood in Court Square, knowing that years ago black men like himself and women like Jeneva had been bought and sold like cattle on the same ground, their spirits spilling into the soil where the two now stood.

When Mecan suggested dinner, pointing to a Cracker Barrel restaurant not far from their last stop, she was glad to go. Glad to let the day be over. The food was good and welcome, hunger having filled the pit in her stomach, and she ate well, putting away a thick pork chop with stewed apples. When they were finished, Mecan excused himself to use the restroom, stopping to kiss her forehead before he left.

An elderly white woman seated at the table beside them gestured for Jeneva's attention. She smiled sweetly, ill-fitting dentures snapping in her mouth, a tattered wig propped casually atop her head.

"Excuse me, dear."

"Yes?"

"I just wanted to tell you what a lovely couple you and your husband make."

Jeneva smiled. "Thank you."

"My Herbert, rest his soul, used to kiss me like that any time he left my side. Only a man who loves you will bother to do that."

"Yes, ma'am."

"My Herbert was such a romantic man."

"Was he?"

"Yes, yes. And I was the love of his life. I made him very happy."

"I'm sure you did."

"I miss my Herbert, rest his soul. I miss those kisses of his." A line of spittle fell against the old woman's lip as she stared off into the distance, a memory of her deceased husband pulling at her.

Jeneva smiled again, looking over her shoulder as Mecan made his way back to the table.

"Well, you have a very nice evening," Jeneva said to the woman as she took Mecan's hand.

"You, too, dear."

"What was that all about?" Mecan asked.

"She wanted to tell me what a lovely couple my husband and I make."

Mecan rolled his eyes. "Oh, shoot. I thought she'd told you something we didn't already know."

Twenty-nine

The excitement that had filled her at all their other stops had vanished into thin air as they traveled interstate 85 north into Atlanta, Georgia. The drive from Montgomery had taken less than four hours and when Mecan pulled off the exit, smack dab into the hustle of the large city, it only served to aggravate her nerves. Although Jeneva wanted to be excited, wanted to discover all that Atlanta had to offer, she mostly wanted to see Quincy, to pack him and his things in the back of that red Eldorado, and head back home.

Jeneva stared out the large bay window in their suite at the Ritz-Carlton hotel. The room was luxurious and inviting with its mahogany furniture and exquisite decor. The hotel itself boasted an exclusive clientele and superior service. Mecan had chosen it for its magnificent swimming pool and close proximity to Robert's Buckhead home.

"Did you call Robert?"

"Yes. He knows we're here."

"When can I see Quincy?"

"Jeneva, do you trust me?"

"Baby, you know I do. I trust you with my life."

"Then relax. There's a lot we need to do before you

see Quincy, but I promise you won't have to wait long."

"What do we have to do?"

"For starters, you and I are going over to the Children's Hospital in the morning to meet with Dr. Adler. I want her to update us on Quincy's progress, plus I want to see what programs are going to be available to him if and when he's in Atlanta."

"You mean when he's visiting Robert?"

"Yes. How do you feel about that?"

"Robert is his father. I'll have to adjust, I guess."

"That's good. As long as you keep an open mind."

"What else?"

"We're having dinner with Robert and his wife tonight. The four of us have a lot to talk about."

"You really are going to make this difficult, aren't you?"

"No. I'm trying to make it easy. Robert and his wife have been caring for Quincy for three weeks now. Don't you think you should meet her?"

Jeneva heaved a deep sigh. "Then do I get to see my son?"

Mecan smiled. "After we go to the botanical garden and the High Museum of Art."

"Now you're just trying to make me mad," she said with a pout.

Mecan kissed her protruding lips. "I love you too much to want to make you mad."

"Where are we eating?"

"Downstairs, in the Dining Room restaurant."

"We need to go, then."

"Where?"

"Across the street to that mall. I need a new dress," Jeneva said, reaching for her purse, Mecan following closely on her heels.

* * *

When Robert and Fiona Douglas entered the Dining Room restaurant, Mecan and Jeneva were already seated and waiting. Jeneva studied the couple closely as they made their way across the room and over to where she and Mecan sat. Fiona was as beautiful as Bridget had said she was. As tall as Robert, she was long and lean, her complexion a crisp ivory just a touch shy of being too pale. Her red hair was pulled back into a neat ponytail, the length of which was wrapped in gold twine. She wore a gold-tone dress, its classic cut complementing her wispy figure and deep green eyes. She looked nervous, biting her bottom lip, and Jeneva could not help but think that if Robert's hand were not pressed against her lower back, the woman would have dropped through the floor.

Mecan rose from his seat and extended his hand in greeting. "Robert, hello."

The two men shook politely as Robert introduced his wife. "This is my wife, Fiona. Fiona, this is Mecan Tolliver." Robert tilted his head in Jeneva's direction. "And this is Quincy's mother, Jeneva."

Jeneva smiled, a faint bending of her lips that eased her own nervousness. "Hello. It's very nice to meet you."

"It's nice to meet you, too, Jeneva."

"Please, sit down," Mecan said, pulling out a chair for Fiona.

When they were settled in their seats, the moment became awkward as each waited for the other to speak first.

"How's Quincy?" Jeneva finally asked, breaking the silence.

Robert nodded his head. "He's good. He's had a lot to adjust to, but he's done very well."

"He's a very sweet boy," Fiona said, directing her comment at Jeneva. "You must be very proud of him."

"Thank you and, yes, I am."

"I'm sorry I took him the way I did, Jeneva," Robert said, cutting his eyes toward Mecan as he spoke. "I didn't mean to upset you, but I really needed to spend time with Quincy and I was worried that I couldn't get you to agree to it."

"You didn't give me much of an opportunity, did you, Robert?"

"No, I didn't. I regret that, but there were some circumstances that made me feel like I had no other choice."

She shook her head. "From the moment you arrived, you threatened to take Quincy from me. When I agreed that you could see him and spend time with him, suddenly you needed to bring him home with you. When I didn't agree, you stole my son and disappeared with him. You did exactly what you intended to do from the beginning. So what now? What extenuating circumstances are there that will allow me to just let this go and trust you? Because I don't, Robert. I don't trust anything about you."

Robert bristled, the tension filling in the lines of anxiety etched in his brow. Fiona pulled her elbows up against the tabletop, her chin resting on her clasped hands. She refused to look at her husband or Jeneva, knowing that the woman had every right to feel the way she did, whether Robert liked it or not. The blanket of silence fell over the table for a second time as Robert struggled to defend himself.

Fiona's gaze fell on Mecan as he wrapped an arm around Jeneva's chair. The man attempted to defuse the situation, which had become potentially volatile.

"Jeneva, Robert has something he needs to tell you."
He turned to the other man. "Robert, I believe you
have information Jeneva needs to be made aware
of."

Robert and Mecan stared intently at one another, a
silent conversation passing between them.

Jeneva's gaze flew from one man to the other.
"What is it?"

Robert cleared his voice, blinking rapidly before
speaking. "Jay, I have colon cancer. It had been in remission for two years now, and right before I came
back to Washington, I learned that it had come back.
When I showed up in Seattle, I just wanted to try and
put my life in order, to make amends for my mistakes
so I could move on and deal with what I have to deal
with."

Beneath the table, Jeneva grabbed Mecan's thigh,
clutching at the man's pant leg. Mecan placed his
hand over hers. "Are you being treated? Is it serious?
I mean . . ." She felt herself stammering, searching for
the right words.

"I'll be having surgery next week to remove the dis-
eased tissue and then I'll start chemotherapy after
that. I beat it once. I'll beat it again. Getting to know
my son has been a wonderful motivator. He's an incredible young man."

Jeneva nodded, catching Fiona's eye as the woman
reached out to hold her husband's hand, fighting
back her tears.

"Why didn't you tell me, Robert? Why didn't you
say something?"

The man shook his head. "It wasn't important.
Being with Quincy and trying to make things right
was the only thing I could think about at the time."

Jeneva shook her head, clutching at Mecan's hand
under the cloak of the tablecloth.

"How do we make this work, Robert? And how do you feel about it, Fiona? I mean, obviously you two have a lot to deal with right now. And you have your own family. How do you expect Quincy to fit in with all that?"

Fiona spoke, her soft voice low and methodic. "Quincy is very important to Robert and that makes him important to me. The next few months are going to be difficult, of course, but we love Quincy. He's part of our family now. We hope you'll let him visit with us and maybe we can come see him in Seattle. I know with him at school and everything that it might be hard, but we want to try.

"What we don't want to do, and what I think Robert has already made the mistake of doing, is overstep your boundaries. You're Quincy's mother. You have been there when Robert wasn't and you have every right to dictate to us what, where, when, and how. You also have the right to trust that we will respect your decisions and won't interfere if you don't want us to. We just want to do whatever you think will be best for Quincy. And we hope that you'll think Quincy having a relationship with his father will be best for him."

The two women stared at each other. Jeneva received Fiona's comments as they were intended, one mother speaking from her heart to another. She looked at Mecan, who smiled down at her, his expression encouraging.

Jeneva looked back at Robert. "I think you should know that Mecan has become an important part of my life and Quincy's. Whatever decisions I make, he and I will be making together."

Robert nodded. "I'll respect that."

"Has he had any more tantrums?"

"No, thank goodness."

Jeneva chuckled. "They take a lot out of you when you don't expect them."

Robert smiled back. "Scared the heck out of me."

Fiona nodded. "Me, too."

The waiter interrupted, bringing a bottle of wine Mecan had ordered. Before leaving, the young man, in his tailored white jacket, took their dinner orders. Polite conversation navigated the balance of the meal. At Mecan's suggestion, Jeneva and Robert agreed not to make any final decisions about Quincy until they'd had an opportunity to talk more. After the meal, the four of them stood in the lobby of the hotel as they said good night. Mecan held Jeneva's hand, caressing her fingers with his own. Robert leaned to kiss her cheek.

"Thank you, Jeneva."

She shrugged, smiling faintly.

Mecan said, "We're visiting the hospital and the school in the morning. We should talk again after that. Jeneva would like to see Quincy, also."

Robert nodded.

"Why don't you two come to the house for dinner tomorrow?" Fiona said, looking from Robert to Jeneva and back again. "We would like you to meet Quincy's brother and his sisters and I'm sure you would want to see our home, where Quincy's been staying. I know he'd like you to see his room, Jeneva."

"Thank you. That's very nice of you," Jeneva responded.

Fiona smiled. "I know this is awkward, but I hope you and I can become friends. I'd like to try."

"I appreciate that. Who knows? Let's take it slow."

The woman nodded, grabbing her husband's arm. "Well, good night. We'll see you tomorrow, say four o'clock?"

Mecan answered. "Thank you. We'll be there at four."

* * *

Jeneva lay with her head resting against Mecan, who lay propped against the lush pillows along the large bed.

"If you had told me six months ago that I would actually be trying to work anything out with Robert Douglas, I would have called you a liar."

Mecan chuckled. "I liked his wife. She's a decent person."

Jeneva gazed up at him. "So did I. And I'll be honest with you, Mac, I didn't want to like her. I didn't want to like anything about her. When Robert first told me he remarried six months after we were divorced, I was bitter. I kept trying to imagine what was so perfect about her that made him willing to stay married for all these years, when he couldn't do that for me. And when he told me they had three kids, I really hit the fan. It was a real blow to my ego."

Mecan hugged her, wrapping his arms tightly around her body. "I don't think it had anything to do with you, or Quincy. Robert should never have married you in the first place. You were both young and he didn't have a clue what he wanted for his life. He had a lot of growing up to do."

"And a year later he did?"

"One year can make a big difference in a person's life. We can discover some amazing things about ourselves in just a few weeks if we remain open to the possibilities. Just look at the last few weeks you and I have had together. Could you have imagined this six months ago?"

Jeneva shook her head against his chest. "No, never." She leaned up to kiss his cheek. "Not in my wildest dreams did I imagine feeling so loved."

Flipping her on her back, Mecan hovered above

her, lowering his body against hers, his torso supported by his arms. He kissed her, a long, deep kiss that took her breath away. "Neither could I," Mecan said, kissing her again. "Neither could I."

Thirty

Located in the heart of the Buckhead community, the Douglas home was a striking stone and shingle residence with an incredible wraparound porch and substantial columns. The architectural details ran through three floors of living space. The entranceway was a welcoming introduction to the comfort and warmth of the rest of the home. Fiona had created an incredibly relaxed atmosphere for her family in a richly detailed house that sat in a community of distinctively wealthy homes. The interior decor was classic French country, but what moved Jeneva and Mecan was the incorporation of ethnic artwork that decorated the walls. It was an impressive collection, each piece meticulously chosen for the areas in which they hung.

Fiona greeted them both warmly. "Hello, please come in," she said, giving both Mecan and Jeneva a warm hug. "Welcome to our home."

"Thank you for having us," Mecan said as Jeneva nodded in agreement.

Robert stood at the bottom of a circular stairwell, a miniature version of himself standing at his side. He smiled, shaking Mecan's hands and hugging Jeneva gingerly as he said hello. "This is our son, Robert, Jr. Robbie, this is Quincy's mom, and her friend Mecan."

"Call me Mac," Mecan said, shaking the youngster's hand.

"Hello, Robbie. My name's Jeneva."

The boy smiled excitedly. "We told Quincy you were coming. He's really excited."

"So am I," Jeneva said. "I've missed him very much."

"He's in his room, Jeneva. Why don't you come on up?" Robert said, gesturing for her to follow him.

"Robbie, I need your help in the kitchen," his mother said, pointing toward the back of the house.

"Mom, I wanted to go with Dad," the boy exclaimed.

"Quincy and his mother don't need your help. Move it. Now."

"Why don't you show me that pool out back?" Mecan said. "If it's okay with your mother."

Fiona smiled. "That's a good idea. You can help me with the lemonade and we can have it by the pool with Mac."

"Okay."

Mecan leaned to kiss Jeneva's cheek. "Take your time," he said as he winked in her direction, turning to follow Fiona and her son down the hallway.

Jeneva smiled and then lifted her gaze toward Robert, who was ascending the stairs. She took a deep breath. At the top of the steps, Robert turned to wait for her to catch up to him.

"Quincy just finished swimming," he said, meeting her eye. "We have a therapist who comes in three times a week to work in the pool with him."

Jeneva smiled, and as Robert turned to continue down the hallway, she grabbed his arm.

"How are you feeling?" Jeneva asked.

The man shrugged, his shoulders jutting toward the high ceilings. "I've been better, but I've also been worse. This is a good day, though."

"I'm sorry this is happening to you, Robert. I've wished some really horrible things on you the last fourteen years, but this wasn't one of them."

Robert chuckled. "I know I deserved at least half the things you might have wished."

This time Jeneva shrugged. "Probably not. They weren't pretty."

Robert took her hand. "I really owe you an apology for what I did. I am so sorry. But I just wasn't ready then, Jeneva. I didn't know how to be a husband, and when Quincy was born, it was just too much for me to handle. I just didn't know how to tell you."

"Robert, I've had a lot of time to think about us, and the past, since you came back. What we shared gave us Quincy, and that's pretty special. But if you and I are honest with ourselves, we both know that what we had wasn't anywhere close to the love we deserved to have. Since I met Mecan, I've found that love, and I think you've found it with Fiona. What's done is done. What I need from you right now is to be well so that you can be a father to Quincy. He's the only one you owe anything to as far as I'm concerned."

Robert reached out to hug her. "Thank you."

Jeneva nodded. "And for the record, if you ever take my son like that again, I'm not going to be satisfied until your testicles are hanging from that flag pole out front. You understand me?"

Robert laughed. "You've been spending far too much time with Roshawn."

Jeneva smiled. "Where's my baby?"

Robert led her down the massive hallway to the third door on the right. He pushed the door open and called Quincy's name. "Quincy, Mommy is here."

Quincy stood in the center of the room, fighting

to get his arm into a white T-shirt. As Jeneva stepped into the room, the boy clapped excitedly, jumping up and down with glee.

"Ma . . . ma. Hello."

Jeneva smiled widely, pulling her son into her arms for a deep hug before stepping back to help him with his shirt. "How are you, baby?" she asked, repeating it twice.

"Quin . . . cy . . . hap . . . py!" he answered, clapping his hands.

The tears blossomed as Jeneva cupped his face in the palms of her hands. "Mama's happy, too!" she said.

"The speech therapist has been in constant contact with the doctors at Hewitt House. I've tried to make sure they've followed the program that was established for him. He's doing really well," Robert interjected, dropping down onto the side of Quincy's bed.

Jeneva looked around the room as Quincy pulled her along by the hand, showing her the toys that filled the chests and spilled out onto the floor. An oversize plastic sportscar was his favorite for the moment as he demonstrated for his mother how it ran, complete with sounds and background noises. Jeneva laughed. It was obvious that the room had been decorated especially for Quincy, and as Jeneva took in her son's surroundings, she could feel the tears threatening to fall.

The walls were bright white, the room's furnishings filling it with color and warmth. A full-size bed sat in the corner, a denim-blue duvet covering the comforter. On the wall at the head of the bed there was a framed fourteen-by-sixteen-inch photograph of Jeneva and Robert, taken the year before they'd been married. Both were smiling, their faces reflecting a happier time. It had been one of Jeneva's favorite shots of them together, the one that had disappeared with Robert. As she stood staring at it, Quincy climbed atop the bed and tapped his fingers against the glass.

"Quin . . . cy . . . Ma . . . ma . . . Da . . . dee. Mine."

Jeneva nodded. "That's right, baby. That's your mama and your daddy."

Quincy grinned broadly, clapping his hands.

Fiona and Mecan sat in the lounge chairs by the side of the pool. When Jeneva, Robert, and Quincy stepped outside, Mecan was engaged in deep conversation with Robbie and his twin sisters. He came to his feet as they approached the sitting area.

Quincy's grin was wide as he raced forward, throwing himself into Mecan's arms.

"Mac. Hel . . . lo . . . Mac."

"Hello, Quincy. How's my buddy?"

Quincy clapped his joy, spinning around in circles with excitement. When he dropped to the slate floor, laughing, his brother and sisters joined him, all of them giggling and being silly. Jeneva joined Mecan, wrapping her arms around the man's waist. She smiled and he nodded and both knew that all was well.

They ate dinner on the patio and Jeneva marveled at how well Quincy interacted with his siblings. They played and fought like children do and he was happy. Fiona's love for them all was evident, and the first opportunity Jeneva had, she pulled the woman aside to say so.

"Thank you, Fiona," Jeneva said as the two women stood in the kitchen, clearing away the dishes.

"I should thank you. I know this hasn't been easy for you."

"It hasn't been easy for any of us." Jeneva smiled. "You know, I didn't want to like you," she said with a deep laugh.

Fiona laughed with her. "That's okay. I didn't want to like you either."

Through the glass doors, they could see Mecan and Robert eyeing them curiously.

"That's one heck of a guy you've got there," Fiona said, crossing her hands across her chest as she leaned against the countertop. "Mecan loves you very much. You're a very lucky woman."

Jeneva joined her, both staring back out at the two men. "You know what? I think we're both lucky, Mrs. Douglas. Because your guy isn't half bad either."

Jeneva and Mecan took the next four days to explore Atlanta, making the most of their trip there. From the galleries to the mall, they packed as much as they could into the time they had left, including taking all four Douglas children to the Children's Museum and the Atlanta zoo to see the giant pandas of Chengdu. Jeneva had even ventured a shopping spree with Fiona, the two women discovering how similar their tastes were when both stepped out of the Nordstrom dressing room wearing the same designer suit.

The day before they were scheduled to leave, Jeneva and Mecan woke early. There was a mild chill in the morning air but the sun was shining and Jeneva had an intense desire to run. Lacing up her Nike sneakers, she tried to lure Mecan to the streets to join her.

"You are really going to let me go run by myself?"

"Yup."

"You really aren't going with me?"

"Nope. Morning cartoons are on."

Jeneva laughed. "What if I get mugged?"

"You won't."

"What if I get seduced?" she said suggestively, raising her eyebrows ever so slightly.

"You better not." Mecan laughed, pulling her down to his lap to kiss her mouth.

Jeneva pressed her cheek to his, inhaling the scent of him. "When I get back, we need to do something or I'm going to go stir-crazy."

"Whatever you want, baby."

Jeneva sprinted in the direction of Buckhead, slowing to an easy jog as she admired the landscape of expensive homes. Two dogs greeted her with yips and barks and an elderly black man even lifted a hand to wave in her direction. Circling the block, she headed back toward the hotel before her legs cramped up on her, retaliation for having slacked off on her running. Although she enjoyed the time alone, she missed being with Mecan and was glad to see the hotel's entrance and the elevator to their room.

"So what are we doing today?" Jeneva asked, showered, dressed, and ready to move.

"I thought we'd go to the National Black Arts Festival at the Greenbriar Mall. I want to pick up some prints for the school, and we might find a painting or two for the house."

"Whose house?" Jeneva asked.

"Our house."

"I guess that's something we need to talk about."

"It is. We need to make some serious decisions about our living arrangements, our finances, everything."

Jeneva wrapped her arms around his neck. "I just want to be wherever you are, Mecan. I don't care where that takes me as long as you're by my side."

Mecan kissed her, pressing his face against her

neck. "You keep that up and we might not make it out of this hotel room."

Jeneva laughed. "Yes, we will. We're buying paintings for our home. I've never bought artwork before and I think I'll like this much better than that horse."

There were more than fifty artists participating in the festival and Jeneva was awed as they lingered among the original works and intricate creations. Each of the artists had a story, something they were willing to share, and before she knew it the day had flown by and they had three paintings being shipped to Mecan's address on San Juan Island. The prints for Hewitt House were rolled into a neat corrugated tube they carried with them.

Mecan had indulged her, insisting she take two paintings by a Miami artist that had captured her attention. The dreadlocked brother worked as a Miami police officer, but it was clear from the artwork around them where his true passion lay. Mecan extended his hand in greeting, introducing himself, as Jeneva stood staring at the collection of oil paintings and graphite drawings.

"Very nice work. We're very impressed. My name's Mecan Tolliver and this is my fiancée, Jeneva."

"Thank you. I'm Antonio Roberts, and it's nice to meet you both."

"I love this one," Jeneva said, pointing to an image of a young black girl staring at them from a window, her expression pensive.

Antonio laughed, his smile engaging. "She's very popular. I can wrap her up for you."

Mecan laughed with him. Jeneva rolled her eyes at the two of them.

"I like that one also," she said, lifting up an image of four little boys sitting side by side on a porch stoop.

The artist had captured their ethnicity in a rich shade of blue and Jeneva found it captivating.

"Why blue?" she asked.

Antonio smiled again. "The blue reflects the mood of their environment. The images I translate onto canvas are scenes I witness daily in my work. Some of the neighborhoods aren't so nice or the people that friendly. Their grief, their fears, even their joy lingers with me, and when I paint it, blue seems most fitting."

Jeneva continued to study them, losing herself in the stories captured in paint. Mecan pointed at both, pulling a platinum Visa card from his wallet. "She'll take both, Mr. Roberts. I think they'll be great in our son's room."

The woman smiled at him, passing the artist the painting in her hand. She reached up to kiss Mecan, wrapping her arms around his waist.

"Thank you," she said. "I love them."

Their last night in Atlanta was bittersweet and they all enjoyed a steak dinner at the Douglas home after packing Quincy's clothes and his favorite car into the back of the Eldorado. "Vroom . . . vroom . . . vroom," Quincy had chanted as he and Mac put the boy's luggage into the trunk.

Laughter rang around the dinner table as the children chattered back and forth, promising to come visit Quincy and making Jeneva promise to let Quincy come back. The adults struggled to keep the mood light, not wanting any of them to become upset by Quincy's departure. At the door, Mecan and Robert shook hands, pulling each other into a half hug as they patted one another on the back.

"You take care of my son, and his mother," Robert said, a tear rising to his eyes.

"You have my word," Mecan responded. "You take care of yourself."

Fiona gave Quincy a big hug, kissing his cheek while he giggled. As they turned to walk out the door, Quincy jumped up and down excitedly.

"What's the matter, son?" Robert asked.

Quincy smiled. "Quin . . . cy . . . fam . . . lee. Mine."

The drive was pleasant as they crossed from one county line to another, leaving Atlanta behind them. Quincy sat in the backseat, humming to the radio. Every few minutes, Jeneva would spin around in her seat to look at him, assuring herself that he was still there and that he was well. When he finally lay back, closing his eyes to fall asleep, both Mecan and Jeneva smiled.

"Are we going back the way we came?" Jeneva asked.

"We don't have to. After we leave Shreveport, we can take any route you want."

"I feel like taking the long route."

The man looked at her curiously as she grinned in his direction. "How long is long?" he asked.

"Well, I figured if we can build love one state at a time, imagine what we could do with building a family."

Mecan smiled.

"Quincy and I have never seen Texas, or New Mexico," Jeneva said.

Mecan laughed. "We won't be far from Arizona either. I hear Phoenix has some great spots for families."

"You ever drive the California coast?"

Mecan shook his head. "I'd like to see San Francisco. I think our son would get a real kick out of that big bridge."

"Think this old car can handle it?"

"Without a doubt. This is what she was meant for."

They sat in the quiet of traffic for a brief moment, oblivious to the sounds of racing engines and honking horns. Jeneva shifted her body closer to Mecan's, her hand running along his leg.

"I don't want a long engagement," Jeneva said. "I've already wasted too much time."

Mecan winked at her, pulling her hand to his lips as he kissed the back of her fingers.

"Besides," Jeneva continued, "Quincy needs a playmate and you're not getting any younger."

Mecan laughed. "I always wanted a big family."

"Do you think you can handle one more?"

"With you by my side? I can handle anything."

Epilogue

The men were in front of the home playing basketball, Quincy, David, and Uncle Jake going up against Darwin, Robbie, and Robert. The noise was thunderous as they cheered and chased after the ball. Inside, the women were setting up in the kitchen, getting everything ready for the rest of the Tolliver clan expected to arrive. In the living room, Ming was showing Jennifer and Elizabeth her new belly-button ring.

Frances opened the lid on the large box Paris had just brought back from the Dough-Rei-Mi bakery. She nodded her head approvingly.

"Jeneva, did you see this? They did a nice job," the woman said, gesturing for Jeneva to look where she was pointing.

Glancing over the woman's shoulder, Jeneva smiled. "Oh, it's beautiful!" she said, the words *Happy 16th Birthday Quincy* engraved in yellow-tinted, cream-cheese icing on top of a chocolate-fudge sheet cake. "I hope it tastes as good as it looks."

At the kitchen counter, Roshawn, Fiona, MaryAnne, and Bridget were giggling with Paris.

"What are you girls up to?" Frances asked, eyeing them suspiciously.

"I'm sure it's no good, Mama Frances," Jeneva said, giving them all the evil eye.

Paris laughed. "Mama, did you know about Jeneva and Mecan making out in the back of Daddy's old car?"

Jeneva blushed profusely. "I don't believe you!" she said, giggling.

"I swear, Paris," Mecan said, entering the room. "You are the biggest tattletale. If I want to make out with my wife in the back of my car, I can. I'll have you know our daughter was conceived in that backseat." He pressed a kiss to Jeneva's mouth, wrapping his arms around her body.

Frances shook her head. "I can remember your daddy and me necking in that car once or twice, if I do recall. It's got a nice big backseat."

"Now that's what I'm talking about," Roshawn exclaimed, giving Bridget a high five.

Paris winced. "That was more information than we needed to know, Mama."

Her mother fanned a hand in her direction, laughing boldly at the memory. "Mecan, did you tell Darwin I said to come check these potatoes? He wanted to make fancy potatoes and his behind is out playing ball. I could have done these potatoes myself by now."

"I'm sorry, Mama. I sure didn't. I'll go tell him right now."

"What have you been doing?" the woman asked.

"I was just checking on Alexa."

Jeneva swatted him on the behind. "Mac, don't you wake that baby up. I just got her to go to sleep."

Mecan laughed. "I didn't, but she's going to have to wake up to sing happy birthday to her brother."

Roshawn hummed. "Mmmm. Six months old and that girl has him wrapped around her finger already." She pointed at Jeneva. "Don't you ever say another word about Ming and her daddy."

"Or Robert and those two spoiled princesses of his, either," Fiona added with a laugh.

Jeneva gave them a look, rolling her eyes as she leaned her body against Mecan. The man kissed her neck.

One by one the men began to file into the house, the boys dropping down in front of the television where the girls sat watching BET's *106 & Park*. Heads were bobbing up and down to the music.

Robert winked an eye at Fiona, wrapping his arms around Mecan's mother. "Thank you, Mrs. Tolliver. I really appreciate that beautiful card you sent me last month."

"You're welcome, baby. I just thought you being in remission for a year was something we needed to acknowlege."

"Yes, ma'am. It made me feel really good," Robert said.

"God is good, God is good," Uncle Jake said as he lifted the lid on a pot that steamed on the corner of the stove. He took a deep inhale, poking at the contents with a wooden spoon. "Darwin? Boy, what's this mess in this here pot?" He turned to stare at his nephew. "What you cookin' now?"

"Why can't you leave my food alone?" Darwin said, pulling the spoon from Uncle Jake's hand. "You'll know what it is when it's done."

Quincy bounced into the kitchen, throwing his arm around Uncle Jake. "Want . . . play ball?" he asked, barely stuttering at all.

"Boy, don't you ever get tired?" Uncle Jake asked.

The room laughed.

"You've met your match, Uncle Jake," Mecan said. "Quincy never gets tired."

"I can vouch for that," Robert added. "All he wants to do is play."

"Is Quincy coming back to Seattle with you, Jeneva?" MaryAnne asked.

"No. He's going back with Robert and Fiona for a few weeks, then he's back at school."

"Do you want to take David, too?" MaryAnne said to Fiona. "That boy is about to wear out my nerves."

Fiona laughed. "We'll trade you David for Jennifer and Elizabeth. But I bet you'll want to send them home before you get back to Seattle."

"I have an idea," Roshawn said. "Why don't we just leave all the kids here with Uncle Jake and Mama Frances?"

Frances laughed, swinging a dish towel at Roshawn's head. "I don't think so. That's why they call them grandchildren. We send them home when we get tired of them."

"And Lord knows 'um tired," Uncle Jake said, following behind Quincy and the ball.

Laughter swept through the room.

"You people need to get out of the kitchen so Mama and I can finish up," Darwin said, "or we won't be eating any dinner in this house tonight."

"I know that's a lie," Bridget said. "Mama Frances will feed us even if you don't."

Darwin cut his eye at the woman, pointing a finger in her direction. "Keep messing with me, Bridget. I have no problems beating you with this spoon," he said with a wide grin.

"Promises, promises," she said, grinning back.

Roshawn laughed. "Now we're getting freaky. First the car, now the kitchen."

The noise spilled out into the family room and the rear yard. Thirty minutes later, a crowd had begun to gather. A deck of cards was being shuffled for a game of rise and fly, youngsters were racing across the grass, the bang of the basketball hitting the garage vibrated through the house, and the smell of good food was making them all hungry.

Upstairs, Mecan and Jeneva had locked themselves in the rear bedroom, shutting the paneled door against the noise. Mecan's large hands had eased beneath Jeneva's blouse and were racing up and down her bare back as he kissed her passionately. Pulling away, he smiled down at her.

"I love you, Jeneva Tolliver."

Jeneva grinned. "I love you, too," she said, bringing his mouth back to hers. As they fell into the moment, Jeneva could feel her spirit smiling widely. *I can kiss this man forever,* she thought, knowing that the love they shared had *forever* written all over it, and the possibilities of forever were burned deep into her heart.

Dear Friends,

   This has been such an exciting journey for me. I can't begin to express the magnitude of this experience. I truly hope that you enjoyed *The Right Side of Love* because I truly loved writing this story. Finding love is such a phenomenal experience. I hope that you all have or find such a glorious expression in yourselves and those around you.
   I pray that this story makes you laugh, smile, and reflect on the love of family, and the enchantment of passion. Thank you so much for your support and please visit me at my website and continue to send me your comments.

With much love,

Deborah Fletcher Mello
www.deborahmello.com

More Arabesque Romances by
Donna Hill

ABOUT THE AUTHOR

Deborah Fletcher Mello is a writer, poet, and inspirational speaker whose experience encompasses twenty-plus years of scripting technical documentation for corporations worldwide. Born and raised in Stamford, Connecticut, she now calls Hillsborough, North Carolina, home, where she resides with her husband, son, and three dogs.

ATHENS REGIONAL LIBRARY SYSTEM

3 1001 00102150 1

Madison County Library
P O Box 38 1315 Hwy 98 West
Danielsville, GA 30633
(706)795-5597
Member Athens Regional Library System

__TEMPTATION	0-7860-0070-8	$4.99US/$5.99CAN
__A PRIVATE AFFAIR	1-58314-158-8	$5.99US/$7.99CAN
__CHARADE	0-7860-0545-9	$4.99US/$6.50CAN
__INTIMATE BETRAYAL	0-7860-0396-0	$4.99US/$6.50CAN
__PIECES OF DREAMS	1-58314-183-9	$5.99US/$7.99CAN
__CHANCES ARE	1-58314-197-9	$5.99US/$7.99CAN
__A SCANDALOUS AFFAIR	1-58314-118-9	$5.99US/$7.99CAN
__SCANDALOUS	1-58314-248-7	$5.99US/$7.99CAN
__THROUGH THE FIRE	1-58314-130-8	$5.99US/$7.99CAN

Available Wherever Books Are Sold!

Check out our website at **www.BET.com.**